POWER COUPLE

Dear Reader:

Allison Hobbs continues to create novels demonstrating that she is a prolific and talented writer.

This time she delves into the cooking reality show world and stirs up controversy with a couple, Cori Brown, hostess of *Cookin' with Cori*, and her former NFL star husband, Maverick. The popular chef who once owned a soul food restaurant in Harlem finds herself entrenched in scandal and sex, while Maverick seeks pleasure—with sidepieces. But she must ensure that a clean image remains in the headlines. Her ten-year marriage is at stake, and the two are challenged to maintain their brand they've fought hard to protect.

Throughout the story, Cori moves through life with flashbacks and memories of her deceased Grandmother Eula Mae, a former madam and a key influence. Along with Cori's glam squad, the show's quirky competitors make a wildly entertaining cast of characters as they concoct dishes for the winning spot.

As always, thanks for supporting myself and the Strebor Books family. We strive to bring you the most cutting-edge, out-of-the-box material on the market. You can find me on Facebook @AuthorZane or you can email me at zane@eroticanoir.com.

Blessings,

Zane

Publisher
Strebor Books
www.simonandschuster.com

ZANE PRESENTS

POWER COUPLE

A NOVEL

ALLISON HOBBS

SBI

STREBOR BOOKS

NEW YORK LONDON TORONTO SYDNEY

Strebor Books
P.O. Box 6505
Largo, MD 20792
www.simonandschuster.com

ISBN 978-1-59309-674-8
ISBN 978-1-5011-1937-7 (ebook)
LCCN 2015957696

First Strebor Books trade paperback edition June 2016

Cover design: www.mariondesigns.com
Cover photograph: © Keith Saunders/Keith Saunders Photos

10 9 8 7 6 5 4 3 2 1

Manufactured in the United States of America

For information regarding special discounts for bulk purchases, please contact Simon & Schuster Special Sales at 1-866-506-1949

The Simon & Schuster Speakers Bureau can bring authors to your live event. For more information or to book an event, contact the Simon & Schuster Speakers Bureau at 1-866-248-3049 or visit our website at www.simonspeakers.com.

For Jason Frost
Book Connoisseur and Dear Friend

CHAPTER 1

Maverick and I were not ready to become parents. But after ten years of marriage, the pressure was on us, not only from our families, but also from the media and our fans.

While Maverick was in Los Angeles filming a Lexus commercial, I had the task of interviewing potential candidates that the surrogacy agency considered good matches for us. We'd both agree on the final candidate, but I wanted to get the ball rolling and at least start vetting the women.

There was no medical reason that prevented me from carrying a baby full term; I simply didn't want to put my body through that kind of trauma. Also, my husband and I were still building our brand and there was no way for me to fit a pregnancy into my hectic schedule.

God forbid if I suffered a bout of morning sickness and vor while tasting some of the disgusting food the contestants r on *Cookin' with Cori*, my food-based reality show.

Unlike other celebrities, I decided not to fake my wearing prosthetics. I was going to be fully tıng menting and sharing my journey every step ɹould

If the blogosphere exploded with accus when I my way out of morning sickness, labor r boobs, and postpartum depression, th I suffer through any of the inco didn't have to?

There would be controversy over our decision, but I was certain my husband and I would stand together, hand-in-hand, and face the critics. We'd argue that Maverick's career wouldn't have to be interrupted by a pregnancy, so why should mine? People could say and think what they wanted, but I felt it was empowering for a woman to keep her career intact—like a man—and still bring a child into the world.

Though the haters would probably say: *Cori Brown is so selfish! So shallow! So unwomanly!* I had so much influence over women in the age range of twenty-one through forty, I was certain that many out them would agree with me and come to my defense.

Nonetheless, controversy sold and I was looking forward to all the free publicity my husband and I would receive once the news got out that we were using a surrogate and were proud of it!

The media had dubbed us, "Mavcor," a blending of our first names, Maverick and Cori. Maverick earned the lion's share of our income, but I was no slouch. Though we were already worth tens of millions, our goal was to become billionaires. The way things were going, it was entirely possible that we'd reach that goal within the next five years.

Maverick Brown and I had been inseparable since college when he was the star quarterback of the school's football team, and I was his devoted girlfriend who'd won her way to his heart with perb cooking skills.

averick received the Heisman Trophy and of course, various eams were pursuing him. I wasn't about to let him leave me nd so I persuaded him to marry me a few weeks before Although I would have preferred a big, dream wed- to a simple ceremony before he ran off to training tely, his newly hired agent butted in our business erick to hit me with a prenup. It was the worst prenup in history with nothing in it that benefited me, but I signed it, anyway. I had to if I wanted to marry Maverick Brown. From the day I signed that horrible prenuptial agreement, I made a decision that Maverick and I would be permanently joined at the hip. No separation, ever. And absolutely no divorce. We were going to stay together, forever—no matter what it took.

Before being sidelined by a knee injury, Maverick had a stellar nine-year professional football career that included two Super Bowl wins and numerous lucrative endorsement deals. With Maverick's money, I opened a soul food restaurant in Harlem called Bay Leaf, made it a success, and then made a hefty profit by selling it. The rest of my story became history: three bestselling cookbooks and a series of instructional DVDs. I also had my own reality TV show where I whipped up Southern cuisine while blindfolded contestants, who were not told any of the ingredients, had to rely on their palates and sense of smell to duplicate the dish I'd prepared.

The contestants on my show were mainly untalented assholes with huge egos, but their obnoxious personalities combined with my sassiness, killer wardrobe, sexy apron, and stilettos had helped make my show a smashing success during the first season. I was set to begin taping season two in a few days.

Back in the early years of our relationship, I used to keep Maverick happy with the soul food recipes passed down by my grandmother, Eula Mae Barber, a former madam from back in the forties. After her brothel was shuttered, she opened a restaurant and a hotel and was able to earn a good living. Though she was considered successful, she didn't want her twin daughters to ever have to hustle the way she had, and she sent them off to college to find good husbands—preferably doctors. Grandma Eula Mae had a thing about doctors. Even before she became senile, she spoke of doctors as if they were gods and the only men worth marrying.

She was sorely disappointed when both her girls became college professors and married businessmen. She was even more disappointed when they put their careers first, allowing their marriages to crumble.

Out of all of Eula Mae's descendants, I was the only one who had an interest in cooking. I was the only one in the family who was interested in braising short ribs or frying catfish to perfection. For me, standing next to Grandma Eula Mae while she eyeballed the measurements for banana-blueberry pancakes was fascinating, like watching a scientist at work. Everyone else sat at the table and gobbled up her food, but couldn't care less about the masterful skill it took to prepare the meal. While my cousins ran out of the house, holding their noses and complaining about the stench of chitterlings, I had my hands immersed in water, helping my grandmother clean those pig guts.

I was raised on soul food, but rarely touched the stuff, anymore. Maverick and I were extremely picky about what we put into our bodies. We practiced a healthy lifestyle, and neither of us would dream of stuffing ourselves with the high-fat food that had made me famous. But we didn't share that information with the public.

With maturity, my husband had become even more smoking hot than he'd been back in college. At age thirty-three, Maverick Brown was increasingly sought after to promote not only the usual sports gear and custom brews but also luxuries that most viewers could only imagine. Currently an analyst for a major sports network, Maverick was in negotiations for his own Sunday evening show.

Recently, a Hollywood casting director had offered him a juicy role in an action movie. That deal hadn't been finalized yet, but it was only a matter of time before my hubby was showing off his ripped body on the big screen.

We were indeed a power couple, living our dream, and the idea of me slowing down for a pregnancy was unthinkable.

En route to the hotel where I would conduct interviews with potential surrogates, I tweeted to my 5.85 million Twitter followers that the search had begun for the perfect gestational surrogate for Maverick's and my future bundle of joy. Within minutes of posting the tweet, my assistant, Ellie, was ringing my phone.

"Your fans don't need to know about your plans to hire a surrogate. You should delete that post, immediately," Ellie said, sounding panicked.

"I'm not deleting the post, so get your panties out of a bunch. My fans are going to love being included in my pregnancy journey."

"But you're not pregnant, and there's nothing wrong with your reproduction system."

"That's the beauty of it all. I'm going to start a movement. After a certain age, women are badgered to put their careers on hold and start a family, but men don't have to deal with that kind of pressure."

"Men *can't* have babies, Cori. There's a difference in equal rights and what mother nature intended."

"True, but before the women's movement, people believed that a woman's place was in the home—cooking, cleaning, and popping out one baby after another. And those who did go out into the workforce had to cater to their male bosses while on the job."

"I agree that things were bad for women back in the day, but what does that have to do with your going public about your search for a surrogate?"

"Everything! Did I mention that my grandmother was one of thirteen children? My great-grandmother was a human breeding machine. Can you imagine having that many kids?"

"No."

"Having thirteen kids is insane. God only knows the condition of her poor tummy. And with no surgery to fix it, it must have been a sight to see."

"It was a different era, Cori. Women accepted the effects of childbirth as natural. Having a large brood of children was normal before there was safe and effective birth control," Ellie commented.

"That's my point. Do you think my great-grandmother would have given birth to all those goddamn babies if she'd had a choice?"

"Of course not."

"Right. She would have been on the pill or using an IUD if they'd been invented back then, right?"

"I agree."

"Their homemade birth control practices were pitiful. Between you and me," I said conspiratorially, "my Grandma Eula Mae ran a whorehouse. She used to make her girls stuff their coochies with globs of Vaseline as a form of birth control. Now, how primitive is that?"

"Sounds pretty antiquated."

"But it goes to show you that women have always sought methods to have control over their bodies. The invention of the pill was revolutionary, and for a long time, only the privileged had access to it. Just like abortions. Do you think the wealthy elite didn't have unplanned pregnancies? Their asses got pregnant just like common folk. But only the poor were stuck with the stigma of having illegitimate children because rich people could terminate pregnancies discreetly."

"I'm not following you, Cori. What do abortions have to do with your using a surrogate?"

"Currently, only a privileged few can afford to hire a gestational surrogate, but I believe that in the future, the option to carry a child or pay someone to do it for you will be as common as butt injections."

"It's still not a good idea," Ellie said worriedly. "Going public with your plans to hire a surrogate when you have no medical issues will make you appear vain and…" Ellie paused. "Never mind."

"No, finish what you were saying. I'll seem vain and what?"

"You'll seem vain and heartless!"

"I don't agree. My target audience is sophisticated, progressive thinkers."

"Wrong! You're striving to expand your brand to include sophisticated, progressive thinkers, but at the moment, your average fan can't get rid of the extra weight she picked up during pregnancy. She prepares your Southern-style recipes for her own comfort and also because she believes the food will keep her husband from straying. Your target audience believes in your motto…*Food is the way to your man's heart and don't you forget it*," Ellie said, mimicking the slogan I used at the conclusion of each episode of my TV show.

"Well, it's a true statement. As you are well aware, I snagged Maverick with my food. The man was addicted to my cooking, among other things," I said in a mysterious voice, alluding to naughty sex tricks.

"Sure, you initially enticed Maverick with your cooking, but now that both of you subsist on kale juice, bean sprouts, and arugula, your catchphrase is deceptive, and it's my job to make sure that no one finds out that you two have become vegetarians."

"I'm not completely deceptive. I taste the cooked food that's prepared on my show and I've been known to eat a hog maw or two for promotional pieces. Only last month, Maverick ate a ton of burgers while he was filming that commercial for Five Guys."

Ellie sighed audibly. "You and Maverick are greatly admired. You're considered America's sweetheart couple, so why risk ruining your popularity by revealing an aspect of your private life that many may find offensive? Let me put out a story about your failed pregnancy attempts and several heartbreaking miscarriages. Let's get some sympathy for you instead of contempt."

"You're wrong, Ellie. My gut tells me that the public is going to eat this up. And I always go with my gut." Before my assistant could utter another word, I blurted, "Listen, Ellie, my driver is pulling into the parking lot of the agency, so I'll have to talk to you later. Ohmigod, this is so exciting. Wish me luck in finding the perfect carrier for my baby!"

CHAPTER 2

I tweeted that Maverick and I were using a surrogate to carry our child, and fans assumed I couldn't get pregnant. After the Internet exploded with sympathy over my plight of being barren, I had no choice but to allow Ellie to put together a statement that expressed how heartbroken Maverick and I were after suffering through three miscarriages. Though we prayed to one day be blessed with a full-term, natural pregnancy, we intended to use a gestational carrier in the meantime.

"Those fucking fans get on my nerves with their narrow-mindedness," I complained to Maverick while sitting in the massive dining room of our exclusive Upper West Side apartment. Our personal chef, Tamara, quickly cleared the table of leftover appetizers and hastily exited the room as she was supposed to do.

"I can't believe I have to live a big lie to appease fans that aren't as enlightened as I'd believed."

"You can't blame the fans for assuming that a supposedly down-to-earth woman like you would opt for a surrogate if you're healthy and able-bodied," Maverick said.

"Was that a dig? Sounds like you've been talking to your mother."

"It wasn't a dig; I was merely making a comment. And yes, I did speak with my mom after she saw your tweet. She can't imagine why you'd allow a stranger to carry her grandchild. Frankly, I didn't know what to tell her."

"You should have told her the truth. I have too much going on in my life to put up with swollen ankles. I wear fucking stilettos on my show and it would ruin my image if I had to waddle around the set wearing orthopedic shoes."

"My mom is old school, and she can't wrap her head around using a surrogate without a medical reason. To her, it's like misusing a human body."

"Your mom needs to become a part of the twenty-first century."

Before Maverick could speak in defense of his mother, our chef reappeared in the dining room, pushing a cart with steaming covered dishes. Maverick and I put our conversation on pause while she served us.

"Tonight, we have herb-grilled cauliflower with sautéed Portobello mushrooms and kale. And also a pine-nut pesto sauce and black pepper-cabernet reduction," she announced with a smile. Then she poured more wine into our imported Italian crystal goblets.

"Thank you, Tamara," Maverick said graciously.

I gave our chef a tight smile that meant, *stop grinning at my husband, bitch.* Taking a hint, Tamara scurried back to the kitchen.

"This is delicious," Maverick commented.

I nodded after sampling the grilled cauliflower. "The organic wine is a perfect pairing with the dish," I added, taking a sip.

"Maybe you'll let our newest chef stick around for longer than a few weeks," he said with a chuckle.

"Nope. I'm not allowing any female to get comfortable enough in my home that she starts feeling entitled to sharing my husband. It happens all the time with celebrities. The nanny, the maid, the yoga instructor, or the private chef always ends up having an affair with the husband. I don't know how those dumb broads keep letting the sidechick win. I'll be damned if that's going to happen up in this piece," I said, twisting my neck around, and completely abandoning the cheerful persona I presented to the public.

"You act as if I would throw away the life we've built together over an erection."

I stared at him. "Are you saying that your dick gets hard over the hired help?"

"Of course it does; I'm only human. But I don't act on it. I don't do anything outside the bounds of our agreement."

"Our agreement is an entirely different subject, something we need to modify, but right now I'm focused on the fact that our new chef has you lusting for her. I want that bitch out of here, tonight. This will be the last meal she cooks for us."

"You're overreacting, Cori."

"No, I'm not. How would you feel if I told you my pussy got wet from looking at another man?"

"Does it?"

"No!"

"Men are different than women. And the dick is a strange creature. It can brick up over the oddest things and during the most inappropriate circumstances."

"For example?"

"At the dentist's office last week—"

"Your dick got hard at the dentist's office?" I stared at him in astonishment.

"The dental hygienist ran a gloved finger across my gums and my dick got hard."

"Was she deliberately trying to—"

"No," he said, cutting me off. "It was a completely innocent act. She was merely doing her job, yet my dick responded as if it had been caressed. That's the thing about being a man, you never know what will arouse you."

"Did the hygienist notice your erection?" I asked with irritation.

"I don't think so. I was covered with a dental drape, so I doubt it."

"Jesus, you're so perverted," I said, looking at Maverick with repugnance.

"I disagree. I'm a normal, red-blooded man who experiences dozens of erections in the course of a day."

"Dozens? Jesus, over what—big titties and asses?"

"Can we have an open and honest conversation without you getting upset? If I can't be honest with you, I'll keep my thoughts to myself."

"All right, go ahead—I'm listening."

"A man can get aroused by what he sees, what he hears, as well as what he feels."

"You get a hard-on over what you hear?" I asked, incredulous.

"Sometimes. A woman might have a sexy sound to her laughter, and my dick will respond."

"That's utterly ridiculous."

"That's only one example. Exposed cleavage is a big one for me. Also, the sway of a woman's hips when she walks. There are so many triggers, I can't name all of them. But the thing I want to impress upon you is that I don't cheat. I abide by our agreement."

"Speaking of our agreement. I've been doing some thinking, Mav, and I feel—"

"Babe," he said, softly cutting me off. "You have to stop firing the help and have faith that I don't waver from what we agreed upon." He stabbed a forkful of grilled cauliflower. "I enjoy Tamara's cooking and I'd like to keep her around for a while."

"Were you aroused when Tamara poured your wine? Did the sound of its tinkle give you an erection?" I asked sarcastically.

"Remind me to never divulge any more of my private thoughts since you take pleasure in using them against me."

I mimicked playing a violin. "Don't be so dramatic. Answer the question, Mav."

"No, I'm not aroused by Tamara in any way. Her short haircut is a little Butch for my tastes and I don't find her chef uniform particularly alluring."

"Good, keep it that way, and don't let me catch you leering at her."

"I don't leer; I steal glances." Maverick laughed heartily, but I didn't see anything funny.

"Stop playing. You know how jealous I get."

"Have I ever given you reason to doubt my faithfulness?"

"No, but…" I was about to bring up the subject of our agreement, but my heart melted when I looked up and noticed the look of adoration in his eyes.

"In you I found my perfect mate," Maverick said, smiling at me.

"Okay, Tamara can stay on one condition."

"What's that?"

"Her chef pants are too tight around the butt area. I'd like her entire uniform to be a lot looser. Would you please pass that information on to her?"

"There's nothing wrong with her uniform. I'm not repeating anything as petty as that. Get Ellie to speak to Tamara."

"That's not in Ellie's job description."

"Most of what Ellie does for you is not in her job description, but she does it anyway. She's an assistant-slash-publicist-slash lapdog, so get her to do your dirty work."

"Okay, I'll have Ellie speak to Tamara about her attire."

"Speaking of attire, I'd like for you to strip out of yours." Maverick lifted his eyebrows suggestively.

"You want me to strip, right here in the dining room?"

"No, not in front of the help; I'm not that big of a freak. Meet me in the bedroom in fifteen minutes."

"Let's go to the bedroom together and undress each other," I suggested with a sultry smile.

"I'll be there in a few. I have to make a quick call to my agent. He's been having some trouble negotiating my new contract."

"Oh, no," I uttered, concerned for Maverick. Hosting his own show was a cherished dream of his.

"Nothing to worry about. Some minor details have to be worked out, that's all." He gave me a lingering look. "Don't even bother to put on anything sexy. I want your ass waiting in bed for me, naked."

A shiver went over me. After ten years of marriage, I was still hot for my husband. Luckily, I hadn't had to kiss a lot of frogs to find my Prince Charming. I had met Maverick during our freshman year of college. He wasn't even a star player yet, but realizing he had potential, I held on to him and never let go.

Feeling loved and desired, I pushed away from the table and advanced toward the hallway of our huge apartment. I suddenly whirled around, intending to remind Maverick to bring the organic wine to the bedroom.

In a gilded mirror hung near the entryway, I caught sight of the reflection of my husband and Tamara. He was pointing to the wine bottle on the table, probably telling her to put it on ice. I chuckled because I didn't even have to verbalize my wishes; Maverick and I were always on the same page. But in the brief moments of his verbal exchange with Tamara, I saw a flicker of something wild and unrestrained in both their eyes.

As I proceeded down the hall, I told myself I was imagining things and being overly jealous as usual. There was no way that my devoted husband would look at another woman with such undisguised lust burning in his eyes. And he especially wouldn't do it in the sanctity of our home.

But…imagination or not…that bitch had to go. I closed the bedroom door and called Ellie. "I need you to give our chef her walking papers first thing tomorrow."

CHAPTER 3

Through the magic of television, a rundown old warehouse in Brooklyn, New York would be transformed into a studio where a group of judges would interact with the potential contestants for my show. But until the work crew had completed the job of altering the space, the seventy-five contenders that had been selected from hundreds had to stand in line outside the building, clutching their signature soul food dishes that they hoped would be tasty enough to earn them a spot on *Cookin' with Cori*.

Forty people would make it inside the warehouse to actually plate their dish, and from that number, only twenty would be selected to compete. A group of chefs, a few producers, and people from the casting agency were at the warehouse weeding through the hopefuls and tasting the food that had no doubt, curdled, congealed, wilted, and fermented during the many hours that had elapsed since the signature dish had been prepared.

Far from the madness of first-day filming, I was in my posh dressing room at Chelsea Piers where we filmed all the episodes except the Signature Dish premiere and the season finale. My beauty team flitted about, getting me ready to tape the segment where the twenty remaining contestants would have to compete against each other and duplicate one of my signature dishes. Along with two other esteemed chefs, I would judge the fat-laden cuisine and four people would be sent home, kissing goodbye their dream of winning a hundred thousand dollars and a spread in a major food magazine.

Only God knew what those casting idiots were looking for in a contestant because the ability to cook certainly wasn't a requirement. I was still baffled as to how last season had turned into such a huge success with so many colossally bad cooks competing. Casting must have known what they were doing by selecting wacky and weird personalities over those with true culinary skills.

Last season there was the raunchy, biker grandmother who dressed in biker gear, and who used so much profanity, every other sentence had to be bleeped. I was appalled by her, but she was a big hit with the viewers.

We also had a stutterer last season. Whenever it was time for him to describe the dish he'd prepared, he'd hold up a finger, signaling us to wait for him to gather his words. That fucker had truly tried my patience. Being forced to smile for the cameras while listening to all the stuttering and stammering had been pure torture, but for some reason, his struggle with self-expression made for good TV. Go figure.

En route to the Brooklyn warehouse, Ellie joined me in the Town Car. My beauty team that included Gina, my hairstylist, Clayton, my makeup artist, and Robin, who dressed me, rode in a van behind us. Although I would only be on camera for approximately twenty minutes of the season premiere, it sometimes took up to four hours or more to get my segment right.

If a contestant didn't gush or grovel enough upon meeting me for the first time, we'd have to shoot the introduction over and over until the jackass got it right and either curtsied, bowed, or yelled at the top of their lungs, "Oh, my God, I can't believe I'm face-to-face with Cori Brown."

"How's the surrogate search going?" Ellie asked as the car glided along the streets.

"Not so good."

"What's the problem?"

"I asked to be matched with a vegetarian, but the so-called vegetarians I met all had crappy diets. One woman was thirty pounds overweight due to a diet that included Oreo cookies, Red Bull, and a bunch of junk food that she felt was okay because it didn't contain animal fat. People are so stupid. Another dumb cunt held the idea that it was okay to pop Xanax for her anxiety issues. I never realized how difficult it would be to find a health-conscious surrogate."

"Maybe you should have your own baby. There's no one who'd take better care of your fetus than you."

I felt every muscle in my body tense. Ellie was paid to keep me feeling cheerful and optimistic, not to upset me by disagreeing with my decisions. "I thought you understood my position, Ellie."

"I do."

"Doesn't sound like it. Did I mention that Maverick's mother has been trying to poison him against the idea, and I can tell he's beginning to waver…and now you?" I pursed my lips and shook my head, demonstrating my displeasure.

Ellie looked away guiltily. Biting her fingernail, she gazed intently out the window. When she returned her focus to me, she was grinning excitedly. "Pregnant women have a beautiful glow and… and…" Ellie stammered, trying to think of the benefits of being a human blimp. "Think of all the magazine covers you and Maverick could get if you carried your own baby. I could probably get you both a Diane Sawyer interview after the baby is born."

"Really?" Pregnancy was starting to feel a little more desirable.

"I'm sure of it. Your baby will be like American royalty, and after all the difficulties you bravely endured while trying to conceive a child, the world will want to see your baby and also get a glimpse of you and Maverick in your role as new parents." Ellie was nodding her head and grinning almost maniacally, as she attempted to convince me to ditch the idea of hiring a surrogate.

I envisioned a whimsical nursery with our little mocha-colored prince or princess grinning at the camera from its canopy crib.

"Can't we get the same kind of media attention if a surrogate carries our child?"

Ellie wrinkled her nose. "The public doesn't warm up to children born from surrogates. It doesn't seem like the kid is actually yours if it lived in the womb of another person."

Sulking, I didn't bother to respond. It was my turn to stare absently out the window while Ellie scrambled to rearrange her thoughts in a manner that was more in alignment with my plans. I wanted that Diane Sawyer interview badly, but I didn't intend to have to struggle to lose baby weight in order to look good during the filming.

The sudden trill of my cell phone startled me. I was pretty certain it was Josh, the executive culinary producer of my show, calling with an update on the chaos ensuing at the warehouse. He was probably frantic for me to hurry and get there. Josh was such a control freak. He organized every single detail of a given episode, including what went into the cabinets and fridge; what was cooking on the stovetop and even what utensils and pots needed to be on hand for each segment.

Viewers would be shocked to discover I had little influence over what happened on the show. Josh had the final word on everything, including the food I prepared on the show. I was still brooding over the fact that he had rejected my smothered chicken, broccoli, and bacon casserole, stating that the dish had too many components to fit into the show's format.

I didn't bother to grope inside my purse for the phone; I let it ring, preferring to enjoy a few moments of peace and quiet before I entered the chaotic world of reality TV.

The aggravating sound of the phone stopped and then started again. This time an obnoxious jingle emanated from Ellie's pocket. She answered quickly and before I could protest, she passed her phone to me, whispering, "It's Maverick."

"Hi, sweetie," I sang into the phone, relieved that it was my darling husband calling and not Josh.

"After we discussed keeping Tamara, you went behind my back and fired her. Why would you do that?" Maverick sounded livid and I couldn't figure out how to tell him that I got rid of our chef over what appeared to be a look of lust.

"I'm working, Mav. Can we discuss this when I get home tonight?"

"No. I want you to answer a couple of questions right now. First, what did Tamara do that warranted getting fired? And second, why did you think it was okay to dismiss her and bring another chef into our home without discussing it with me?"

"I didn't hire a new chef, yet. I was going to talk to you about it, tonight."

Maverick seethed silently for a few moments, and then said, "Your irrational jealousy is getting out of hand."

"I know, I know," I whined, hoping to win some sympathy points. "It's just that…well, I could tell that Tamara wanted to do more than cook for you."

"Dammit, Cori. You have to get a grip. Last night, Tamara told me confidentially that she tries out all her recipes on her fiancé before cooking for us, and that she never prepares anything for us unless it passes the test with him. I could tell by the way she spoke about him that she's very much in love."

Apparently, I'd misinterpreted the look that had passed between Maverick and Tamara, and I felt embarrassed. Moments later my embarrassment turned to irritation. "Why doesn't the bitch wear an engagement ring?"

"She told me she doesn't like to wear it while she's working with food."

"She shares a hell of a lot of her personal life with you," I said with an edge to my voice.

"Maybe she'd share more with you if you didn't treat her with such disdain. I find myself having to be extra friendly to make up for your coldness."

"In what rule book does it say that I have to be chummy with the hired help?"

"She was recommended by one of the network execs, and you're making me look bad."

"I'll be nicer to the next chef. I've decided to hire a man this time."

"Oh, *you* decided," he said in a vexed tone. "Well, I don't want another chef. Tamara didn't do anything wrong, and you need to apologize to her and ask her to come back."

"You can't be serious. Look, there's something about her that rubs me wrong, and I don't want her around."

"You're being ridiculous, and you should be ashamed of yourself." He hung up, leaving those derogatory words echoing in my ears.

Despite his manly, super-jock image, my husband could be such a bitch sometimes. After ten years, he should have been more understanding of my insecurities. Perhaps it was irrational, but I didn't like the way Tamara interacted with him. The way-soft voice she used when she spoke to him and the way she made extra comments about the food, irked me to my soul. If getting rid of Tamara gave me peace of mind, then so be it.

Maverick would forget all about Tamara when he tasted the scrumptious food that her replacement prepared.

"How's the search hunt going for my new personal chef?" I asked Ellie as I returned her phone.

"I have three candidates to interview while you're filming to-day."

"Great." I stepped out of the car and braced myself for the insanity that awaited me inside the warehouse. In the course of the next few months, I would neglect every other aspect of my life—including my marriage—as I put in twelve-hour days on the set, and sometimes longer.

CHAPTER 4

With Ellie at my side and the rest of my team behind me, I sauntered onward with my usual self-assurance. But the closer I got to the door, the more panicked I felt. Suppose last season's good ratings were merely a fluke and this time we ended up getting canceled? How would that affect my cookbooks and DVD sales? And what about the Cori Brown cookware collection deal that my agent was working on—would that fall through? What would I do if my career took a huge hit while Maverick's continued to soar?

I hated it when I couldn't control the negative chatter inside my mind.

Ellie moved forward and opened the door for me. I entered the warehouse, awed that the interior of the dismal building had been converted into a bright and beautiful studio set. There were shimmering hardwood floors, a raised platform that was decorated with gorgeous flower arrangements and lush greenery, and of course, the fanciful letter "C," the logo for *Cookin' with Cori*, was festooned in various places throughout the vast space.

I was pleased, but didn't let it show. Then I smelled the stale odor that seeped from beneath the new flooring. An unpleasant scent that was embedded in the ceiling and in the walls of the old warehouse. It was a musty, dank scent that all the razzmatazz in the world couldn't disguise. I was certain that none of the other major cooking competition shows filmed their premieres in an old warehouse. I hated the way the network cut corners with my show. Suddenly irate, I began barking orders at anyone unfortunate enough to cross my path.

Totally ignoring the group of contestants who were gawking at me, I headed to my designated dressing room. The place was a shithole and hadn't been spruced up like the set. Luckily, I was camera-ready and only needed a quick touchup from hair and makeup.

Clutching a digital tablet, Josh followed me into my dressing room and shooed away my glam squad. He pulled up images and videos of the twenty competitors who had made the cut.

A few of the contestants looked normal, but there were plenty of wacky ones, like the Asian chick who wore blue contact lenses and matching blue hair with yellow ends. Another oddity was a white guy named Angus who had a shaved head with colorful tattoos decorating his scalp. Josh assured me that Angus wasn't a white supremacist, but was merely a young man expressing his individuality. There was a Wiccan chick who chanted while cooking and who wore black everything, including jewelry, nail polish, and lipstick. We also had a white Baptist preacher on the show who wore his hair in a fifties-style, Elvis pompadour.

You'd think that a soul food show hosted by a black woman would have a heavy concentration of African American contestants, but like all the other reality shows, *Cookin' with Cori* had only a token few. Josh's explanation for this slight was that the show had to appeal to the masses. Of our three token blacks, there was one woman and two men. The black woman, LaTasha, was average-looking, and on tape, she seemed bubbly and likeable. Of the two black men, one was a dwarf who had to stand on a crate to reach the stove. The other, Michelangelo (his real name), was so fucking gorgeous, I was certain he was an aspiring actor, using my show as a platform to get into the film industry. His handsomeness was slightly edgy with his jet-black hair styled in a short Mohawk with natural curls from the nape of his neck all the way up to his hairline. His dark hair contrasted nicely with his russet-brown skin tone, and his penetrating light-brown eyes.

According to his bio, Michelangelo was twenty-four years old. I watched his introductory video and got the impression that he was somewhat full of himself. He probably thought he'd win with his looks, but I had news for him.

"So, who's going home?" I asked Josh. It didn't matter that the contestants hadn't even begun the "Replication Round" where they tried to imitate my food with at least three of the top ingredients. Based on their lack of showmanship and TV appeal, Josh had already decided who would be the first to go home.

"Honestly, the cheerleader from Texas—Doralee Harper—should be going home," he admitted. "She doesn't know an apron from her asshole, but she's perky and the camera loves her, so we're going to keep her around for a while."

I peeked at her testimonial on the tablet. Cobalt eyes, tall and leggy with big, fake boobs, Doralee was conceited as hell, talking a mile a minute while flipping waves and waves of long flaxen hair. The sound of her Texas twang grated on my nerves, and despite not having met her personally, I instantly hated everything about her.

Josh took the tablet from my hand and quickly swiped through images. "This one is probably going home tonight."

I gazed at the video of a puny, dorky, white kid named Ralphie. Twenty-two years old and rather effeminate. He was the nutty professor type with buck teeth and large-framed glasses on a narrow face. During his testimonial, Ralphie fought his emotions as he tearfully expressed that his love of Southern cooking came from the African American foster mother who raised him. There was a montage of photos of him through the years, embracing his foster mother during important events such as Christmas, Thanksgiving, birthdays, and family reunions where lily-white Ralphie stood out like a sore thumb amidst a pack of hood rats. The foster mother, a roly-poly woman, smiled broadly in all the photos, revealing approximately four missing teeth in the front.

"Can Ralphie cook?" I inquired.

"He can cook his ass off. His food rivals yours," Josh replied, shaking his head ruefully.

"So, what's the deal? Why do you want to give him the ax?"

"Our behind-the-scenes test audience doesn't like the visuals of him with the black foster mother and the hood rat family members. The foster mother's look is so…well, it's so stereotypically black. And her butt is so humongous, it's distracting."

"His foster mother isn't the one competing," I said snippily, giving Josh the side-eye after his harsh criticism of so-called black characteristics.

"But she's a huge part of his storyline, and if he makes it to the finals when the families come on the show, there's not a thing wardrobe can do with that massive butt of hers. And I doubt if the execs would be willing to pay for any emergency dental work for her."

"Hmm," I murmured thoughtfully as I swiped though the numerous images of Ralphie with his family.

Josh continued pleading his case against Ralphie. "The foster mother seems to be the loud, boisterous type and the test audience doesn't think she'll be able to turn down enough to fit in with the other, uh, more dignified families." Josh giggled conspiratorially as if he were in the privacy of his own home, poking fun of blacks with his white friends.

Livid, I cocked my head to the side and stared at Josh.

"Why're you looking at me like that?"

"You find it funny, huh? It's okay when white people rescue unwanted black kids, but it's an aberration for a black family to help an unwanted white child. Since it's too uncomfortable for you and your test audience to watch, you all decided to make fun of Ralphie's loving foster mother and call her all kinds of crude names."

"No, you're missing my point," he said, assuming a look of innocence.

"You enjoy laughing at the shenanigans of low-class blacks, don't you? Hell, you probably laugh at me behind my back."

"That's not true," he protested. "I admire and adore you—and you know it, Cori."

"I'm not convinced. I believe you lump all blacks in the same boat as Ralphie's foster mother. You perceive us as ignorant coons, and utterly primitive people, with big butts that viewers find distasteful and insulting."

"I shouldn't have said those things, but you have to believe me, I didn't mean anything by it."

Unforgiving, I sneered at him. "I was always aware that you were racist, Josh, but I never realized you were a confederate flag-waving, neo-Nazi-type racist."

Josh gasped and his face drained of all color. "How can you say such a terrible thing about me? I'm the most liberal person you'll ever meet, but I have to do what's best for the show. Forgive me for sounding racist. It's not what's in my heart."

"You pretend to be liberal, but your hatred of black people is glaring, and quite terrifying. I bet you're a secret, card-carrying member of the Klan or the Tea Party. You could be an undercover white supremacist for all I know." I looked at him with all the disdain I could muster.

"Oh, Cori, you know that's not true. I'm Jewish and gay—a

double minority, myself. I would never…" His voice trailed off as if overcome by deep emotion.

Technically, Josh was my boss and he had the final say on important issues, but since he was blubbering one apology after another, I figured I might as well milk the situation for all it was worth. Hell, the buffoonery and heathenishness I saw on those videos of Ralphie's foster family made me cringe. But I disagreed with Josh and his test audience. A white boy speaking with a heavy 'hood dialect, along with a ghetto family would be the kind of train wreck entertainment that viewers wouldn't be able to tear their eyes away from.

"What do I have to do to prove I'm not racist?" Josh asked in a hoarse tone.

"Get rid of the Texas cheerleader with the snatched waist and fake tits. I find her boob-job to be distracting," I said, emphasizing the word, "distracting."

"Touché. But you have to admit that Doralee is gorgeous. The test audience loved her. Our ratings will be through the roof with her on the show. Her mother is a former beauty queen, and having the two of them together on camera during the finals will be such a boon for the show."

"I want her out of here." I made the cutthroat gesture. "I don't even care who the other three rejects are, as long as Ralphie isn't one of them. For once, I'd like the pleasure of tasting food prepared by someone with a smidgen of cooking ability."

"Getting rid of Doralee is a big mistake," Josh said gravely.

"I'll take the risk," I retorted.

Josh groaned.

"By the way, what's the story of the hunk with the brawny chest and the dreamy light-brown eyes?" I softened my tone, indicating that I was over my hissy fit.

"Michelangelo?"

I nodded. "He's hot."

"Smokin'," Josh agreed. "All of the members of the crew are crushing on him."

"And what about you?"

"I'm happy with the man I have at home, but I have to admit, Michelangelo is delicious eye candy."

"Does he know his way around the kitchen or is he simply a pretty face, using the show as a vehicle for his acting debut?" I hoped he was a serious cook because I was already thinking of hiring him to work for me after the show wrapped. Since I only kept personal chefs for a few months, by the time Michelangelo was available, he'd be right in time to replace whoever was Tamara's replacement's replacement. I hoped Dreamy Eyes would be able to prepare tasty vegetarian cuisine. It was time for my husband to experience what it felt like to have hot male competition walking around the place where he should have been most comfortable—his own home!

"Not only does Michelangelo have movie star good looks, but he can also throw down," Josh said, trying to endear himself to me by using black slang. I tossed him a tight smile. I had to get along with him in order for the show to run smoothly, but now that he'd revealed his racist side, I'd definitely be giving Josh the side-eye from now on.

CHAPTER 5

Behind the scenes, two chefs who worked for me when I owned the Harlem restaurant, prepared the county-style potato salad, garlic green beans, and grilled boneless ribs that would be placed in front of the blindfolded contestants and presented as the Cori Brown dish that they had to replicate, using the three main components of the meal.

While the contestants were sequestered off stage, I stood in front of the camera. Gina, my hairstylist, was nearby and armed with a container of hairspray and other tools of her trade, watching like a hawk for an errant strand of hair. In the midst of preparing the dish, I spoke about the importance of pan-searing the ribs before putting them on the grill. For the sake of ratings, I angled a warm smile toward the cameras as I fondly recalled how this particular dish had become my husband's favorite back when he was playing college football.

"And it's still his favorite meal," I added with a wink that told the female viewers that my recipes would help them get a man like Maverick or assist them in keeping the one they had.

"Cut!" the director yelled. "That was perfect, Cori."

Though all I'd done was chopped vegetables and rubbed seasoning on meat, I was relieved the cooking segment was over for me. The area I'd worked in would be cleared and a beautifully plated, completed dish of potato salad, grilled ribs, and garlic green beans would be brought out from the kitchen that was hidden behind the scenes.

I ripped off the mustard-colored apron with the swirly "C" in the center. I didn't have to be present for the next segment where the contestants tried to duplicate my dishes.

There would be a two-hour wait before it was time for me to return to the set, joining two judges who would help me decide who stayed and who got the boot. Even though I would only ingest a tiny portion of the soul food, I dreaded having to taste any amount of the gruel the contestants had thrown together.

After an exhausting thirteen-hour day, I looked forward to crawling into bed and snuggling against Maverick's hard, masculine form. Being close to him, even when he was asleep, would be such a comfort after the long day I had. Hell, I needed to do more than cuddle up. I was stressed the fuck out and the relief I needed could only be achieved from a hard dick, plowing into me vigorously.

When I arrived home, the lights were dim in the hallway and living room. Our bedroom was pitch-black and I could hear Maverick snoring as I made my way inside. Slipping out of my heels, my feet sank into the soft carpet and I released a sigh. *Home, sweet home!* As my eyes adjusted to the darkness, I gazed at Maverick's silhouette. My big, brawny husband was curled beneath the covers in a deep sleep, but not for long.

A soothing shower was what I needed to get the burst of energy that was necessary to play the role of aggressor in bed.

Maverick usually initiated sex, but tonight I had to atone for the sin of going behind his back and firing Tamara. Tonight I'd have to put on a hell of a performance. Suck his dick down to the hilt. Lather up his balls with my tongue. Pinch his nipples while riding him. Talk extra dirty in his ear, making sure to include at least one of the filthy fantasies that always prompted him to go crazy and completely ravage my insides.

I hated it when Maverick was upset with me, and so tonight, I would do whatever it took to get back on his good side, even take it in the ass if that was what he wanted, even though anal sex was something I did not find particularly pleasurable.

In the shower, warm water sprayed my body from multiple angles, making me feel pampered and relaxed as it cascaded over my shoulders and ran down my back. In my mind, I reviewed the day. The best part had been sending that annoying Texas cheer-leader packing. Judging by the disbelief in her eyes, she wasn't accustomed to being rejected. Later, when the cameramen and the rest of the crew were packing up their gear, I noticed Josh engaging her in a secret exchange. I assumed he was comforting her until her rage-filled, accusatory eyes turned to mine. For a good ten seconds…maybe longer, that bitch stared daggers at me.

Why was Josh coddling her? He didn't owe that Texas slut an explanation for why she'd been booted from the show. There was no earthly reason why Doralee was still hanging around after she'd already been filmed taking the walk of shame down the corridor. All she needed to know was that her food sucked and she was out of there. Yet Josh had felt compelled to tell her that it had been my decision—not his—to get rid of her. There was no plausible reason for him to have confided that information to her.

Apparently, the culinary executive producer of my show was not only racist, but also devious. I'd definitely have to watch his sneaky ass from now on.

After toweling dry, I slathered on Chanel Coco Mademoiselle body lotion, a scent that drove Maverick wild. I slinked into the bedroom, my naked body soft and shimmery, and then slid into bed. Mav's back was to me. I threw back the duvet and discovered that he was cocooned inside the top sheet, and no matter how hard I tugged, I couldn't unsnarl him. Giving up on the notion of touching his bare skin, I ran my hand gently across his sheet-covered shoulder, allowing my fingers to delicately skitter downward over the curvature of his muscled arm.

Changing tack, I ran my hand along the length of his back, and when he still hadn't responded, I smoothed my hand over his hip and down his thigh. He lay there motionless, but I was aware that he was awake. I could tell by the rigidity of his body. Could hear hostility and anger in the sound of his breathing and felt waves of resentment emanating from him.

Determined to entice him into a forgiving mood, I reached over and groped for his dick, which should have been pulsing with readiness, but instead, it was hidden beneath the sheet, defiantly shriveled and limp. He squirmed away from my wandering hand.

"Mav!" I whined his name and then awkwardly began caressing his hipbone and thigh, stretching out my fingers to get to his groin, determinedly trying to bring his dick to life.

"Stop." His voice came out soft and sleepy, but there was a cold finality in his tone that unsettled me.

Stop! Since when did my libidinous husband ever turn down sex? "What's wrong, babe?"

"I'm tired."

"You don't have to do anything except lie there; I'll do all the work." Eager to feel his dick swelling and stretching inside my mouth, I yanked at the sheet vigorously, but it was tucked around his body tightly, practically mummifying him. "Come on, babe. You know you want it." I licked my lips with the realization that once I swirled my tongue around the head of his dick, Maverick would begin helplessly moaning and groaning, no longer able to resist me.

Suddenly, he sat up and ripped the bedding away from his body. For a moment, it seemed as though he was about to get rough with me—toss me around—and fuck my brains out. But instead, he stood up, stalked across the room, yanked open one of my dresser drawers and proceeded to grab bunches of my neatly folded lingerie, carelessly flinging panties and thongs down to the floor.

"What the hell?" I clicked on the bedside lamp.

Maverick whirled around and I was stunned to see what he'd grasped from my drawer. Giving me the nastiest smile I'd ever seen on his face, he said, "If you want to get off, you better use this." He returned to bed and thrust my favorite dildo in my hand.

Speechless, I stared at the object in horror. It wasn't a secret that I had adult toys—we sometimes played with them together—but the malicious manner in which he'd rebuffed my sexual advances was rather unnerving.

"Maverick," I said softly. "You made your point. I get it. But is it necessary to be so disrespectful?" I released the dildo and it hit the thick fabric of the duvet with a thud.

Maverick flopped down on his side of the bed, picked up the pink dildo, and flung it at me. "Man, go fuck yourself!"

I've never been the wimpy type. I would describe myself as being more like a tigress than a kitten. But I was so caught off guard by Maverick's seething resentment, his unmitigated rage, I found myself apologizing. Profusely. Promising to rehire Tamara.

He pointed to the mound of my undies that he'd thrown on the floor. "Man, just clean that shit up and let me get some sleep."

I hopped out of bed. Without uttering a word of protest or scoffing at the audacity of him ordering me to clean up the mess he'd made, I began picking up the scattered underwear. I shocked myself by behaving in such a weirdly submissive manner. It was fucking surreal, like I was in the midst of an out-of-body experience.

Looking over my shoulder, I glimpsed Maverick settling back in bed. Getting comfortable, he gathered the covers around his body and then drew them up to his neck.

After I'd returned all my lingerie to the drawer, I crawled back into bed and stared at my husband in dismay. Maybe if I gawked at him long enough, he'd feel compelled to offer an explanation for his reprehensible behavior. Feeling my gaze and apparently annoyed by it, he pulled the bedding completely over his head. "Turn off the light," he demanded, his muffled voice, contemptuous.

I turned off the light and placed a cautious hand on his shoulder. "Can we talk about this?"

He uttered a sound of discontent and scooted as far away from me as possible, quietly informing me that there'd be no more talking tonight. No getting to the bottom of why he was so irate.

What the hell is going on? My eyes darted around the room as if the darkness held the answer.

I'd always considered it my prerogative to hire and fire the help as I saw fit, and although Maverick had complained, he'd never overreacted like this before. Dear God, it was bad enough that I was constantly worrying that my career was on the brink of collapse. Did I now need to be concerned that my marriage was headed for disaster?

I could feel Maverick leaning over me and stroking my face, and running his fingers through my hair. Believing that I was in the midst of a dream, and wanting to hold on to the good feeling for a little while longer, I kept my eyes closed. His hand moved away and I accepted that the sweet dream had ended.

"Cori."

My lashes fluttered lazily. Dreading any form of condemnation or criticism, my lids lifted begrudgingly.

"Cori, baby. I'm sorry," he said, sitting on the edge of the bed and clenching my hand. "I don't know what got into me last night. I was wrong to treat you like that. Being in negotiations for the new show is starting to mess with my head. I want that show so bad I can taste it."

"It's all going to work out, Mav," I said, sitting up in bed.

"I don't know. My agent flipped when he found out Tamara had been fired. He said she has a close friendship with Kevin Berenbaum's wife."

"Really?" Kevin Berenbaum was one of the executives at Maverick's network and Maverick had a lot of respect for the man. I couldn't imagine how Tamara had developed a friendship with his wife.

"Was Tamara the Berenbaums' chef before she came to work for us?"

"Kevin's wife and Tamara went to the same culinary school. They've been close friends for a long time."

"Kevin Berenbaum is married to a chef?"

"Actually, she was *his* chef until he married her. Now she's also the mother of his only son. She's about twenty-five years younger than him and he's crazy about her and their kid. My agent's so pissed about the timing of Tamara's firing. He can't understand why we didn't wait until after the deal was done."

A wave of guilt washed over me. "Wow, I had no idea about any of this. I'm surprised you never mentioned that you and Kevin had something in common, with both of you having great cooks for wives." I laughed a little, trying to bring some levity to the situation. But Maverick didn't crack a smile.

"Yeah, we married great cooks who never put on their aprons again once we put a ring on it." He gave a bitter laugh.

Feeling defensive, I said, "I don't know about Kevin's wife, but I'm not a kept woman. I work hard and wear my apron at the studio where I earn a living. I can't believe we're having a discussion about me cooking for—"

"Look, I don't want to put Kevin in a weird situation at home, so you need to fix this."

"All right."

"No games, this time, Cori."

"I don't play games."

"Yeah, you do. Even after I called and told you that Tamara was referred by a head honcho at the network, you still didn't give a damn about the position you were putting me in; you said you were going to hire a male chef."

I looked away in embarrassment because Maverick was right. "I had no idea that firing Tamara would cause this kind of trouble for you."

"Nor did you care. You can be really callous when you want to be. I've been thinking…maybe a trial separation would give us both an opportunity to reflect on the marriage."

Startled by his suggestion, I blinked rapidly. Then I laughed, although I was not amused. "You can't be serious."

"I'm dead serious."

"If you want to fucking separate, why'd you wake me up with tender caresses and that meaningless apology?" Growing angry, I threw a pillow at him. He didn't flinch as it collided and then bounced off of him. "Why, Mav?"

"I am sorry that I lost my temper with you. And…" He paused and swallowed. "I love you, Cori." He dropped his eyes briefly and then looked up and locked his gaze on mine. "But I don't like you anymore. I can't stand the coldhearted person you've become."

"Maverick, this is crazy. We can't separate. It'll ruin our brand and you know it."

"I don't care about the brand. I'm sick to death of the whole Mavcor thing. I'm not happy, and I haven't been for a long time."

His admission ripped through me like a serrated blade, cutting away at my self-worth and my womanhood. I winced and placed a hand on the nightstand to steady myself. "I had no idea you were unhappy."

"How would you know? After all, in this house, it's the Cori show. All you think about is yourself."

There was a modicum of truth in Maverick's words, but what he didn't realize was that I had no choice but to put myself first. If I hadn't, it would have been all about him, and I would have ended up without an identity. He was such a big presence, so beloved and revered, if I hadn't placed myself front and center, I would have been swallowed up by his image. Throughout our marriage, I'd been fighting to stay afloat. Fighting to keep up with him. Doing everything in my power to be deemed worthy of being his wife.

"If I only cared about myself, then why do I turn a blind eye every year when you go to Brazil?"

"That's part of our agreement."

"That stupid agreement doesn't benefit me in any way, but I go along with it," I yelled. "And what about your special birthday present that I get you every year? A selfish wife wouldn't go to the extremes that I go through to make sure her husband is happy. Listen, Mav," I said, lowering my tone. "I don't want to separate. We can work this out, together," I said pleadingly with tears running down my face. I snatched a tissue out of the fancy holder on my nightstand and tried blotting my eyes, but the tears kept falling.

"I'm so sorry, Cori, but this marriage is beginning to suffocate me," he said in a gentle tone.

"What about the baby?"

"There is no baby." The tenderness left his tone and was replaced with annoyance.

"The process is already in motion. There's a fetus that was created from my eggs and your sperm. I finally selected a surrogate the other day." The surrogate part was a lie, but I was grasping at straws, trying to hold on to my marriage.

"We haven't signed any papers, yet…no harm, no foul. Whoever you spoke to can keep it moving and be an incubator for another couple."

"But it'll look bad if you walk away, now."

"It's better to leave now than to wait after a kid has been brought into the world. As far as I'm concerned, that kid is a weird lab experiment. Any child that's chilling in a Petri dish and waiting for a womb doesn't stand a chance at a normal life."

I had no idea that Maverick held such disdain for a surrogate birth. Obviously, his mother had forced her outdated viewpoints on him. "Using a surrogate doesn't impact a child's mental or physical health."

"It's still weird as hell. Look, I've changed my mind. If we can't have a child the traditional way, then I don't want one."

My hands trembled and my voice came out shaky. "Okay, forget the surrogate for now. But for the sake of both our careers, we need to stick together."

"Are you saying we should stay together in name only?"

I was horrified by his implication of an open marriage. I'd already thrown away enough of my pride by giving him permission to go to Brazil once a year where he fucked as many Brazilian beauties as he could. After he returned home and after getting a physical where he was tested for STDs and HIV, our marriage resumed as if the vows hadn't been broken.

"Mav, all I'm saying is that neither of us can afford bad publicity, and after putting in ten years, we shouldn't simply give up."

Maverick folded his arms. "Ten years is long enough for me…I want out!"

Though I was on the brink of erupting into more tears, I remained calm. Maverick was not thinking rationally and I had to control my emotions in order to fix this shit.

"Mavcor is the brand of a wholesome and virtuous married couple," I reminded him. "A big part of your attractiveness to the network is based on the brand that we've both worked so hard to build. I doubt if any network would be interested in you if you were a bachelor or a separate entity from the Mavcor package."

"If memory serves, Mavcor wasn't out there on the football field winning back-to-back Super Bowl rings; I did that shit all by myself," he bragged, poking himself in the chest.

I brought up a few more reasons why separating would sabotage both our careers, but going back and forth with Maverick was getting tiring and I had to be on set in another hour.

"I realize I put you in a vulnerable position with the network, and I don't blame you for being upset, but I can fix it. I *will* fix it," I promised. "Tamara will be back to work tonight—I'll give her a raise. Everything is going to work out." Giving him a reassuring pat, I got up and began getting dressed. I sighed as I mentally prepared for a long day.

CHAPTER 6

The filming of the competitors waking up in their hotel rooms hadn't gone well. With cameras in their face, the group of nineteen had to repeatedly fake waking up. I had no pity for them. They wanted to be on television, and reshooting scenes was part of the game.

According to Ellie, who was present during the disastrous early morning taping, one of the male contestants—the dwarf—repeatedly and vigorously scratched his crotch, like he had a bad case of crabs. When he wasn't scratching his pubic area, he was clutching his dick as if holding onto a security blanket. He was asked to be mindful of keeping his hand out of his drawers, but it required about fifteen takes to get him to comply.

The producers loved kooky characters, but vulgarity and outright gross behavior was frowned upon.

Another contestant, fighting off sleep, had groggily insisted that she had to say her morning prayers before interacting with people, and of course, anything overtly religious was also a no-no. Her unwillingness to forgo her morning ritual had wasted an enormous amount of time, according to Ellie.

With the show running behind schedule, there was no point in me rushing to the Chelsea studio. I called the surrogate agency and told them to set up an appointment for me with a candidate who lived fairly close to Manhattan. Instead of meeting with the individual at the agency or at a hotel, I said that I preferred to conduct the interview at her home. I deliberately gave the impression that I wanted a more personalized visit, when in all actuality, it was more convenient for my driver to take me to the surrogate than to sit around waiting for her to get to the city.

With Maverick threatening to leave, I didn't have time to be picky anymore. I needed to get that bun in the oven ASAP. It no longer mattered whether or not the surrogate ate meat—as long as she didn't drink alcohol or use drugs during the pregnancy.

Her name was Sophia Gainer, thirty-three years old and Caucasian. I knew she'd be the perfect gestational carrier the moment I entered her modest apartment in the Bronx and spotted a box set of my DVDs among her collection. There was a framed poster of me in her kitchen and she had copies of my three cookbooks displayed on the countertop.

"I'm your number one fan, and I'm so delighted to meet you," Sophia gushed. "I can't believe that a big-time celebrity is standing in my humble abode."

"Your apartment is lovely," I commented.

"Thanks. I read about your inability to have a child on one of the blogs, but never in a million years did I think I'd be in the running to carry your child," Sophia said, grinning and shaking her head in disbelief.

So far, I liked Sophia, but I needed to dig a little deeper to find out if I trusted her to carry my child. "Aside from wanting to help women who are unable to bear kids, what's the other reason for your interest in being a surrogate?"

"Well, Cori, I'm a military wife. My husband, Paul, is overseas in Afghanistan. Our boy, Ryan, is twelve-years old and he wants to follow in his daddy's footsteps, but he aspires to go even further. He wants to become a general one day, and as a parent, it's my responsibility to help him achieve his goals. Ryan attends a prestigious military academy in Pennsylvania—on scholarship. He'll be in the eighth grade in September. Even though his education is covered, we have to pay for his room and board and other miscellaneous expenses. And those miscellaneous expenses can really add up. He's currently attending the academy's summer program, taking advanced classes. We had to pay for summer school out of pocket.

"I want my boy to have every opportunity in life, but the rising cost of education makes me concerned for Ryan's future. He's not guaranteed a full ride when he's ready for college and we don't have any money saved."

I nodded empathetically.

"As you're probably aware, the military doesn't pay a lot," Sophia continued. "With Ryan's expenses and trying to buy a house in Pennsylvania, so we can be close to our son's school, we can use all the financial support we can get."

Without a doubt, Sophia was a conscientious parent. I felt I could trust her to be as careful with my baby during gestation. But I had another question before making a decision. "How does your husband feel about your decision to become a surrogate—particularly for an African American couple?"

"He's all for it. He views it as another way for our family to serve our great country. As far as race goes, Paul and I don't see color."

Good answer!

Sophia and I chatted for another thirty minutes and then I checked my watch and stood.

"The agency will be in touch with you soon, Sophia."

"Will they let me know one way or another?"

I'd already made up my mind that Sophia was the one, and it was difficult keeping that information to myself. "You'll hear something by the end of the week," I assured her.

During the drive to Chelsea, I called Ellie and instructed her to rehire Tamara. "Tell her it was a huge misunderstanding and offer her ten thousand more a year. Let her know that Mav and I should both be home by eight tonight, and I'd like dinner served precisely at eight-fifteen. She can pick up a key from the concierge."

I was grateful that Ellie hadn't asked why I'd changed my mind about Tamara. Not that it was any of her business, but I wasn't in the mood to think about my marriage crisis, let alone discuss it.

Next, I called the surrogate agency and told them I'd decided that Sophia Gainer was a good fit and asked that the paperwork be emailed right away. I'd have to forge Maverick's signature, but that wouldn't be difficult. In the course of our marriage, I'd signed his name hundreds of times. Whether Maverick liked it or not, we were going to have a baby with a surrogate. It was easy for him to insist upon a traditional birth when he didn't have to worry about ruining his body.

In a matter of minutes, Ellie called me back to let me know that Tamara had accepted my offer. "She was really happy and grateful," Ellie said.

She was happy now, but her days were numbered. She'd be on the unemployment line the moment Maverick inked his new deal with his network.

"It's been crazy here on the set. Josh is in rare form," Ellie confided.

"What's going on, now?"

"They've been giving the kids ("kids" was our nickname for the contestants) champagne to enliven them, but they're all acting a bit too loopy to film. A lot of them aren't following instructions, and it's really slowing down production."

"Please don't tell me we're going to be working past eight because I can't stick around that long—not tonight." With my marriage in crisis, my dinner date with my husband was too important to miss.

"There's also a bit of a problem with one of the celebrity judges," Ellie informed.

"Which one?"

"Enrique. He canceled at the last minute, and I overheard Josh saying that he's probably hung over or lying up in bed with his latest boy-toy." I groaned. "They're waiting for his replacement to arrive."

"Who's the replacement?"

"I don't know, but I can find out if you want."

"That's okay. I'm cool with whoever fills the spot as long as it's not Baxter Sinclair with his funky cologne and heavy British accent."

"Should I remind casting of your aversion to Baxter?"

"They're well aware."

"Is there anything you need me to do until you get here?" Ellie asked.

"No, not really," I said absently. My mind was on Maverick and the seduction I planned for him after dinner tonight. Even though I wasn't exactly in the mood for anything kinky, desperate times called for desperate measures, and I couldn't think of a more appropriate time to make one of his filthy fantasies come true. I usually only contacted an escort service on Maverick's birthday, but I needed to indulge my husband's freaky desires. Too bad I couldn't delegate the task of contacting an escort service to Ellie, but some matters were simply too sensitive to entrust to others—even someone as loyal and discreet as my assistant.

The driver rolled into the lot, parked, and opened the door for me. Sauntering into the studio I wondered if the rest of the day would go smoothly or if there'd be one calamity after another. Having a heads-up on Josh's mood, I was braced for a long day of chaos and turmoil. But come hell or high water, I was getting out of there by seven-thirty.

The contestants were hanging around idly while a scene was

being set up, and they all murmured excitedly when I made my entrance. I waved at them without breaking my stride. I made it a point to limit my interactions with the kids. Not knowing them on a personal level made it easier not to care when they were discarded like yesterday's trash.

Ellie, along with my glam squad, hurried toward me. "Not now, not now," I said, holding up a hand. "I need something in my stomach before we get started."

"Would you like a green smoothie and walnut-kale salad with sesame dressing on the side?" Ellie quickly suggested.

"Sure, that sounds good."

While Ellie was busy gathering the ingredients from the *Cookin' with Cori* kitchen, I visited the website of an escort service I'd used last year on Maverick's birthday. The service was known for its discretion, so I didn't have to worry about anything being leaked to the press, but God forbid if a hacker ever got hold of their files. I shuddered to think of the scandal!

I perused the photos and studied the face of a Russian, blue-eyed blonde named Katya, who was listed as bisexual. Perfect! Pussy-eating bitches drove Maverick wild. I wasn't into chicks at all, but I went along with it strictly to please my husband.

I looked at Katya once more, and decided that there was something about her close-set, blue eyes that bothered me. I checked out some other girls on the site, but for some reason, I went back to Katya. Those eyes of hers made her appear to be extra freaky. If Maverick's nasty fantasies were satisfied, he'd be less outraged when he discovered that I'd taken it upon myself to go ahead with the surrogacy plans.

After keying in all the pertinent information and paying the fee for the prostitute to make a house-call, I logged out of the escort service site and checked my email.

I smiled when I noticed an email from the surrogate agency. I printed the form, signed both my name and Maverick's and then faxed the form back. My husband had better think again if he thought I'd allow our budding empire to crumble over his momentary bout of marital boredom.

After being stuck in that miserable warehouse yesterday, I had a newfound appreciation for my massive dressing room with its bright-pink desk, comfy furniture, and every amenity I could hope for. Despite the bedlam that was ensuing on the set, my world was peaceful.

There was a knock at the door that I assumed was Clayton, anxious to get started on my makeup. The door cracked open and an exquisitely beautiful face with flawless makeup peeked in. "Hi, Cori!" From her tone, one would think that the spectacular-looking, leggy woman who entered my dressing room was a dear friend of mine, but I'd never met her.

"I'm Azaria Fierro; we met at the Emmys after-party last year. It's an honor to get the opportunity to work on your show. I'm one of the behind-the-scenes chefs at The Food Network."

All of our behind-the-scenes chef positions were filled on my show, so this slut needed to get the hell out of my dressing room and go back to The Food Network.

"After working behind the scenes, you can imagine how super anxious I am about getting in front of the camera."

"What?" I scowled at her.

"I'm filling in for Enrique." She threw a wrist up to her forehead, mimicking nervousness, but there was nothing nervous about this aggressive woman. Today was her big break thanks to Enrique for not being able to hold his liquor. I wished I had a bucket of water for Azaria's thirsty ass. It was clear to me that she was going to try to outshine me and milk her moment for all it was worth.

From head to toe, she looked exquisite. Versace sunglasses pushed back on a head of thick, russet hair. She wore a stunning red dress that accentuated her prominent breasts and clung to her curves. A Chanel jumbo classic was slung over her shoulder and she wore strappy sandals that I could tell cost a mint. Who was this chick, and why had Josh replaced Enrique with her?

It was *my* goddamn show, and I didn't appreciate having female competition. Though I was attractive enough, I wasn't a sex goddess, not by a long shot. At five-feet-four and wearing a size eight, I was in excellent shape, but was considered short and chunky by Hollywood standards. Although I worked hard at being glamourous, I couldn't light a candle to this incredibly beautiful woman with a feisty personality to match.

"Nice meeting you, Azaria, but if you don't mind, I'd like some privacy before my glam squad team comes bursting through the door."

"Oh, sure," she said, looking wounded from my abrupt dismissal. Then, recovering quickly, she affixed a fake smile to her lips. "I simply wanted to say hello. I'll get out of your way. I'm sure your glam squad has their work cut out for them," she added snidely before exiting.

Fucking bitch! I snatched up my phone and called Josh. "I don't want that Azaria chick on my show. I don't understand why you'd pick an unknown chef to be a judge?" I barked at him.

"Azaria is a person to watch, and some of our network bigwigs are hoping to steal her from the Food Network."

"What do they plan to do with her?"

"There's talk about a pilot for a thirty-minute daytime show."

"But no one has ever heard of her."

"Well, between you and me, Enrique's going to rehab and she's a shoo-in for his spot on *Cookin' with Cori*."

"That damn Azaria must be sucking a lot of network dick to be able to slide in here and take Enrique's job."

Josh chuckled, and I could tell he was enjoying my anger. "Listen, play nice with Azaria. She knows people in high places," he cautioned.

I let out a sound of displeasure. "Last I heard, *Cookin' with Cori* was my show. That bitch better figure out a way to play nice with *me.*"

"Did Ellie tell you that we're shooting some promo stuff with you and the judges after we wrap up this evening?"

"No, she didn't. But I can't do it…not tonight. Mav and I have big plans, so you'll have to postpone the promo shoot."

"Everything has already been arranged," Josh whined.

"I have plans with my husband! Besides, I don't want to interact with that obnoxious Azaria Fierro."

"Okay, we'll shoot around you and fit your piece in with the rest of the cast. Are you available Sunday?"

"That's my day off and I'm not giving it up."

"Well, what's a good day for you?"

"Anytime except tonight and Sunday."

"Okay, I'll get back to you." Josh gave a groan, not bothering to hide his irritation with me. I didn't give a damn about his pissy attitude.

By the time Ellie returned with my food, I'd lost my appetite. I could feel it in my bones, Azaria was going to be a thorn in my side, and I had to figure out a way to get rid of her.

CHAPTER 7

That goddamn temperamental Josh was such a backstabbing cretin. I despised him with every fiber of my being. Well aware that it would infuriate me, he asked Azaria to stand in for me while the promo material was being shot. She was more than happy to take my place in front of the camera. She performed my famous double-flip of food in a skillet so damn well, I wondered if she'd been rehearsing my moves.

Unable to bear watching that hussy wearing my apron and standing in my spotlight, I agreed to work late. Azaria wasn't supposed to be in the promo piece at all, but she finagled her way into a segment with Norris Buckley. The two of them sat at a table, nodding and smiling as they enjoyed crispy fried chicken, okra, and buttery corn on the cob. Viewers would assume the judges were eating a meal that had been prepared by me, but the food had actually been whipped up by our in-house chefs.

Enjoying herself immensely, Azaria hammed it up, teasingly licking her fingers while batting her eyelashes. Even while acting silly, her stunning beauty was apparent. The bitch looked absolutely radiant and I hated her with a passion for outshining me.

When she began sultrily dabbing at her lips with a napkin, I couldn't take any more of her bullshit. "This is a family-oriented show—not a porn channel," I chastised.

The director of the piece had been grinning at Azaria and clearly enjoying her antics, but after I voiced my complaint, he sheep-ishly told her to tone it down.

Already, Azaria was pretty well-liked, and it was clear that I was going to have to hatch a hell of a diabolical plan if I wanted to get her ousted from the show.

We didn't finish shooting until after eleven. I'd been trying to talk to Maverick all day, but my calls had all gone to voicemail. I'd left several messages, informing him that I had to work late and apologizing for missing our dinner date. I didn't mention the escort because I had every intention of canceling the appointment with Katya.

Unfortunately, filming became so intense and hectic, I never got the chance to contact the agency. As close as I was with Ellie, I didn't dare assign her the task of calling the agency and cancel-ling. The decadent threesomes that Maverick and I occasionally partook in were nobody's business, and were something I'd take to the grave.

Upon arriving home, I heard a low groan coming from our bed-room, and I placed a hand over my heart as dread crept into my chest. A part of me realized there was a possibility that I might find Maverick in bed enjoying the little gift I'd mistakenly given him, but my heart sank anyway. I had hoped that after hearing my messages explaining that I'd been detained, he would have had the good graces to tip the hooker and send her on her way. But no…his selfish ass went right ahead and indulged.

Moving down the hallway, I was so upset, I didn't realize I was holding my breath until I began to feel lightheaded. I paused briefly, forcing myself to fill my lungs with large gulps of air.

I stood outside the closed bedroom door for a few moments

and listened to the moans and groans. Maverick was dead wrong, but what could I say when I was the one who'd arranged for the prostitute's services? Resisting the urge to flee, I bravely gripped the door handle and pushed it open.

The smell of sex was thick in the air. Maverick's and the hoe's comingled scent was so pungent, it made me queasy, almost causing me to retch.

The scene inside the bedroom hit me like a gut punch, nearly bringing me to my knees. But I kept myself standing upright by pressing a palm against a wall. My eyes went from the two naked bodies on the bed and then down to the jumble of clothes on the floor. Intermixed with Mav's clothes were a red dress, black panties and bra, and one red stiletto. The other stiletto had been kicked away from the pile of clothing and was resting against an African sculpture.

Unable to look at the disgusting scene that was taking place right before my eyes, I found myself focusing on the floor, staring at my husband's shirt, his shoes, his tie. Clothing that was as familiar to me as my own attire. Yet, the man who had shed those clothes seemed like a total stranger to me.

I'd always known my husband had unusual sexual desires, but I thought the fetishes he mentioned while in the throes of love-making were merely fantasies—twisted shit that he'd never act upon in real life.

But there he was on his hands and knees, his face pressed into Katya's buttocks.

It took a few moments for my brain to register what was going on. At first I thought he was burrowing his tongue deep into her asshole, and I gawked at him with my face crinkled in disgust.

Then I felt a huge wave of relief when I realized he was biting her butt cheek, not licking her ass. Had I stumbled upon my husband being in the midst of licking a dirty whore's ass, I'd never be able to stomach kissing him again.

The escort service had charged an exorbitant sum of money for Katya to fuck and suck my husband and to eat my pussy afterward. But here she was—doing a lot extra—facedown with her golden hair splayed out around the pillow, and her skinny ass tooted upward in Maverick's face.

Using both hands, he palmed her buttocks, holding them in place as he bit into her flesh.

Loving the savage mauling she was getting, she moaned, bucked her hips, and cried out in passion as Maverick covered her ass and thighs with bite marks. His wedding band glimmered mockingly in my direction.

I wanted to shield my eyes from the depravity. I attempted to run out of the room, but I was transfixed. My husband, the father of our unborn child, was groaning in ecstasy as he sank his teeth into a stranger's ass.

"Mav." I spoke his name in a quavering voice.

He didn't answer me. The way his body tensed and his refusal to respond informed me that my presence was an irritant. He was finally living out one of his twisted fantasies, and he was too caught up to stop and include me in what was supposed to be a ménage à trois.

He and the Russian whore were lost in their own world, completely oblivious or simply uncaring of the fact that I was standing in the bedroom gawking at them.

In shock and disbelief, I could hardly breathe. My voice came out in a choked whisper as I uttered his name, again. He continued to ignore me, and my body sagged against the wall.

I was near tears, but then I suddenly got mad. I became so enraged, I was about to leap on the bed and start fucking up both of them. I eyed the lamp on the nightstand, thinking about knocking Maverick over the head with it. Then I imagined myself yanking that skinny ho out of my bed and stomping the shit out of her.

On the verge of acting the damn fool, I had to remind myself that Maverick wasn't technically cheating. I had hired the prostitute that was writhing around in our bed.

My hands wouldn't stop shaking from the overwhelming urge to wring a bitch's scrawny neck, so I tried to convince myself to get a grip and focus. I glanced at my watch and smiled with jubilation when I realized that the two hours I'd paid for had elapsed. The bitch was working overtime and I wasn't having that.

I cleared my throat. "It's time for Katya to go," I said to Maverick, digging my nails into his shoulder as I tried to pull him off of the hooker. He was in a weird zone and was no longer behaving like a rational human being. Ignoring me, Maverick continued gnawing on her bony ass. Then he flipped her over and sank his teeth into her shaven pussy.

Apparently, getting her pussy lips ravaged was a major turn-on for Katya. "Oh! Ooo! Maverick, baby. You bite the cunt so very good for me," she purred in broken English.

"Her time is up, Mav. Get off of her!!" I screamed as I smacked the back of his head. Maverick and I had always been quite civilized and neither of us had ever laid a hand on the other, but he was out of control and clearly required being brought back to his senses in a physical way.

Like an animal fighting for its food, Maverick bared his teeth at me. "I told her I'd pay cash for an extra hour. You're fucking with the vibe, Cori. Are you going to join us or just stand there and watch?" he snarled, practically frothing at the mouth.

To witness my husband reveal such a primitive side of his nature was startling. I shuddered as I took several steps backward. "You know I'm not into that shit." My lip was turned up in disdain.

"You hired Katya so she could show me a good time, right?"

I nodded.

Katya twisted to her side and stared at me, waiting for my response. Seeing her face in person was unsettling. Those close-set eyes of hers weren't the true-blue they'd seemed in her photo on the website. Not that it mattered, but it seemed rather misleading that she was touted as having ice-blue eyes when they were actually a grayish-blue. And they were frighteningly close together, not attractive at all. For some odd reason her eyes reminded me of those of a Siberian husky. I hated those dogs. And I hated Katya.

"Cori, if you're not going to join in, would it be okay if Katya and I had some privacy?" Maverick asked in a pleasant tone.

It was a reasonable request, I supposed, but I felt like I was in an altered state of reality as I awkwardly left the room. At first I stood outside the door, wondering what the hell had just happened. Then I started debating whether or not I should go grab a knife from the kitchen and go back in the bedroom and start slashing up both their asses.

I made my way to the kitchen, but instead of picking up a sharp knife, I ended up leaning against the island, swilling organic wine straight from the bottle. When the wine didn't calm my nerves, I started working on the plate of chick pea salad and creamy avocado spaghetti squash that Tamara had set aside for me.

There was a terrific punch of flavor in the meal, but I couldn't enjoy it. Not with Maverick committing adultery right down the hall. I dropped my fork on the plate and gazed longingly at the knife block on the counter. Though stabbing Maverick in the heart was tempting, I had too much to lose and couldn't allow myself the pleasure of murdering my husband.

The next morning I awoke to the feeling of Maverick's hard body pressed against mine, blanketing me with his heat. With an arm wrapped around my waist, he had molded himself to my spine. His hot hands roamed my body; his fingers seared my skin. Adrenaline flooded through me and I became wet. But when I opened my eyes and realized we were in the guestroom, I remembered the travesty of last night, and I jabbed him in the ribs with my elbow.

"Don't fucking touch me! I was forced to sleep in the guestroom, and you have a lot of nerve crawling in bed with me," I hissed with my back turned to him.

"Why're you so upset? You hired that escort, not me."

"We were supposed to have a threesome, Mav! But I had to work late. I had the shittiest, most grueling day, ever…and then I had to come home to more bullshit."

"But it was your idea. You set the whole thing up."

"If you had listened to any of the messages I left, you would have heard me tell you to tip the damn hooker and send her on her way. I planned to reschedule at a later date when we could all have fun together."

"My bad." He massaged the back of my neck, trying to get me in the mood, but my body stiffened. "Babe," he whispered, inching up on me from behind, pressing his hard-on into my ass. "I had a long, exhausting day at work, too. And when I finally got home, Tamara had an awesome meal waiting. I dug in and wasn't paying any attention to my phone. I really expected you to walk through the door at any moment. When Katya arrived, I figured you'd be right behind her."

I turned around and faced him. "But the way you were acting… growling and biting her. What was that about?"

"You're exaggerating. I wasn't growling." Mav said, laughing.

"Okay, what the hell was all that biting about? It wasn't exactly sensual. You were going at that girl with such ferocity, it was disturbing. Your teeth marks were all over her body."

He shrugged. "She asked me to bite her. At first I thought she was kidding, but she repeated the request and told me she loved having her ass and pussy bit."

"You didn't have to do it, though."

"You know me, always a gentleman, willing to give a lady what she wants."

I glared at him.

"Look, I did what she requested. The chick went crazy, begging me to bite her titties and everything else. I was hesitant, but then I got into it." He leaned closer. "You want me to bite your pussy, babe?"

"Fuck, no, you perverted animal."

"Come on, Cori. Let me bite your pussy. There's nothing wrong with a little experimentation. After ten years of marriage, we need to explore more."

"Kiss my ass! I'm not letting you bite me." Appalled, I tried to get away from him, but he held me tight. "Let me go, Mav. The driver will be here to pick me up in thirty minutes. I have to get ready."

"Can't I get a quickie?" he asked, stroking his dick.

"No! You had more than enough sex last night."

"But I'm still horny."

"Jerk yourself off or take a cold shower."

"Last night with Katya was only about sex. I want to show you my feelings. Don't you want to feel how much I love you?" He took my hand in his and then brought it up to his lips, covering it with soft kisses. I made the grave mistake of looking into his eyes, and my anger instantly melted and was replaced with an unexpected wave of affection.

"Mav, I'm late. I don't have…"

Before I could finish the sentence, his mouth abandoned the

top of my hand and found its way to my neck, and then down to my collarbone. A mixture of irritation and excitement surged through me as his hot mouth sought out my breasts. I could never resist Maverick's lips on my body, and I let out a breath of resignation as I surrendered to him.

I wanted to reach for my phone on the nightstand and text Josh and let him know that I'd be running late today, but with Maverick whispering lustfully and rubbing on my pussy, I relinquished the idea. It was my show, and I'd get there when I got there, I told myself as I spread my legs.

I grabbed Maverick by the shoulders as he pumped dick into me. I opened my eyes and watched the muscles in his arms bulging with every stroke. God, how I loved his strong, beautifully sculpted body. After all these years of being together, I still adored my husband and experienced fireworks and all kinds of explosions whenever he made love to me.

"Do you forgive me for fucking that whore last night?" he murmured as he drove his curved thickness inside me, stroking deeply and caressing my most sensitive places. "Do you forgive me?" he repeated.

I nodded.

"Don't nod your head; say it!"

"I forgive you for fucking that whore last night," I whimpered as sparks of electricity popped off inside me. He began pounding my walls and my toes curled as a familiar warm feeling began to flood my system. On the verge of an orgasm, I cried out his name.

"Can I fuck her again?" he requested, taking advantage of the fact that my brain had turned to mush.

"Yes, baby," I responded, but I didn't mean it. I was in the moment, merely saying what he wanted to hear. Feeling good, I threw the pussy at him, humping and working as hard as he was—desperately trying to get there. Then I felt it. A sensation akin to hot lava gushing through my bloodstream. "Oh, Mav; oh, baby!"

"You ready to cum on this big dick, Cori?"

"Mmm-hmm," I whimpered, almost there.

"Is your pussy juice gonna run down my dick and drench my balls?"

My husband had such a filthy mind and he loved talking dirty, but I was so close to the finish line, I was no longer capable of speaking coherently. I could only grunt out responses.

"I told Katya I was going to let her lick your cum off my nuts. Are you good with that, babe?"

Needing to concentrate on my orgasm, I ignored his question.

"Is it okay if Katya comes back over?"

Maverick could be annoyingly persistent, and for the sole purpose of shutting him up, I uttered in frustration, "Yeah, okay."

Finally, I felt explosives beginning to detonate, and an incredibly intense orgasm skyrocketed through me. "Yes. Mmm. Oh, God, yes!" I screamed the words.

Then Maverick let go. He'd been holding back, waiting for me. At the moment of his climax, he exclaimed, "I'm gonna fuck the shit out of both you and Katya tonight."

Half-crazy from coming, I joined in, ranting and raving about how good he was going to fuck me and his whore. But it was only talk. I didn't mean it. Maverick had to be out of his mind if he believed I'd ever allow that Russian bitch to get back in my bed, again!

CHAPTER 8

I arrived on the set an hour and a half late, and Josh was having a fit over having to film out of sequence for the second day in a row.

"We need you on the set, like, now, Cori," he said with a neck roll.

That bastard had tried it! I couldn't believe Josh had the audacity to bark at me in front of the crew. For his sake, he needed to be grateful that the kids were off-set and hadn't witnessed him disrespecting me. If they had been around, it was highly likely that I would have come out of my nigger bag and cursed him out the way Grandma Eula Mae used to curse out her daughters and grandchildren after she started getting senile.

Mistaking her twin daughters (my mom and my Aunt Chloe) for the hoes that used to work for her back in the day, Grandma Eula Mae would launch into shocking diatribes laced with generous amounts of foul language whenever my mom or Aunt Chloe gently tried to coerce her away from the stove. She was constantly setting off the smoke detector, but that didn't stop her from standing in front of the stove for hours on end cooking up a bunch of bullshit. It was such a pity that she'd lost her amazing cooking skills with the onset of dementia. But you couldn't tell her that she wasn't still the best cook in Philadelphia.

Once when my mom and aunt attempted to escort Grandma Eula Mae out of the kitchen, she yanked away from them and grabbed a huge skillet and began her rant:

"If you black-ass, tar-baby bitches don't get your stank, cum-dribbling coochie holes out of my kitchen and get back upstairs, you'd better. Instead of flapping your thick liver-lips at me, you need to be wrapping them around the dicks of those peckerwoods that paid good money for your services. Now, get the hell out of my muthafuckin' kitchen before I knock some sense into your nappy heads with this here skillet! Get on up those stairs and cater to my customers."

Then she mumbled under her breath, "You heifers need to be grateful that I don't allow nigga men with their big ol' horse dicks inside my establishment. If I let nigga men get ahold of you, your pussy holes would be stretched out of shape and not worth a plug nickel."

Startled, my cousins and I would giggle uncomfortably whenever Grandma Eula Mae forgot she was our grandmother and lapsed into the role of a hell-raising madam. My mother and aunt, however, didn't find it funny. They loathed being reminded that their fine educations and refined ways had been purchased with whorehouse money.

In her final year, as her mental status seriously began to decline, Grandma Eula Mae no longer recognized any member of the family. She mistook my cousins, our mothers, and me as being part of her stable of whores. She would unleash scathing recriminations upon us, her words generously peppered with the vilest profanity I'd ever heard. From listening to my grandmother, I had learned to curse like a sailor, and therefore, Josh was lucky that I'd only given him the finger as I made my way to my dressing room.

If he talked to me one more time out the side of his neck, he was going to get cursed out, Grandma Eula Mae-style.

Gina was inside my dressing room waiting for me. "Morning, Cori. How you feeling?" she asked as she pulled out a flat-iron from her overstuffed work bag.

To be honest, my life sucks! My husband wants to bite a Russian bitch's pussy on a regular basis and additionally, he wants me to participate in the freak show. He wants me to lay back and watch while she licks my cooch juice off his balls.

If I had told Gina the truth about how I was feeling, she would have possibly fainted. So, I simply said, "I'm not having a good day, thanks to that prissy bitch, Josh. It would behoove him to keep his distance from me, today."

Not wanting to get in the middle of beef between Josh and me, Gina wisely refrained from commenting and merely murmured a sound of understanding. As she worked on my hair, Clayton tapped on the door and came in.

"Sorry to barge in on you, Cori, but Josh is having a hissy fit. He said he needs you on the set ASAP. He wants me to get started on your makeup right away."

I didn't like having two people working on me at the same time, but not having a legitimate excuse to go against Josh's wishes, I sighed and nodded in solemn acceptance.

While Gina and Clayton hovered over me with curling irons, makeup brushes, and other beauty tools, my thoughts wandered back to my marital problems. Before I'd left for work this morning, Maverick had confided that he felt completely obsessed with the idea of unleashing his inner freak on Katya. It was on the tip of my tongue to suggest that he get psychiatric treatment, but after giving the idea a little more thought, I changed my mind.

We were part of a culture where surgeons and well-respected medical doctors were known to snap selfies while posing with celebrities who were lying unconscious on operating tables, and there was no way I could trust that a psychiatrist wouldn't run to TMZ with Maverick's perverted sex secrets. If word got out that the beloved, All-American golden boy, Maverick Brown, was going around leaving teeth marks all over a hooker's body, his career would be over. And there was no doubt in my mind that my reputation would be tarnished along with his. As much as I loved Maverick, I wasn't willing to go down with his sinking ship.

In retrospect, I wished I hadn't selected Katya from the dozens of photos that the escort agency provided on their website. I didn't like the bitch's Siberian husky eyes, and I should have followed my gut instinct and skipped past her photo. It took a really demented bitch to encourage a man to put teeth imprints all over her body and beg him to treat her like she was literally a piece of meat.

Never in a million years would I have imagined that my husband had some sort of carnivorous fetish. Maybe his proclivity toward biting had something to do with our vegetarian lifestyle. Perhaps if I reintroduced meat back into our diet, Maverick would get over his newfound biting obsession.

There was a knock on my dressing room door.

"See who it is and get rid of 'em," I ordered.

Clayton and Gina both rushed to the door, eager to see who had the balls to interrupt my beautifying procedure. Clayton opened the door to a mere crack.

"Yes?" he said.

"Can I speak to Cori, please?" said a female voice.

"She's busy," Clayton growled.

"Let her in," I said, curious to see who the hell had the gall to disturb me while I was getting ready for the camera. I was surprised to see the sole black female contestant. I didn't know much about her. Couldn't recall her name or whether or not the meal she had prepared yesterday was appealing. But it took a lot of chutzpah for a contestant to knock on my dressing room door. I looked her over. She was sweaty. Her makeup was dripping off her face and her hair had shriveled into a fuzzy Afro on one side and was limp and lifeless on the other. Maybe this impromptu visit wasn't boldness at all, but was actually an act of sheer desperation.

"My name is LaTasha. I'm from Philly, like you," she said, beaming at me.

"What can I do for you LaTasha?" I replied brusquely, ignoring the fact that we shared the same hometown.

"Being that we're both Philly girls, I figured you'd understand how embarrassed I'll be if I'm seen like this when the show airs." She waved her hand along the fuzzy side of her head. "They've had us holed up in one of the kitchens for hours, practicing various recipes from your last cookbook. There's so much heat in the kitchen, my hair and makeup is ruined," LaTasha complained.

Wondering what in the hell she expected me to do, I looked at her like she was from another planet.

"We're not allowed to bring anything with us from the hotel, and…" She trailed off and cut an eye at Gina. "I was wondering if I could borrow your flat-iron so I can bump my hair."

"Hair and makeup services are only for judges and the host—not contestants," Gina reminded her.

"I know, but look at me!" Grimacing, she gestured toward her hair. "I have to do something about this mess before I go back on set with all those cameras pointed in my face."

"I don't bring extra equipment with me, and I can't let you borrow any of the equipment I use on Cori's hair. That's unsanitary."

"That's okay, let her borrow one of the flat-irons," I said, sounding kindhearted. Being an African American woman, LaTasha was a reflection of me, and I simply couldn't have her hair looking a hot mess on my show.

LaTasha spilled all kinds of tea while she was working on her hair. She gave us the rundown on all the other contestants. We found out that Touki, the petite Asian girl who smiled so sweetly during filming, was a demanding diva off camera. Yancy Dunlap, the Baptist preacher, tended to spread malicious gossip that kept the contestants bickering and at each other's throats. The dwarf was a nasty little bastard who masturbated so much, he was given a single room. Becca, the Wiccan chick who dressed in all black, had a drinking problem, and when intoxicated, she would threaten her cast mates with witchcraft powers and had even alluded to casting spells on the judges and me.

All of that was interesting, but I was more interested in learning who was talking smack about me.

LaTasha had a bad case of diarrhea of the mouth, but I appreciated getting a heads-up on who my enemies were. According to LaTasha, the gay guy, Lionel, who always wore bright-yellow suspenders, said he wouldn't dream of serving my heart attack food to any of his friends or loved ones. He went as far as to say that unhealthy slop like mine should be banned from television.

Although I was deeply offended, the yellow suspenders-wearing guy had a point. I no longer ate the artery-clogging crap I was famous for, either. But still, how dare he come on my show and openly criticize my food among the cast? Colorful and zany, he was proving to be an interesting character on the show. But I didn't care how entertaining he was—Yellow Suspenders was not going to make it to the final four. He could kiss his culinary dreams goodbye; he was out of here!

LaTasha also disclosed that all the female contestants had the hots for Michelangelo, the super-hot black guy, but he didn't pay any of them a bit of attention.

"We think he has a big crush on you, Cori," LaTasha divulged.

"Me?" I was pleasantly surprised.

"He's never said anything, but he's constantly flipping the pages of your cookbooks, committing all your recipes to memory. And you should see the way his face lights up when you arrive on set."

With the insanity going on in my life right now, and having a husband who was obsessed with a skinny Russian prostitute, my ego could use a boost. Discovering that Michelangelo appreciated a chocolate sister with curves lifted my spirit.

Today, the contestants were being challenged to prepare my special meatloaf, glazed carrots, collard greens, and biscuits and gravy. I didn't care if Michelangelo's dish looked like dog food and tasted even worse; he could count on me for a high score.

LaTasha got her hair under control and then touched up her makeup, but instead of leaving, she continued to hang around my dressing room, talking nonstop and helping herself to the coffee that was on hand for Gina, Clayton, and Robin. Personally, I didn't touch the stuff. Green tea was all I needed to get my day started.

Weary of hearing LaTasha's mouth, Gina rolled her eyes. I could tell she was ready to toss LaTasha out of the dressing room. But I found the bubbly contestant to be amusing and encouraged her to give me the four-one-one on all the contestants.

She gulped coffee and smacked her lips. "This stuff is good. You're lucky they don't make you drink the swill they give us. The coffee we get tastes like dishwater. I thought it would be free-flowing considering all the pressure we're under on the show, but the contestants only get one measly cup per day."

I grunted in a noncommittal way. I didn't want LaTasha to get the idea that venting to me would change her circumstances. Suffering was a part of being a contestant on a cooking reality show. Everyone knew that.

Of course, I'd gone from college straight to culinary stardom and had no idea what it was like to struggle. I didn't want to know, either.

"At the hotel, I was sharing a room with Heather. She's pretty cool," LaTasha said. "From what I could tell, she didn't have any annoying quirks or bad habits. Seems like the moment I got used to her, they moved me to a different room with a new roommate. And they did it in the middle of the night. Seems like the people who run this show…" She paused and looked at me sheepishly. "I'm not referring to you, Cori, but those other folks seem to want to keep us disoriented and tired. Now, I'm sharing a room with Becca. Since we're not allowed to leave the hotel, the only way I can get away from her and have some personal space is to either hang out in the group suite or go sit in the lobby. It's like we're in jail."

LaTasha and her complaints were starting to irk me. "You were well aware of the rules when you signed on."

"But you don't understand. That Wiccan chick is such a disgusting slob. I complained to some of the show's staff that she has a drinking problem, but instead of them trying to help her, they give her more alcohol. There's more booze being offered than coffee, and coffee is what we need since they only allow us a few hours of sleep every night."

I'd heard that the contestants were all sleep-deprived. The producers felt that keeping them frustrated and in a state of confusion would trigger high emotional responses when they were involved in stressful situations during the show. To have a contestant completely lose it during an episode ensured great ratings. But they always edited out anything that made the show look bad.

"Becca shouldn't be on this show," LaTasha continued. "She should be in rehab. Sharing a room with her is starting to mess with my sanity. Did I mention that last night she was walking around the room butt-ass naked and drinking straight out of a whiskey bottle? Having her as a roommate is abusive. I shouldn't have to look at her naked, boney ass every night. Could you put in a word and try to get me another roommate?"

I was through being nice to LaTasha. I'd provided her with

beauty products, hair equipment, and coffee. Now she wanted preferential treatment. I swear, give a bitch an inch…

I was on the verge of telling LaTasha to go kick rocks when Ellie walked in.

"Listen, you need to rejoin the other members of the cast," I told LaTasha sharply.

"Why? It's so warm and welcoming in here. And I was having a good time," LaTasha whined.

"You've worn out your welcome, now beat it," Clayton said with bass in his voice.

LaTasha guzzled down her coffee and grudgingly headed for the door. Once she'd exited, Ellie gave me a look that I couldn't read.

"Bad news?" I asked softly.

"Not really." Ellie's eyes shifted from Clayton to Gina.

"Do you two need privacy?" Gina asked.

"Yes, could you and Clayton excuse us for a few minutes," I said in an apologetic tone.

After Gina and Clayton left us alone, I turned expectant eyes on Ellie. "Well?"

"I spent several hours wooing your surrogate. And after appealing to her womanhood, I told her that you feel awful that you can't carry your own child and that you'd feel much more comfortable with the situation if you and Maverick got to know her on a more intimate level. It wasn't easy, but I convinced her to forgo protocol and have sex with your husband," Ellie announced, looking downward.

"Yes!" I squealed, pumping a fist into the air. I felt bad dragging Ellie into such a bizarre mess, but I had no choice. If my husband wanted to squander his seed around, then dammit, I wanted to get a baby out of it. There was no reason for him to know that Sophia was our hired human incubator and had already been paid a portion of her fee to carry *our* child. I'd make him believe she was another bimbo from the escort agency. And when she turned up pregnant... Well, I'd cross that bridge later.

Feeling jubilant, I hugged Ellie. Having been witness to my jealous rages when the thots of the world so much as smiled at Maverick, Ellie gazed at me curiously. She had no idea why I was setting up my husband with the surrogate. Actually, it wasn't any of Ellie's business. She was paid to be my mouthpiece and to handle my business. I wasn't obligated to provide her with an explanation for my actions.

CHAPTER 9

"I smell burned onions." I crinkled my nose as I ventured to Becca's workstation while TV cameras captured the moment.

"I had the flame up too high, and now I have to sauté them again," Becca replied, her face flushed with embarrassment. Or perhaps her reddened complexion was the result of too much alcohol.

There was a lot to hate about a cooking competition show, but contestants particularly loathed having to discuss the components of their dishes while in the midst of cooking. It was distressing to try to appear knowledgeable and personable while keeping an eye on whatever they were preparing. And my cheeky comments didn't help to ease their discomfort.

"Are you using truffle oil?" I inquired in a horrified voice as she drizzled oil into the pan.

"Um, yes. I could have sworn I tasted truffle oil during the blind taste test," she babbled nervously.

"Did you? Hmm," I replied mysteriously, causing her to question her palate.

We were filming the cooking segment of the show, and as host, I was expected to criticize some of the contestants and praise others. It didn't matter how their food tasted; it was simply the luck of the draw.

I roamed over to my next victim, the Baptist preacher. After learning that he was a troublemaker, it gave me wicked pleasure to see him struggling with the glaze for the carrots. Frowning, I stared at his pan. "There's an awful lot of sugar in there, and it's making your glaze sticky and thick. You may want to add another ingredient."

"Should I add more butter?" he asked anxiously.

"You'll have to figure it out, but you're going to have to do it fast. Otherwise, you might be getting the boot tonight. You've been hanging on by a thread, but you're still here. Could it be that your congregation back home has been sending up prayers for you?"

"That's right, Cori. My congregants and I love the Lord, and we strongly believe in the power of prayer."

"That's good, but you may need more than prayer to keep you from having to take that walk of shame, tonight," I added spitefully. Church-going folks annoyed me with their hypocrisy. Always talking about prayer and loving the Lord, all while treating their fellow man like crap.

The preacher nodded miserably and then tossed in more butter, which was a bad move. He had more than enough butter in the pan. What the dumb fuck needed to do was add the tablespoon of lime juice that my recipe called for. If he studied my cookbooks as much as he gossiped, he'd be aware of that.

Hamming it up for the cameras, I stood next to the preacher and spoke in a theatrically hushed and solemn voice. "Reverend Dunlap has been in the bottom three twice. One wrong move tonight, and his luck will have finally run out. Will he be joining the cheerleader from Texas, Doralee Harper, who was the first to go?"

The reverend was an emotional wreck by the time I left his station and sauntered over to Ralphie, who my favorite contestant this season. I wanted so badly to pull him aside and tell him that he would never make it to the final four if his black foster mother didn't lose some weight and do something about her four missing front teeth. But the rules prohibited me from giving the kid a heads-up on the social aspect of the competition.

"How's it going, Ralphie?" I inquired in a somber tone that was meant to distress him.

"It's going well, Cori," he said confidently as he sliced shiitake mushrooms. "My meatloaf is in the oven, and my biscuits are going in next."

I scrutinized his glazed carrots that were simmering in a pan, and tasted them. "Mmm. Tastes exactly like mine. Maybe better," I added. "But I'm curious, what are you going to do with the shiitake mushrooms you're slicing?"

"They'll be added to the gravy."

"So, you tasted mushrooms in my gravy?"

"No, but I wanted to add a component that would give your gravy a little more flair." He smiled impishly.

"That's a brash move, and I hope it pans out for you, Ralphie."

"I'm sure it will!"

Ralphie was self-assured, not boastful, and I liked that about him. It was a shame that Josh considered him an embarrassment to white people and wanted him gone.

I meandered over to handsome Michelangelo while he was rhythmically moving to music in his head as he reached for a whisk. The director decided he wanted a different take of him grabbing the whisk, and he wanted more dance moves involved. The shot took about forty minutes, and by the time they got it right, I'd forgotten the clever line I'd planned for the hot hunk. The only thing that came to mind was, "Do you always dance when you cook?"

"I do a lot of different things when I cook," he responded in a tone that sounded suggestive, to say the least.

At a loss for words, I fanned my face and said, "Whew, it's getting hot in here." There were chuckles from the crew and the other contestants, and Josh gave me the thumbs-up signal. He liked the sexual innuendoes and playful bantering.

"I see you're working on the gravy. May I have a taste?"

"Suuure."

The way he stretched out that one word, seemed to make it ooze with sex. Instead of focusing on his gravy, my gaze was fixed on his luscious lips, and I had to force myself to tear my eyes away. Of course the camera caught it all—my seemingly girlish infatuation and his sensuality and charm.

The way the competitors, the cast, and crew all applauded when the take was finished, you would have thought that Michelangelo and I had successfully completed a torrid sex scene.

After I'd collected myself, I decided that the scene with Michelangelo needed to be reshot. As an accomplished chef, I didn't want to come off looking like a love-struck schoolgirl. I didn't want to personally deal with Josh, and so I texted Ellie and told her to let him know that I wasn't satisfied and wanted to redo the scene with Michelangelo.

I continued my rounds in the kitchen, treating some of the contestants nice and being downright vicious to others—like Lionel. As usual, he was wearing those yellow suspenders that he thought were cool and quirky, but I detested.

Lionel's biscuits tasted amazing, but I told him he'd put too much salt in them. I also informed him that his meatloaf was so dry, and that it was hard to get down. Pretending to choke, I coughed exaggeratedly until one of the contestants handed me a bottle of water.

Looking distraught, Lionel turned several shades of red, which pleased me immensely. The bastard said my food should be banned from TV and I was going to do everything in my power to send him packing.

Josh refused to reshoot my critique with Michelangelo and I refused to vote Ralphie off the show. Following the script, Azaria Fierro wrinkled her nose when she tasted Ralphie's gravy, and said that the shiitake mushrooms gave it a strange, bitter taste. The other judge, Norris Buckley, criticized Ralphie's biscuits, claiming they'd been left in the oven too long, and that the texture wasn't quite right.

Their critique was utter bullshit. Ralphie's food was cooked to perfection, and I was willing to go to bat for him. I'd never claimed to be a perfect human being; Lord knew I had my faults, but I'd always had a soft spot for the underdog. Since it was *my* show, my vote vetoed both Azaria's and Norris's, and I was able to keep Ralphie safe for the time being.

The preacher's prayers were answered, and he was saved. Lionel and his suspenders, however, were sent home.

Surprisingly, we wrapped up at a decent hour. Leaving the studio at seven-thirty in the evening seemed early compared to most nights. In a hurry to get home, I asked the driver to take the quickest route to my apartment.

I'd informed Maverick in a text that Katya was booked and I had set him up with someone else. I told him that the woman I'd arranged for him to fuck wasn't into chicks, so there wouldn't be a threesome. I was rushing to get home so that I could speak with him face-to-face before he went to meet Sophia at the hotel.

He'd have to meet all the escort bitches in hotels from now on. No more hoes in our apartment—that was my new rule.

When I arrived home, Maverick was relaxing in boxers and drinking a beer. He was watching a tape of himself interviewing a rookie football player.

"Why aren't you dressed? Sophia is probably at the hotel by now."

"I'm not going."

"Why not?"

"I'm comfortable with Katya; I'd rather wait until she can fit me into her schedule."

I was stunned. "You're willing to be put on the waiting list of a sleazy hooker who barely speaks English?"

He took a swig of beer. "It's not like I'm hard up for sex. Why're you so eager for me to get with another woman? Seems strange, especially since you're not participating."

"I never really enjoyed that girl-on-girl mess. I only did it for you."

"Well, thanks. I appreciate it. We usually do threesomes on special occasions, and I'm finding it weird as hell that out of the clear blue, you're suddenly hiring escorts like you're ordering take-out. First, Katya, and now this chick, Sophia. What's going on, Cori?"

I swallowed guiltily. "Well…I'm going to be so busy with the show for the next few months, I wanted to make sure that you don't feel neglected. Is it a crime for a woman to want to keep her husband sexually satisfied?" I caressed the back of his neck. "Sweetie, I'm a member in good standing with the Chasity Martin escort service. If you cancel at the last moment, I could lose my membership altogether."

"So what! There're lots of escort services in New York. Besides, it's not as if we hire escorts more than a few times a year."

"But…I thought you wanted to see Katya again."

"I do, but I was hoping you'd be able to make arrangements with her outside of the agency. Pay her under the table."

"I could make that proposal to her, but I don't have any way of communicating with her other than through the agency. After I make contact with her again, I'll be sure to get her personal information. In the meantime, if you want me to keep my gold membership with Chasity Martin, then be a good boy and go meet Sophia."

"What does Sophia look like? Is she hot like Katya?"

I hesitated. "I wouldn't refer to her as hot, but she's attractive. She looks more like the housewife type."

"Why'd you pick a boring housewife?"

I shrugged. "Change of pace. If you're not feeling Sophia, then make it a quickie…or tell her that all you want to do is talk," I said with forced laughter as my insides twisted with anxiety. If Maverick didn't take his ass to the hotel and pump some dick into Sophia, my plan would be totally screwed.

CHAPTER 10

here wasn't a married woman in the world, besides me, who could get a peaceful night's sleep while her husband was across town in a hotel fucking another woman. But I honestly wasn't concerned about a plain-Jane like Sophia stealing my man. My only concern was Katya, with her freaky self. But since I had no intention of ever using her services again, there was no reason to waste another thought on that bitch. With a contented smile, I plumped my pillow and waited for sleep to overtake me.

For some unknown reason, my mind was filled with memories of Grandma Eula Mae. I could clearly hear her voice in my head, divulging secrets about her scandalous past. No one in my family was aware that she'd left a box of cassette tapes in the attic. Voice recordings that she'd begun when she first noticed she was becoming forgetful. She'd wanted her family to understand what her life was like back in the old days.

Despite enjoying the benefits that her immoral lifestyle had provided, my mom and Aunt Chloe considered their mother's past to be an embarrassment. Had they known of the existence of the tapes, they would have destroyed them. They had rewritten Grandma Eula Mae's history, telling their acquaintances that their mother had accrued her sizeable income from her restaurant, hotel, and by making good investments.

According to the fairy tale they'd invented, Grandma Eula Mae

hadn't started out selling dinners in her whorehouse; they pretended
that she had sold dinners from her modest home. According to
their story, a well-to-do client who loved my grandmother's soul
food gave her the down payment to open her restaurant.

Grandma Eula Mae's tapes contained so much wisdom, it was if
she were guiding me from the afterlife. It was a passage from one
of the tapes that was enabling me to rest so peacefully tonight.

*In many cases, my earnings came from not only the customers, but also
their wives. It sounds crazy, but I've counseled more enraged white women
than I can count. In a fit a jealousy, angry white women have come to
the colored section of town to fetch their husbands.*

*Not wanting to lose the husband's business and not wanting the irate
wife to cause a commotion in my establishment, I have taken many a surly
wife aside and educated her on the ways of men.*

*I remember how I had to hold my temper when Marge Tasker slapped
me dead across my face after I told her I was helping to hold her marriage
together by providing whores for her husband. I came close to whooping her
ass, but I realized if I beat on that cracker, I'd have to do some hard time.*

*She was huffing and puffing like she was the one who had been slapped,
and after she calmed down, I explained the true nature of men to that
simple-minded woman. I told her that it was a man's nature to have
perverted urgings. I assured her that her husband's strong sex drive had
nothing to do with a lack of love for her. I asked if she wanted him jumping
on top of her two and three times a night and doing unspeakably filthy
things to her. Looking horrified, Marge shook her head.*

*After I informed her that there was a nasty, animalistic side of men
that a clean-living woman like herself should never have to experience,
she began to get the point. With curiosity getting the best of her, Marge
and many other white women, paid good money for me to let them in on*

menfolk's dirty secrets. I entertained them with naughty tales. Not one to betray the confidentiality of my clientele, I never named names. I simply told them that there was a great deal of cunt-eating, dick-sucking, butt-fucking, titty-slapping, and other forms of perversity that went on within the confines of my establishment.

After the women gasped and turned deep shades of red, I'd ask if they'd put up with such immorality in their bedrooms, and of course they whole-heartedly rejected the idea of engaging in anything other than missionary sex once or twice a week.

I convinced them to let the whores do the dirty work while they led clean lives. And to this day, I am convinced that whores save marriages. When menfolk feel the need to splash their ejaculation into a woman's face, they don't want to have to look at that woman across the breakfast table the next morning.

Women who try to curtail their husband's nasty habits are asking for trouble. A wise woman would turn a blind eye to her spouse's extramarital shenanigans and be thankful that he's not forcing his angry pecker between her lips or trying to shove it inside that very private and restricted back entrance that the Lord did not design for penile penetration.

Imagining poor Sophia enduring Maverick's depravity instead of me, I turned on my side and contentedly drifted to sleep. I awakened briefly when Maverick came home and slid into bed beside me. I felt him brush aside the hair that had fallen into my face, kissing me softly on the cheek. As he placed an arm over me, I snuggled close to his warm body. We lay together, entwined and at peace.

It was a good thing Sophia's husband was deployed in Afghanistan. Otherwise, how would she explain the teeth marks that I was certain now marred her body?

I woke up at five and tiptoed around the dim bedroom, trying not to awaken Maverick as I got ready for work. In case he wanted to share the sordid details of his evening with Sophia, which I wasn't interested in hearing, it was best to get out of the condo before he woke.

Dressed in tights, an oversized, shapeless top, and a pair of flip-flops with my pink Birkin bag looped over my arm, I looked like a homeless person who'd stolen rich lady's handbag. But I didn't care. As long as my team did their jobs and made sure that I was camera-ready in time for my segment, I could look a hot mess when I walked out of my apartment.

Prepared to dart out of the bedroom, I pulled a turban over my head to hide my tousled hair, but to my dismay, Maverick sat up and grinned at me.

"That housewife you hooked me up with was a feisty little freak," he announced.

I plastered on a tight smile. "Glad you liked her."

"I'd like to get with her again."

"It was a one-time deal, Mav."

"No. You and I have a new arrangement, now. I have needs that you don't want to fulfill, so I should be able to have a prostitute whenever I want. I prefer Katya, but if her schedule is still full, then I want you to book Sophia, again," Maverick said, as if it was perfectly normal for a wife to set up fuck sessions for her husband.

"I'll see if Katya's free, but don't get used to this, Mav. You can have one more session with Katya, and then we have to resume our original agreement: you can have new pussy twice a year, during Carnival and on your birthday. You've already exceeded your limit."

"I was hoping we could raise the limit to, uh, maybe six times a year."

"I don't think so. You're getting carried away!"

"Only kidding," he said and flashed that cute smile of his, which made me sigh in relief. I planned to make up a story about Katya being deported back to Russia, and of course, after I put my plan in motion regarding Sophia's unplanned pregnancy, he'd be scared straight. Out of fear and contrition, he'd keep his dick in his pants. At least for a while.

I walked over to a jewelry box where I kept some of my less-expensive pieces. I perused my collection and my eyes settled on a pair of diamond studs that I'd never worn and never planned to. I believe they'd been inside a swag bag from some stupid event I'd attended. I slipped the small box inside my Birkin bag.

"I'll see you tonight," I said and kissed Maverick on the cheek.

"You'll be seeing me a lot sooner than that."

I gave him a curious look.

"You forgot?"

"Forgot what?"

"Don't you remember that your boy, Josh is paying me a lot of money to make an appearance on your show."

"Oh, right." I'd been juggling so many important life situations, I'd completely forgotten that Josh had come up with the idea of including Maverick at the judge's table as guest-judge. Josh felt it was a great idea to have the man who enjoyed my food on a regular basis on the show, weighing in on the decision of which contestant had best replicated my dishes.

I dreaded having Maverick on the show. If Josh thought I was a diva, he was going to find out today who the true diva was in this marriage. After he saw the array of outlandish demands listed on Maverick's backstage rider, he'd think of me as being down-to-earth and a joy to work with.

I laughed to myself imagining befuddled staffers running around attempting to find Maverick's favorite pumpkin seeds that were seasoned with soy sauce and a sprinkling of exotic spices. The healthy snacks that Maverick enjoyed were special-ordered from a Zen center in Detroit and prepared by Buddhist monks. If Josh's gofers had waited until the last minute, they would never find any of Mav's food requests. Maverick would respond by pitching a bitch. Displaying the aggression he used to exhibit on the football field, he was likely to topple tables, kick shit, and maybe punch somebody if he didn't get his way. A part of me wanted my husband to reveal his spoiled-brat ways, which was the complete opposite of his golden boy persona. Maybe if he exposed his true nature, everyone would stop insinuating that I was so lucky to be married to a football icon.

"I'll see you at around noon, babe," Maverick said.

I waved and left the bedroom.

It was bad timing for Maverick to be on the set today. I had so much to deal with, and his presence would stifle me. Sophia was scheduled to have the embryo implanted in her uterus today, and I needed to make sure she kept her appointment at the fertility clinic. Her pregnancy would seal the deal on my marriage for the next eighteen years. Maverick cared too much about our brand to even think about walking out on me and our child.

Sitting in the backseat of the Town Car as my driver cruised along the streets of New York, I sent Ellie a text, instructing her to accompany Sophia to the clinic today. *I want Sophia to feel special, so use a car service. When the procedure is finished, see to it that she stays on bedrest for the remainder of the day. Treat her like fucking royalty. Rub her feet, order takeout, and spoon-feed the bitch if necessary.*

When I arrived at the Chelsea studio, I was informed by an androgynous-looking person from the production staff that there would be a delay in filming today.

"Are you sure?" I asked, not knowing whether I was talking to a man or woman.

"Yes, Josh told me to let you know."

"Damn," I murmured. I had planned to surprise Sophia with a visit after work—woo her with the diamond studs that were much too small and cheesy for me. I couldn't accomplish that if I was stuck filming late into the night.

"What's the cause of the delay?" I asked.

"One of the kids had a meltdown at the hotel."

A part of me was relieved that a contestant was showing their ass and holding up production. The fact that someone was having a meltdown meant that once again, Ralphie would be spared from getting the ax. I didn't care what Josh wanted; I was going to insist that the troublemaking contestant be kicked off the show no matter how good or bad his or her food was.

"Who's having a meltdown?"

"That skinny kid, Ralphie."

"Ralphie?" I couldn't imagine impish, self-confident Ralphie having a meltdown. "What happened?"

"No idea," the staffer replied. "I heard he's threatening to walk. Josh is at the hotel trying to convince him to at least finish filming today."

Most of the emotional breakdowns among the cast were caused by too much drinking or heated arguments between cast mates. Ralphie didn't drink and he got along with everyone, so I was perplexed as to what the problem could be. Although I was genuinely concerned about him, there was no way I was going to miss out on an opportunity to show myself in a favorable light. I gazed around the large room and noticed one of the cameramen laughing and goofing off during the delay. "Are there any cameras at the hotel?" I asked the androgynous staffer.

"Not that I'm aware of."

"Okay, thanks." I pulled out my phone as I rushed toward my dressing room. I called Gina, who was no doubt using this free time to take a cigarette break. I told her to round up the rest of my glam squad and to get to my dressing room ASAP.

Next, I called Josh. "Whatever is going on with Ralphie, I'm sure I can fix it. Give me ninety minutes to get myself together. Have the camera crew meet me at the hotel. Filming me talking Ralphie down from the ledge, so to speak, will make good TV. Don't you think?"

"It would make excellent TV if that scrawny piece of white trash would open the damn door to his room and allow someone to reason with him."

"What exactly is going on?"

"We got a call late last night. His foster mother had some sort of diabetes crisis and was hospitalized. From the kindness of my heart, I personally informed Ralphie, and I also assured him that we'd keep him updated on her progress. But that little ingrate insisted on leaving the show to be by his so-called mother's side," Josh said with undisguised revulsion.

"If the kids were allowed even minimal contact with their family, maybe we wouldn't be having this issue," I said.

"Rules are rules and he's being irrational. He locked his roommate out of the room and he's having a meltdown because he can't afford to buy a plane ticket home—not with the twenty-dollar daily stipend the show pays the talent." Josh sounded cocky and insensitive.

"But I thought we paid for the contestants' flights back home."

"We do. But only after they've completed their contractual obligations."

"I'm confused. You don't even want Ralphie on the show, so why are you forcing him to stay?"

"He's free to leave after I get the footage of his shocked face when the judges vote him off tonight."

"That's low, even for you, Josh. You'd actually do that to him while he's going through a personal crisis?"

"I'd do it with a smile," Josh retorted. "Locking himself in his room and refusing to communicate is not going to resolve the issue. He's being childish, and he's costing the network a ton of money by holding up production."

"Well, if you knew how to talk to people, maybe he'd cooperate."

"I'm not kissing Ralphie's ass or anyone else's," Josh spat. "It was on the tip of my tongue to tell that little twerp that all he had to do was cook one more meal and then he'd be free to pack his bags. But of course, I couldn't do that. Giving him a heads-up about his doomed fate would take away the element of surprise."

I hated the fact that the producers and not the judges had the final say in who stayed and who got sent home. I could intervene every now and then, but Josh was so hell-bent on getting rid of Ralphie, it wasn't likely I could save the poor kid.

"I can get through to him, Josh. I know I can. But you're going to have to bend the rules a bit and allow him to video chat with his family. Is his mom conscious? Is she able to talk?"

"Hell if I know—or care," Josh said irritably.

"I need you to arrange for him to Skype with his family."

"Does that heathen family of his even have Internet access?"

Running out of patience with Josh, I sighed in exasperation. "Everyone has a cell phone these days. Your attitude toward Ralphie's family seems downright racist."

"I'm sick of you pulling the race card, Cori. I'll have you know, my ex-boyfriend was black."

"Loving black dick doesn't mean you're not racist," I retorted.

"You can be such a vile person sometimes, Cori."

"I call it like I see it."

"Whatever," he said sullenly.

Winning even a small battle with Josh filled me with satisfaction. "I'll be at the hotel as soon as possible," I said and then hung up.

It warmed my heart to think of the high ratings we'd get for tonight's show, and it was entirely possible that I'd be nominated for an Emmy after the performance I planned to give.

CHAPTER 11

Although the show was technically unscripted, there were writers on the payroll who crafted plot lines, twisting and tweaking footage to create conflict. But the writers had nothing to do with the important scene that was about to be filmed between Ralphie and me. It had been created from my own brilliant mind.

Looking sensational in a Balmain jacket and a black-and-gold-toned beaded mini skirt, I arrived at the hotel and rode the elevator to the tenth floor with the camera crew trailing behind me.

Holding an iPad, I knocked on the door. "Ralphie, it's Cori. Can I speak with you?"

"Unless you have a plane ticket for me, go away," he responded harshly.

I frowned.

"Don't worry, that part will be edited out," one of the camera guys assured me.

"I have wonderful news for you, Ralphie. Your mom is doing much better."

He opened the door and I eased inside with the cameras closely behind.

"I hope you're telling the truth," he said, his voice raspy and his eyes red from crying.

"I wouldn't lie about something as serious as your mom's health. But you can see for yourself." I tapped the screen of the iPad and a few moments later his foster family appeared. A group of rough-necks were gathered around his foster mother's hospital bed.

"Mama!" Ralphie cried out excitedly. "Mama, I was so worried. They told me you were in a diabetic coma."

It was weird as hell hearing a white boy sounding exactly like a black person from the 'hood.

"I wasn't in a coma. I had a seizure, but I'm doing much better, baby," the woman in the hospital bed answered. "What's this I hear about you leaving the competition?"

"I got upset when they wouldn't let me speak with you."

"I wasn't in any shape to talk while the doctors were working on me, but as you can see, I'm doing fine. You don't have to worry about me; I have the whole family by my side. I want you to get back in that kitchen and burn! Cook the way yo' mama taught you. I want everybody in America talking about the way my boy throws down."

"I will, Mama. I promise, I'm gonna make you proud. I'm gonna win this thing…for you!"

"Now, that's my baby boy!"

Ralphie sniffled and wiped away tears of joy. The love I witnessed between Ralphie and his foster mother was strong and sincere. I was genuinely touched and had to dab at a tear trickling from my eye.

After Ralphie finished chatting with other family members, he disconnected from Skype and gave me a hug.

"Thank you, Cori."

"Ralphie, I've watched you put your heart on the plate in every cook-off since the beginning of this competition."

"I try."

"Tonight, I want to see you try even harder. You need to put both your heart and your soul on the plate."

"I will. I promise."

"No more talk about going home?" I asked with a lifted brow.

"No," he said, shaking his head. "I was feeling emotional about my mama, but now that I know she's okay, I'm going to give two hundred percent."

"You've got stiff competition, Ralphie. Getting to the top five isn't easy, but if you use all the knowledge your foster mother shared with you, I'm sure you'll get there. With your talent, you could make it to the top two!"

"You think?"

"I'm sure of it. Especially if you keep cooking the way you have so far."

Ralphie brightened somewhat and I stared at him, angling my head in a way that ensured the camera would capture my best side. In a serious, melodramatic tone, I said, "But my belief in you won't mean a thing if you don't have faith in yourself."

For added drama, I gripped his shoulders and gazed soulfully into his eyes. "Do you believe in yourself, Ralphie? Do you believe you can win this competition?"

He nodded. "I know I can. I'm not going anywhere, Cori. I'm gonna kick butt in that kitchen tonight!"

"That's the kind of confidence I like to hear," I said and gave Ralphie a high-five.

I was proud of myself. Today, I'd done the writers' job for them. The footage of me comforting a distraught Ralphie and then convincing him of his greatness was an award-winning performance. I could feel the Emmy in my hand.

My job was done, and I gave the camera crew the thumbs-up, letting them know we had enough footage of my one-on-one with Ralphie. I would personally see to it that heads rolled if anyone dared to cut out even a millisecond of the segment of me successfully restoring Ralphie's faith in himself.

Although Josh was livid with Ralphie and wanted him gone, there had to be a way to convince him to keep the kid around a little longer. In my opinion, America would be quite entertained by Ralphie and his foster family.

Phone in hand and prepared to call Josh, I exited Ralphie's room. I was startled to see Michelangelo coming out of the room next door. He was wearing clingy briefs and my eyes inadvertently wandered down to his ample package, which couldn't be ignored. The man was fine as fuck. He was built like a damn gladiator and had the audacity to have the added bonus of a big dick. It didn't seem fair for one man to possess so many attributes.

Dressed in only his underwear, it was obvious he was slipping out of another contestant's room. I wondered whose bed he'd recently finished heating up. I thought about LaTasha, but quickly shook my head. She seemed a little too rough at the edges for a suave brother like Michelangelo. He was probably the kind of black man who only dealt with women outside of his race. He'd probably been running through all the white coochie on the show, as well as the Asian and Hispanic chicks. I reminded myself to get the tea from LaTasha since she seemed to know all the dirt on her fellow cast mates.

As Michelangelo swaggered toward me, I gave him a snide look. "Do you always roam the corridors in your underwear?"

"It's not the way it looks."

"How is it?"

"My roommate was going through some sort of crisis. My man was flipping out, and so when Becca knocked on the door to find out about the commotion, I stepped outside the room to speak to her privately. That's when Ralphie locked me out. Becca was kind enough to let me chill in her room. Her roommate, LaTasha, didn't seem too thrilled about me being there, so I chilled in the suite where the contestants mingle together. I was relieved when Josh called and said I was free to return to my room. Is Ralphie okay, now?"

I nodded and Michelangelo knocked on Ralphie's door.

I'd completely forgotten that Josh had said that Ralphie had locked his roommate out. Ralphie and Michelangelo was such an odd pair, I couldn't even picture them conversing, let alone rooming together.

As Michelangelo raised his fist to knock on the door again, Ralphie swung it open. "Sorry for acting like an ass," Ralphie apologized.

"It's cool, man. Is everything okay on the home front?"

"Yeah, my mama's doing much better."

I glanced at Michelangelo's tight butt as he entered the room, fanned my face, and then made my way toward the elevator. If contestants weren't off-limits, I would have found a way to sneak Michelangelo out the hotel and invite him out for drinks, simply for the opportunity to stare at him and drool.

t was nerve-wracking having my husband on set. I found myself constantly worrying about his comfort level. Male diva that he was, I expected Maverick to drive everyone nuts with his over-the-top demands. But thanks to Azaria's constant flirting with him, he was content and on his best behavior. I wasn't the least bit worried about any hanky-panky between the two of them. Sure, my husband was going through a whore phase, but he didn't want any ol' whore—he was only interested in the rare type that enjoyed being bitten. Azaria didn't strike me as the type to let someone maul her.

While the contestants were filming individual confessionals, I used the downtime to hide out in my dressing room and make an important call to the fertility center. I was elated to find out that the transfer of my fertilized egg to Sophia's womb had gone well. Hopefully, I'd be able to personally thank her later tonight.

Coddling a bitch for nine long months didn't sit well with me, but I had to do what I had to do. After hanging up from the clinic, I got Sophia on the phone and asked how she was doing. She gave me a sarcastic laugh that I found annoying.

"Are you okay? Did anything out of the ordinary happen?" I inquired with concern, despite the fact that she was pissing me off with her inappropriate laughter.

"No, nothing out of the ordinary happened. I simply did what I seem to be doing a lot lately."

"I don't understand." Sophia and her cryptic messages were starting to bug the shit out of me.

"Last night, I spread my legs for your pervert husband, and this morning I spread them for the doctor who inserted you guys' baby inside me. I'd say that all of it is out of the ordinary, don't you think?"

I flinched when she referred to Maverick as a pervert, but since she was successfully carrying our child, I figured I could overlook her attack on my husband's character. "So, everything went okay?" I asked, although I was already aware that the procedure had gone perfectly fine.

"As well as can be expected," she said with a sigh. "The doctor wants me to stay off my feet for a couple weeks, but I can't take that kind of time off work. I have bills to pay."

She was hinting for more money. I couldn't believe she had the gall to try and swindle me.

"You were paid a large sum up front and you'll get the remaining balance when the baby's born."

"The money you paid me is being used as a down payment on a home. I didn't expect to be laid up for two weeks, but since that's what the doctor ordered for the safety of *your* child, I hoped to be compensated. But if you want to risk a miscarriage, then so be it."

Sophia had seemed so sweet when I'd initially met her, but she was now showing her bitch colors. But I sucked it up. "I'll pay you two thousand dollars for the time you miss from work."

She made a huffy sound as if she thought she deserved more money. Then she said, "The doctor was concerned about the bite marks on my inner thighs."

Is this bitch trying to blackmail me? "What did you tell him?"

"I didn't tell him anything. But when he insisted on giving me a tetanus shot, I allowed it."

"Could that be harmful to the baby?"

"No, he assured me the baby will be fine. But I'm not so sure if I'm okay."

"I'm sure you'll survive a few little love bites."

"Yeah, physically. But who knows the degree of emotional damage your husband has caused me?"

I pretended not to notice the threat that was clear in her voice. Sophia was a sneaky bitch, and I'd have to be mindful to stay several steps ahead of her until she delivered. After she popped the baby out, I planned to give her my entire ass to kiss.

There was a twist of the door handle followed by a sharp, authoritative knock.

I was tickled that Josh had tried to barge in, as usual, but was thwarted by the double locks on my dressing room door. *Ha, ha, bitch!*

"Cori! I need you on set right now," he yelled from the other side of the door.

I wasn't due to film for at least two hours. "Why?"

"Open the door so we can speak privately." He sounded flustered.

Geez! What has Maverick done? I assumed someone had forgotten to stock my husband's dressing room with bottled rain water or perhaps he hadn't been provided with the exclusive brand of organic kale chips he'd requested. No doubt, Maverick was showing his ass, and Josh wanted me to calm him down. I sighed as I made a mental note to never, ever invite my spouse to my show again.

Reluctantly, I opened the door, and Josh charged in, red-faced and clearly agitated. He was clutching sheets of paper.

"What's wrong?"

"We have a situation with one of the kids."

Thankful that Maverick wasn't acting up, I exhaled. "Don't tell me Ralphie is having another meltdown."

"No, this time it's Michelangelo."

"Really? He's usually so cool and calm. What's the problem?"

Josh shook his head grimly and took a seat in my pink cushioned chair that was reserved solely for me. I gave him a forbidding look that he chose to ignore. "Michelangelo had a mishap with a blender, and tomato sauce exploded all over his face and his clothes. The cameras didn't get the full incident, and we've asked him to do a retake, but he refuses. Says he's here to cook and not to play the role of a buffoon."

"I can't blame Michelangelo for not wanting to reenact an un-flattering scene."

"I reminded him that he signed a contract stating that he'd follow the rules of the show, but he's threatening to walk out if we force him to make a fool of himself. Says he doesn't care if we sue him."

"And you want me to try and convince the guy otherwise?"

Josh nodded. "Remind him of this highlighted part of his contract." He handed me the papers and I perused them, shaking my head.

"Look, I already dealt with Ralphie this morning; I don't have the energy to put out any more fires. Don't you have people on payroll who're supposed to indulge the kids when they get huffy?"

"The contestants have tremendous respect for you, Cori. They want to *be* you. Now, use your influence and get Michelangelo to repeat the tomato sauce fiasco. Convince him that being covered in sauce is food art."

"This is low, even for you, Josh."

"It'll be good for ratings."

"It'll be terrible for Michelangelo's credibility as a chef."

"Who cares about his credibility?"

"He does!"

"Oh, fuck him! He's not that great of a chef."

"I disagree."

"Well, he's definitely not on the list to win the show."

"Who is?"

Josh gave me a snide look. "I can't divulge the show's secrets with you."

"Why not?"

"Look what happened to the Texas cheerleader after I told you she was a top contestant. You went over my head and got rid of her."

"She deserved to go. Josh, I really wish there was more integrity on the show. The people you select can't cook and I resent them using my name to gain entry into the culinary field where I'm well respected."

Josh looked at me pityingly. "What does it matter, Cori? No one cares about the winners of cooking competition shows after the first few weeks. Their cookbooks don't sell. They blow through their prize money on restaurants that have no clientele, and then they go back to oblivion, where they came from."

"Well, I'd like my winners to become household names—even if that means mentoring them personally. Don't you think it would make good press if we did some follow-up on the winners?"

Frustrated, Josh let out a groan. "Can we discuss this at a more convenient time? Right now we have a camera crew waiting to shoot a red sauce explosion."

"So, you want me to convince a self-respecting young man to make a fool of himself for ratings? You're asking me to help you ruin the image of someone who doesn't stand a chance of winning, despite his incredible culinary skills?" I shook my head. "I don't know how you sleep at night."

"You won't feel that way when you win your first Emmy."

After speaking the magic word, *Emmy*, Josh rose from my pink chair, looking confident that I'd do his bidding. I wanted to smack the smug look off his face. But picturing an Emmy in my hand, I followed him out of my dressing room.

I approached a tomato-sauce-covered Michelangelo, who stood seething inside his workstation. All the other contestants had been hustled off set and were sequestered behind the scenes.

Michelangelo had wiped the messy sauce from his face, but his apron and clothes were dripping red sauce. "Mike," I said, taking the liberty of shortening his long, pretentious name. "I understand why you feel that reenacting your blender disaster would be demeaning, but I see it as an opportunity for you to stand out from the rest of the pack."

"I refuse to be filmed, looking like a bumbling idiot," he said firmly.

I glanced down at the papers in my hand. "If you recall, when you agreed to appear on the show, you signed a strict contract that gave away all rights to how you'd be represented on the show."

"I didn't think the producers would deliberately try to make me look like a fool."

"This is what you agreed to," I said, and then read the highlighted paragraph aloud. *"The rights granted to Producer also include, but are not limited to, the rights to edit, cut, rearrange, adapt, dub, revise, modify, fictionalize, or otherwise alter the Material, and I waive the exercise of any 'moral rights.' I understand that my appearance, depiction, and portrayal in connection with the series may be disparaging, defamatory, embarrassing, or of an otherwise unfavorable nature, may expose me to public ridicule, humiliation, or condemnation, and may portray me in a false light."*

"I was so excited about being on the show, I barely read the contract."

"I hate to say it, but ignorance is not an excuse. Listen, it's your call. You can quit and the network will sue you. You'll be throwing away any chance of getting on the fast track of becoming a celebrated chef. But if you're smart, you'll embrace your blunder."

"How do I embrace an embarrassing tomato sauce explosion?"

"I don't know. Use your assets. You're a good-looking guy, so do something sexy. Lick the sauce off your fingers and say something clever. Listen, you have a real shot at winning this thing, Mike. Don't quit."

"You think so?"

"I know so," I assured him with an earnest expression.

"I trust you, Cori. So, all right, I'll do it," he conceded.

There was no time for Michelangelo to whip up another batch of homemade tomato sauce for the retake, and so he was instructed to pour a jar of Ragu into his blender. The cameramen moved in close, and I backed far, far away when he loosened the top of the blender and turned it on, full-speed.

"Oh, crap," he exploded as he was splattered with tomato sauce. Then he broke into a grin and swiped his face. He licked his finger and uttered, "Mmm, my sauce is too tasty to waste!"

"And...cut," the director yelled, and the crew applauded.

"Mark my word, that expression is going to trend on the day this show airs," Josh said with a big smile. "Hashtag, *My sauce is too tasty to waste* is going to take over social media."

Once again, I'd saved the day. I passed Maverick in the corridor as I made my way back to my dressing room. He grasped my wrist and whispered in my ear, "I used an alias and contacted Chasity Martin Escort service. They assured me that Katya is available tonight. I booked an appointment with her. Are you cool with that?"

"I suppose," I said reluctantly. "But not at our apartment, Mav."

"Not a problem. I already set it up to meet her at a hotel."

"Okay."

"You're the best, baby," he exclaimed, pulling me toward him and planting a big, sloppy kiss on my lips.

Onlookers gawked at us with admiration and uttered, "Aw, what a cute couple."

They had no idea that my husband was showing appreciation for the fact that I'd given him permission to fuck a bitch outside of our so-called perfect marriage."

Somehow, I had played myself and had ended up in an open marriage. A wide-open marriage! But I was determined to slam that door shut once I had our baby in my arms.

CHAPTER 13

When Maverick asked me to join him for a lavish, multi-course dinner at an Italian restaurant with a few of his cronies from the network, I had no idea I'd be sitting through a four-hour meal listening to endless talk about football. Kevin Berenbaum, one of the head honchos at Maverick's network, along with his lawyer and his management team, were trying to woo him into signing an exclusive deal that would lock him in for the next ten years. They wanted him to venture into covering other sports such as tennis, soccer, and golf, and to continue covering football.

Maverick didn't know shit about any sport other than football and basketball, but the execs didn't care; he was their golden boy. They figured that charismatic, handsome, and well-spoken Maverick could succeed at anything. Kevin offered him a salary that made my eyes nearly pop out of my head, but Maverick balked at the idea of taking on more responsibility.

"You guys are forgetting about my impending film career," Maverick said. "My agent is in the midst of working a deal to get me the main part in an action flick. I've always wanted to be a superhero," Maverick added with laughter, giving the impression that he wasn't serious about taking the role, but I was well aware that he had his heart set on being a film star.

It didn't matter that he couldn't act a lick…he simply wanted to put on a stupid costume and show off his muscles as he performed amazing feats on the big screen.

"You don't want to get involved with Hollywood," Kevin offered with a sage expression. "The film industry is a fickle business. One day you're the toast of Hollywood, walking red carpets and hob-nobbing with A-listers, then the next thing you're on the D list and nobody will give you the time of day. You have a great career with us, Mav. An investigative journalist won't be taken seriously if he's dancing around like a fairy in tights and a cape. I'd hate to see you throw away a lifetime career to hobnob with those phonies in Tinseltown."

"Yeah, but—"

Kevin cut Maverick off with the wave of his hand. "We plan to send you to Pamplona, Spain to not only cover the big sporting event but to also participate," Kevin said, pouring Maverick a glass of expensive tequila.

"What's in Pamplona, Spain…soccer? I hate that boring-ass sport. Nah, I'm not feeling it, Kevin, man. Soccer puts me to sleep."

"It's not soccer. We want to send you to Spain to run with the bulls. Strapped with a mic pack, you'll cover the story in an exciting, interactive way."

"What do you mean?"

"You'll report the event while running with the bulls."

"The hell if I will! I'm not running with any goddamn bulls. That's not even a real sport. What makes you think I'd do some-thing that stupid, and risk getting gouged in the balls?"

At that point, one of Kevin's flunkies put a glass of red wine in front of Maverick, trying to improve his mood and loosen him up. He offered me a glass as well, but I shook my head. The strong tequila was enough for me.

Our final course arrived, and I must say, I was very impressed with the way the chef had prepared a vegetarian version of every course that had been served for Maverick and me.

But Maverick, totally intoxicated, seemed more impressed with the two magnums of 2009 Bond Estates St Eden Napa Valley Red, and two bottles of 1942 Don Julio tequila that the network had spent a whopping $2,500 on.

Before the evening concluded, Maverick and Kevin were laughing together and shaking hands. "We have a deal, man," Maverick slurred as he drunkenly pumped Kevin's hand up and down.

A good wife would have intervened on behalf of her intoxicated husband and told him to wait and discuss such an important matter with his agent. But I didn't want my husband gallivanting around Hollywood with A-listers. I didn't want to risk him being cast opposite a megastar like Angelina Jolie or Halle Berry. I understood New York celebrities and knew how to deal with them, but those Hollywood hoes were a totally different breed. They didn't abide by any established rules. They'd claim your man as soon as they shot a love scene with him. Then before you knew it, he'd hit you with divorce papers and marry his costar-side bitch. She'd tie him down for life by adopting a bunch of foreign kids and then get knocked up with triplets. Your man would end up with eight or nine kids—all at the same time.

No, honey. Maverick did not need to be making any new friends in Hollywood.

Kevin's lawyer pushed papers in front of Maverick and with my encouragement, my inebriated husband signed his name, unwittingly agreeing to forget about becoming a film star, and staying his ass at the TV station in New York.

When we exited the restaurant, a horde of paparazzi were swarming outside the venue. Obviously, someone had tipped them off as to where Maverick and I were dining.

Having gotten what he wanted, Kevin Berenbaum didn't hang around. He dashed inside his waiting limo with his lawyer. His management team scattered in different directions, leaving me alone to guide my staggering husband to our car. The short walk to the car seemed like a long distance while in the midst of being hounded by the media with their ridiculous questions and asinine comments.

One photographer remarked, "Looks like you had too much booze, Maverick. Are you dealing with alcohol issues?"

Before I could formulate a sarcastic reply in my head, another photographer asked, "Are you planning on checking into rehab, Maverick?"

Maverick muttered something unintelligible, exposing himself to be as drunk as a damn skunk. Infuriated, I clutched Maverick's arm possessively and spoke for him. "My husband does not have a drinking problem. We were out celebrating a special life event and he overindulged. But what man wouldn't allow himself to have a good time after discovering he has fathered a son?" I flashed a victorious smile.

The uproar from the paparazzi was deafening as they asked a million more questions. "Are you pregnant, Cori? It's been reported that you're using a surrogate; is that true?"

"I don't have anything else to say at this time, but my husband and I will make an official statement after he sleeps it off." I laughed gaily and allowed the photographers to take a few more pictures of me as the driver helped Maverick into the car. "What I can say is that my husband and I have wanted a child for a very long time, and we're particularly happy that we're having a boy—a son to carry on the Brown last name as well as his father's sports legacy."

In the backseat of the car, Maverick was already snoozing. And that was fine with me. With Maverick dead to the word, I had an opportunity to call my assistant and speak openly.

Ellie picked up on the first ring. "How'd it go?" she asked.

"Perfect. The tip you gave the paparazzi worked out better than I imagined. The media will probably run with the Mavcor baby story in less than an hour, and my darling husband will wake up in the morning to the amazing news that he's going to be a father."

Hung over and grouchy, Maverick was taking longer than usual to get dressed for work. Luckily, I didn't have to film today and was looking forward to lounging around and having the apartment to myself. But the way he was slow-poking around and bothering me with a bunch of questions, was beginning to steal my joy.

Seeming not to know his ass from a hole in the ground, he kept asking me one question after another. First, he wanted to know if I'd seen his newest watch, a TAG Heuer Aquaracer.

"You left it on the hall table," I told him.

Then he asked me to make him a cup of coffee.

Damn! I got up and plodded to the kitchen. I wasn't his goddamn personal maid, and it felt like he was taking full advantage of the fact that I had the day off, trying to work me like a mule.

My network was trying something new this season. They were taking the kids on a field trip to Harlem, where they'd be filmed cooking in various home kitchens of the local residents. Having the kids compete outside of the normal environment at the studio and in unfamiliar houses seemed like a disastrous undertaking to me, but Josh thought it would give the show an intriguing new twist.

Josh had tried to get me involved in the bullshit, but I refused, and when he attempted to throw his weight around and insisted I join the cast and crew, I lost my temper and cursed him out. I wasn't about to sit up in some funky kitchen shooting the breeze and swapping recipes with some ol' bitch who probably cooked with old chicken grease she kept stored in a coffee can next to the stove.

After my tantrum, Josh saw things my way. With the magic of television, I didn't have to step foot into one kitchen in Harlem. I would be filmed later, sampling replicas of the food, prepared by our in-house chefs. And by plugging in voice-overs, it would seem as if I had appeared in the same segments as the contestants.

"Cori, my head is killing me and my stomach is upset," Maverick called out from his private bathroom.

"Take an aspirin or something." I was back in bed, propped up with luxurious pillows and secretly reading what the bloggers had to say about our pregnancy, and I didn't want to be disturbed anymore.

"I checked the medicine cabinet, but I don't see any in here."

Grudgingly, I got out of bed, again. I checked the medicine cabinet in my bathroom and grabbed a bottle of ibuprofen and tossed it to him. I whirled around to leave, but Maverick struck up a conversation, holding me captive.

"I can't believe Kevin went out of his way to keep me at the network for the next ten years. Hell, for the kind of money he offered, he didn't need to get me drunk with expensive wine and tequila." Maverick chuckled and fixed his lips in a crooked smile that I detested. He only smiled like that when he was feeling cocky and full of himself.

"Kevin's a smart man. He came out of pocket to keep that Hollywood producer from stealing you."

"As badly as I wanted to play a superhero, I'm not foolish enough to turn down millions of dollars to appease my ego. But then again, maybe I should have squeezed an extra ten million out of Kevin. After all the blood, sweat, and tears I left on the football field—"

The blare of my cell phone cut him off, thank God. Any minute, he was going to start quoting his football stats. Happy to escape having to stand there and watch Maverick slap aftershave on his face while he bragged about his former career, I hurried out of his bathroom and went to retrieve my phone from the nightstand.

Expecting it to be Ellie, I was surprised to discover it was the concierge of our building calling.

"Good morning, Mrs. Brown," the concierge said. "A package has arrived for Mr. Brown. It was hand delivered. I'd bring it up personally, but I'm unable to leave the front desk at the moment. If you'd like, I can bring it up when I get a break. Or I can put it aside until either you or Mr. Brown comes downstairs."

"Is the package light enough for me to carry?"

"Yes, it is."

"Then, I'll be right down to pick it up." My curiosity had gotten the best of me and I wanted to see what was in the package. I hoped that bitch, Katya didn't have the gall to send my husband a present. It was bad enough that they'd started seeing each other on a regular basis. Since I booked the hotels where they rendez-voused, I was well aware of their numerous hookups.

Wearing a plush robe and slippers, I dashed to the elevator and rode down to the lobby. When the doors opened, the concierge was standing there and handed me the package. During the ride back up, I ripped open the stylish wrapping and was impressed by the beautiful wooden box of Cohiba Luxury Selection Cigars.

I didn't know much about cigars, but I'd heard that a box of Cohibas cost around $4,000, and I doubted if Katya would spend that kind of money on a gift for a trick.

Beyond curious, I open the enclosed card and smiled with relief when I read: *Congrats, I know you're going to be a great father. Best Wishes, Kevin Berenbaum.* I doubted if Kevin had personally written the note, but it was a classy gesture.

In my head, I went over the pregnancy story I planned to tell Maverick, but as I exited the elevator, I was startled to find him standing outside our apartment, wearing only his briefs. I froze and briefly pondered the situation. I thought about stashing the cigars under my robe to buy myself more time, but the box was too big to conceal.

"Why'd you run out the apartment without saying anything? I didn't know what happened. I thought you'd been kidnapped or something." Maverick searched my face, waiting for me to explain why I'd suddenly gone down to the lobby in a bathrobe.

He ushered me inside the apartment and then noticed the package. "What's that?"

Caught like a motherfucker, there was nothing I could do except hand him the box. "It's a gift from Kevin."

"I signed the contract, so why's he still kissing my ass? Damn, I should have held out for more money." Maverick gazed at the insignia on the outside of the luxurious box and whistled. "Cohiba cigars—Luxury Selection! These are the shit!" He opened the box and ran a finger over the collection of luxury cigars. After perusing the gift card, he looked up at me, confused. "Kevin's congratulating me on becoming a father. What's that about?" Maverick handed me the card and I scanned it, pretending to be reading the message for the first time.

"It's all over the Internet, honey."

"What is?"

"The news that we're going to be parents."

"Don't tell me you went behind my back after I told you I wasn't feeling that in-vitro bullshit?"

Fast on my feet, I began blurting out the story that I'd come up with. "I didn't have a choice, Mav. That hooker, Sophia was pissed that you bit up her thighs. She said the condom broke and you gave her an STD and—"

"That's a lie! The condom didn't break, and I don't have any STDs."

"It's her word against yours. She threatened to sue us and she was going to go to the press with the story. She said she has evidence that she was in that hotel with you. I had to do something to keep her quiet."

"So, you offered a lying, scheming whore the opportunity to carry our child? That's ridiculous, Cori."

"I doubled the original price for a surrogate and agreed to pay her tuition to nursing school after the baby's born. She wants to get out of the sex peddling business and lead a normal life."

Maverick snorted. "Oh, yeah? She wants to lead a normal life on my dollar, huh?"

I caressed his arm. "Our dollar," I corrected. "But we have so much, Mav, we won't even miss that little bit of money."

He looked at me with suspicious eyes. "You're slick, Cori. You figured out a way to get exactly what you wanted. I hope you're happy now."

"Maverick, sweetie, we both should be happy. We're having a son."

"Whoopty-doo! We're having a fucking test tube baby, and everyone will be wondering if the kid is really mine. With the messed-up way it's coming into the world, I'll be wondering my damn self if the kid is actually mine."

"We can get DNA testing later in the pregnancy, if you'd like."

"Believe me, I insist on DNA testing."

"Okay, not a problem."

"I can't believe you trapped me into this shit. In vitro fertilization is for white folks. A virile brother like me has more than enough healthy sperm to make a kid the right way. I'm not happy about bringing a Frankenstein baby into the world. It's not a good look for me."

"You should have thought about your image when you were mauling that escort and ramming her so hard you burst through the condom," I countered with a hand on my hip.

CHAPTER 14

We were behind schedule and had to film three episodes in one day. It was grueling work, and watching the kids getting kicked off the show, one after another in the course of a day wasn't fun, either. One of the departed had been my girl, LaTasha, and her teary-eyed exit had been heart-wrenching.

What the audience would see was the prerecorded exit scene of each of the departing contestants, but what actually happened on set was loud sobbing and emotional outbursts that often escalated to anger, profanity, and even violence. When the dwarf had been booted off the show, he kicked one of the cameramen in the shins. That dwarf was a mean little son of a bitch.

Josh would have loved to showcase the contestants showing their asses, but he couldn't use the footage since the kids often blabbered about their mistreatment and other dirty little secrets of the show while in the midst of their tirades. For example, one of the contestants, Touki, the blue-eyed, blue-haired Asian girl, left the show screaming, "It's not fair! How could the judges be expected to properly critique my food when it's been left sitting on a tray for two hours while you assholes did like a zillion retakes?"

Sadly, Touki's words were true. The reason the judges took such tiny bites of the dishes set before them was due to the fact that while the crew made changes and shot retakes, most of the food was often cold and unpalatable by the time it reached the judges' table.

On the day that Maverick appeared on the show, he refused to chew or swallow the food. Off camera, he spat the food into a napkin, but when the camera was on him, he smiled charmingly as he launched into his critique, often praising the awful food that had been placed before him.

Down to our final five, I'd managed to keep my favorite, Ralphie, in the competition despite Josh's fear that an appearance by Ralphie's ghetto-fabulous foster mother would bring down the ratings. When I'd informed Josh that the foster mother had managed to get a set of dentures, he had no choice but to give up the idea of kicking Ralphie off the show. Little did Josh know that I had secretly arranged an emergency dental visit for the woman and had spent money out of my own pocket to get her teeth fixed.

But my motives hadn't been purely altruistic. A part of me wanted America to see what the network wanted to hide. It wasn't only poor little black kids getting rescued by good white people; there were heroes in the 'hood, too. There were black folks out there who opened their hearts and homes to unwanted white children.

After being flown to New York, the mothers of our five finalists were herded to a hotel in midtown Manhattan, away from the madness taking place on the Chelsea set. It was brought to my attention that Ralphie's foster mom was running up a hell of a tab at the hotel bar, and I made a mental note to give her a call and encourage her to arrive at tomorrow's taping sober.

I had to tape one-on-one pep talks with the final five that consisted of Ralphie, Michelangelo, Yancy, Becca, and Angus, the tattooed-covered asshole whom I was convinced was a white supremacist.

There were only three real contenders: Ralphie, Michelangelo, and unfortunately, Angus. But Angus with his neo-Nazi self would win over my dead body.

During the taping of my one-on-one with Michelangelo, I was

nearly moved to tears. Exhibiting his sensitive side, he spoke in a somber tone as he mentioned wanting to win the competition to honor his dad, a New York firefighter who had died tragically while trying to rescue victims during the 9/11 terrorist attacks.

"I thought you were from Ohio," I said, looking down at my notes.

"Yes, that's where we relocated after my dad's death. My mom was originally from Cleveland, and she wanted to be close to her family after losing my pop. I was only nine years old at the time," he said, looking down and pausing in an effort to compose himself. "One of my fondest memories," he continued, "is going to the fire station with my pop and helping him prepare his famous, spicy chili for the other firefighters. Hanging out with my pop at the fire station was how I developed my love of cooking. My dad was an American hero," Michelangelo said, wiping away a tear. "If I win this competition, I'm going to open a restaurant called The Fire Station to honor his memory. His chili and some of his other favorite dishes will be included on the menu."

I had officially gone from rooting for Ralphie to wanting Michelangelo to win. No doubt, he'd be an audience favorite based on his looks and sex appeal, but after viewing his emotionally charged one-on-one session, I was sure the producers of the show as well as the viewers at home would root for him based on his unexpected display of sensitivity.

"We started out with twenty amateur cooks and now we're looking at the final five," I said in an enthusiastic voice and widening my eyes in a way that I hoped would add the twinkle that my audience had come to adore. "Woo-hoo, final five," I yelled, pumping my fist in the air.

The kids cheered along with me and pumped their fists.

"All of you should be extremely proud of yourselves, and I know the last thing any of you want is to go home."

On cue, the kids shook their heads, agreeing that they didn't want to go home.

"Well, contestants, it's time to put your best foot forward. In young people's terms, it's time to turn up because it just got real here at Cori's kitchen!"

After I delivered my spiel, one of the producers told me that the moms had arrived and were hidden off camera. Their arrival would be a surprise to the kids. With my segment complete, I went backstage to greet them.

The only two black women in the group were as different as night and day. There was Ralphie's foster mom with her cheap clothes and obviously fake Louis Vuitton bag. Michelangelo's mom, on the other hand, was an elegant and stylish woman with good bone structure and beautiful salt-and-pepper hair. She had the exact reddish-brown complexion as her son.

I looked the women over and couldn't believe Josh had been worrying about Ralphie's foster mother when he should have been more concerned about Angus's mom. Angus's mom had an unkempt look and thinning, dirty blonde hair. Even worse, she was covered with tattoos, like her son. And one of the tattoos was a swastika. Being Jewish, Josh, I was sure, was not pleased about the tattoo.

Confirming my suspicion, Josh sent his assistant in and had Angus's mom hustled off to makeup to get the offensive symbol covered.

I excused myself, telling the moms I'd meet with them individually in a short while. I bumped into Josh in the corridor, and I could tell by his frazzled appearance that having a Nazi supporter on the show had upset him.

But I had no mercy on Josh. I gave him a smirk and couldn't help rubbing it in his face. "I told you Angus was a white supremacist, but you were so concerned that a black woman would be an embarrassment to the show, you welcomed someone who's sporting a big-ass swastika," I taunted.

"Please, Cori. I can't do this with you right now. I have a show to run, and I don't have time to eat crow," he said as he pushed past me.

Feeling smug, I returned to the room where the moms had gathered and listened briefly while one of the producers explained to them that they were going to be doing a blind taste test and would not be informed which dish had been prepared by their kid.

With the moms being briefed and with Angus's mother being made presentable for TV, I had time for a quick break. Before entering my dressing room, I listened and laughed as Josh barked orders at the crew. He was such a temperamental diva, taking his frustrations out on the innocent production team.

Eager to slip off my heels and give my feet a break, I pushed open the door. To my surprise, my dressing room was decorated with balloons and party streamers. Azaria Fierro and Norris Buckley crept up behind me.

"Congrats, new Mommy," Azaria said, smiling and holding a beautifully decorated box. I had a thing for nicely presented presents, and even though I loathed the woman, I gladly accepted the gift.

"We realize it's a bit early, but we wanted to do something special for you," Norris said.

"Thanks, guys," I muttered as I carefully unwrapped the gift. Inside the Nordstrom box were Burberry cashmere and cotton rompers, an assortment of adorable boy-themed infant sleepwear by other top designers, and a plush, stuffed bunny that Azaria said was identical to one that Kate and William's little prince was given when he was born. I had no idea where she'd gotten that information, but I was impressed with the quality of the stuffed animal.

Although Azaria and I would never be BFF's, I appreciated the gesture. Some of the gossip bloggers had been insinuating that Maverick and I had selected in vitro fertilization to produce a "designer baby" with athletic ability, a specific body type, and precise hair and eye color. The accusations were ridiculous. Our son would no doubt inherit his father's athleticism, and with us both possessing brown hair and brown eyes, why would we make our baby's physical traits different than ours? The media could be so ridiculous at times.

But, still, their attacks hurt, and with Maverick acting sullen and barely speaking to me, I was in need of a little pampering. I thanked Azaria and Norris profusely and then ushered them out. I appreciated their thoughtfulness, but I still wanted to get out of my heels and relax in private before returning to the set.

My marital problems troubled me. Maverick had increased the amount of time he was whoring around with Katya, and it worried me that he might be getting emotionally attached to her. If the media caught on to his indiscretion, our image would be destroyed. And God forbid if he had actually caught feelings for the prostitute and decided to leave me. Everything in my spirit balked at the idea of having to raise our child as a single parent.

On one of her tapes, Grandma Eula Mae had said that a man would share more of his soul with a whore than with his own wife. She said that lots of men had fallen in love with her girls and were willing to forsake their families, their careers, and their reputations to bask in the joy of licking whore-pussy for the rest of their lives.

Imagining the shame of such a betrayal, I cringed. Still, I knew my husband like the back of my hand, and he wasn't like those men back in Grandma Eula Mae's day. For starters, his network would be mortified if he broke up with me and tried to pass off a hooker as wife material. Furthermore, Maverick was much too image-conscious to allow a broken-English-speaking, cheap slut destroy our lives. I was certain that his network had an ethical expectation of Maverick, and had put a morals clause in his contract, prohibiting him from engaging in disreputable conduct.

But I had to take some kind of action to improve our relationship. Maybe if I allowed him to bite me a little, he'd leave Katya alone. On second thought, no, I couldn't have that. Pain was not a turn-on for me and being left with bruises covering my body was out of the question.

Maybe if I found him a new prostitute who enjoyed being bitten, I could keep him away from Katya. There were plenty of sick bitches out there, who'd do most anything for money, including going along with Maverick's twisted fetish.

One thing was for sure, Katya had to go.

I called the agency and lodged a complaint against Katya with the manager. I told her that I forbade Katya to be allowed to hook up with my husband ever again, and went so far as to threaten a lawsuit against the agency if they sent that bitch out on another date with my husband.

Although it was hard to get the words out, I swallowed my pride and divulged my husband's predilection for biting. I agreed to pay double if they could find another girl who'd go along with his twisted desires. The manager assured me that she'd find someone suitable for my husband and that she'd be very discreet.

Clayton, Robin, and Gina came to my dressing room to touch me up before I went in front of the camera, again. The moment they opened the door, I could sense the chaos that was occurring outside my peaceful environment.

The three of them made a big fuss over the presents that Azaria and Norris had given me and began rattling tissue paper as they opened the gift boxes.

"Look at this cute little Burberry romper," Gina exclaimed, taking it out of the box and holding it up.

Feeling cranky over the behavior of Maverick and his whore, I was snappish toward Gina. "Please don't touch the baby's things. I didn't give you guys permission to go through those gifts."

"Sorry," Gina muttered.

Not wanting to get yelled at, Clayton and Robin quickly replaced the lids on boxes they were about to investigate, and the two of them exchanged a glance that I clearly read as: *Someone must be on her period!*

It irritated me when people used their eyes to talk about me right in my face, but I let it go—this time! But if I ever caught Clayton and Robin doing it again, I'd be interviewing a new makeup artist and wardrobe supervisor.

"What's going on out there?" I asked.

"The kids were being filmed as they prepared to cook. They were running around grabbing ingredients from the panty, and someone spilled olive oil on the floor. The preacher slid in it. He ripped his pants and his chef's jacket was streaked with oil. Josh has halted production until the preacher cleans up and changes his clothes."

"Hmph. The way Josh thrives on drama, I'm surprised he didn't leave the slip scene in," I replied. "Hell, I'm shocked that he didn't make the good reverend do multiple takes of sliding in oil."

"Well, with the moms scheduled to be on set, Josh wanted it to appear that everything was running smoothly," Robin offered.

I sucked my teeth. "Josh is such a phony. He made Michelangelo retake the red sauce explosion over and over, but he's choosing to edit out the klutzy preacher wallowing around on the floor in oil." I gave a bitter laugh. "I wish I'd seen it."

"It was hilarious," Clayton offered.

"It really was," Gina concurred. "Yancy claims that Becca had something to do with it. He's accusing her of working dark magic."

"That silly girl doesn't know anything about witchcraft," I said, shaking my head. "But it's a good thing we're not back in the days of the Salem witchcraft trials. If we were, Reverend Yancy Dunlap would see to it that Becca was burned at the stake."

Clayton applied blush to my cheeks. "Hopefully, Becca will go home today. It's tense enough on set, but her hocus-pocus bullcrap is starting to make the remaining contestants nervous."

I knew exactly who was being eliminated, and it wasn't Becca. It was the tatted skinhead. Angus could thank his swastika-covered mother for him not making it to the end.

At this stage in the competition, the amateur cooks were supposed to replicate any of my Southern meals of their choosing, but there was a twist. They had the task of elevating the meal by adding a side dish, made from secret ingredients stored in a mystery box. The producers had borrowed the idea for the twist from another cooking reality show. Cooking competitions stole ideas from each other all the time, and therefore our lack of originality didn't bother me.

What bothered me was that Josh's staff hadn't vetted Angus thoroughly. Having a hate monger on the show wasn't a good look. Maybe I could use Josh's oversight as a reason to wrangle the title of executive producer from him. I would instruct Ellie to schedule a conference between me and the network big brass as soon as possible. Once I had control of the show, and was able to instill my creative ideas, I'd be guaranteed to win that fucking elusive Emmy.

CHAPTER 15

When I had conversed with Ralphie's foster mom, backstage, she was fine—personable and rather charming despite her bad grammar and boisterous laughter. Trenell Carter cracked jokes and discreetly whispered her appreciation for the new teeth I'd paid for. We talked about Southern cooking, and I was surprised to learn she prepared canned corn exactly as Grandma Eula Mae had—with lots of butter in a black skillet, thickening it with flour, and then adding a sweet and savory mixture of brown sugar, salt, and lots of black pepper. Delicious!

An hour later when the contestants were off set, the moms were brought in. A quick glance at Trenell and I was instantly concerned. Her eyes were squinted, and her lips were pressed together severely, giving her an unfriendly look. I wondered if she'd gotten into an argument with one of the other moms. But before I could determine what was wrong with her, the contestants were brought out, and there was a hum of excitement as mothers were reunited with their grown children.

Noticing Ralphie and Trenell locked in a warm embrace, I relaxed, figuring I'd been wrong about her emotional state. Five minutes into the segment, when the group of mothers was given the first dish to taste, Trenell suddenly jumped up and shouted, "What the fuck is this shit? Is y'all tryna poison me? I ain't saying any names, but I heard that a certain somebody was tryna keep me from participating in this lil' get-together tonight. You muthafuckas ain't gotta like me, but y'all taking shit too far if you think I'ma let you poison me and send me outta this bitch on a stretcher."

Stunned by Trenell's outburst, there was a chorus of gasps from cast and crew. It was clear to me that she was intoxicated. Before leaving the hotel, she'd probably slipped a bottle inside her bag and had sneakily gotten wasted while backstage.

A few moments after her verbal outburst, possessed with the strength of ten men, Trenell lifted the sizeable table and angrily toppled it, sending plates of food and cutlery zooming in all directions. The mothers shouted in alarm, and their offspring raced across the room to protect them from the flying daggers and broken glass.

It was a mess. All I could do was close my eyes and ask Jesus to take the wheel.

As security rushed to restrain Trenell, the bawdy woman had the audacity to stoop down and grab a steak knife from the wreckage. While wielding the knife, her eyes darted from side to side like a cornered animal trying to decide which man to slice into first.

At that point, I heard a thump, and I'm sure it was Josh, passing out from the shock of it all.

Then Ralphie's skinny little white ass decided to get involved in the skirmish. "Y'all mufuckas bet not even think about laying a hand on my mama. I will fuck urbody up if any one of y'all lays a hand on her," he ranted while balling his fists and biting down on his lip in a feral, intimidating way. Part of his unique identity was that he was a harmless-looking, skinny white dude who sounded black. But I'd never seen him take on the persona of a straight street thug. Bobbing his narrow shoulders and moving his body rhyth-mically, Ralphie was giving an impressive demonstration of an angry black man who'd been born and raised in the heart of the ghetto.

The chaos was unbelievable. So scandalous, I covered my eyes in shock and humiliation. I'd gone to bat for Ralphie and his heathen mother, and now this was how they repaid me. Disgusted, I walked off set and let Josh handle the bullshit.

That buck-wild bitch, Trenell, had played me. She'd pretended to be nice and friendly backstage, knowing all the while that she intended to get wasted before taping began. Overindulging in alcohol was the reason the bum-bitch had been stricken with diabetes in the first place. Had I known her appearance on the show would come to this, I would have never allowed her to communicate with Ralphie when she was lying up in the hospital at death's door. Had I foreseen this calamity, I would have never put those teeth in her mouth. She'd be gumming food for the rest of her disgraceful life.

I should have listened to Josh and kept Trenell's trashy ass off my show. None of this would have happened if I had used my powers of persuasion to convince Ralphie to let us hire a respectable actress to play the role of his foster mom.

Now the entire episode would have to be scrapped. I was furious. In that moment, I made up my mind to stop protecting Ralphie from his inevitable fate. Despite his culinary ability, he was now facing elimination, and I could no longer help him. After the pandemonium and commotion that both he and his hell-raising foster mother had caused, he deserved to be gripped up by the scruff of his neck and tossed out the door.

Times like this, I needed Ellie's calming voice to help me get through this disaster. Unfortunately, Ellie was busy accompanying Sophia on a shopping trip for maternity clothes. Sophia said she tended to show early in her pregnancies and she needed a more comfortable wardrobe. Sophia, with her cheap taste, had jumped at the opportunity to purchase discounted items at a maternity outlet in New Jersey, so I had no problem granting her wish. But her timing sucked; I needed Ellie here with me.

With production at a standstill, I sat in my dressing room waiting for the producers to do damage control. I had no idea how any amount of editing could salvage the scene, and I imagined that the entire segment would have to be reshot—minus Trenell.

I scrolled through my messages, and saw that there was one from Maverick requesting that I set up a date with Katya for tonight. *Fuck you, Maverick!* He was in for a big surprise when I informed him that Katya was no longer available to him. I planned to tell him that she was booked up, forever as the exclusive date of an Arabian billionaire.

Maverick would be distraught, but I would assure him that I was doing everything in my power to find him another hooker who was willing to be gnawed on.

I kicked off my heels, again and relaxed on my pink couch. Closing my eyes, I tried to imagine life as a parent. There'd be so much positive media coverage, both our careers would benefit. While envisioning the Brown family gracing the cover of multiple magazines, there was a soft rap on my door. It was much too light and too tentative a knock for it to be Josh, bothering me with an *I told you so* lecture regarding Trenell Carter.

"Come in," I said, sitting up. I was beyond surprised when Michelangelo entered my dressing room. For some reason, I felt exposed, and I tugged on the hem of my dress, covering my knees as if they were intimate body parts. He was so hot-looking, my nipples went rigid, and I self-consciously folded my arms across my chest to conceal them.

"Sorry to bother you, Cori. I know your private dressing room is off limits to us, but I'm kind of desperate and was hoping you could help me out. I tried to speak to Josh, but he's running around like a chicken with its head cut off."

"I bet he is," I replied. "What's the problem besides all the chaos out there?"

"The producers are sending our moms back to the hotel, but with everything that's happened, my mother doesn't feel safe being in the room next to Ralphie's foster mother. Would you ask someone from management to please switch her to a different room on another floor?"

"Sure. I'll have my assistant make the arrangements," I volunteered. I pointed to my desk. "Write your mother's room number and other pertinent information on the notepad on my desk. I'll make sure she gets a different room."

"Thanks. I appreciate it, Cori."

He strode over to my desk and my eyes followed him, lingering on his broad back and then sliding down to his ass. As he bent his torso to write the information, I found myself wondering what he looked like beneath his clothes. Then I grimaced, instantly ashamed of myself for lusting after a contestant. I had a fine-ass husband at home—a sports icon—who possessed a gorgeous, athletic body, and had recently signed a multimillion-dollar contract, ensuring that we'd continue living our luxurious lifestyle for another ten years. There was absolutely no reason for me to yearn for an amateur cook who was trying to win meager prize money in order to jumpstart a career that most likely would never get off the ground.

But then again, with Michelangelo's looks, I could see a career for him as a returning guest-chef or judge on any of the numerous cooking shows that dominated national TV.

Not wanting him to catch me gawking at his muscular physique, I quickly averted my gaze when he finished writing on the notepad and turned to face me.

"Ralphie's mom was doing the most. I wonder what that was about." Michelangelo made a face, which made him look adorably handsome.

"I have no idea what was going on with her, but we lost an entire day of filming due to her shenanigans," I said, feeling suddenly world-weary as I envisioned all the extra time I would have to devote to the show instead of being home trying to fix my marriage. My facial expression must have betrayed my emotional exhaustion because Michelangelo gazed at me with concern in his eyes.

"Is everything okay, Cori?"

I plastered on a smile and nodded.

"Are you sure?"

I nodded again, but this time my bottom lip trembled the way it tended to do whenever I tried to fight back tears. For some odd reason, the concern that was evident in Michelangelo's voice was bringing out weird emotions in me. I couldn't remember the last time Maverick had genuinely inquired about my well-being. It made me sad that another man was more concerned than my own husband.

Thinking about the condition of my marriage was heartbreaking. Sure, Grandma Eula Mae had always said that a woman should look the other way when her man's catting around with a whore, but she'd never said that the wife should get involved and personally manage her husband's hookups.

Naively, I'd thought that being open-minded about my husband's activities outside our marriage would strengthen our relationship. But I was losing him, anyway. His heart simply wasn't in it anymore, and I could feel his love slipping away.

I tried to contain my emotions, but a strangled cry escaped my lips. Coming to my aid, Michelangelo traversed the room swiftly, reaching me in only three strides. He sat down next to me. "What's wrong, Cori?" he asked worriedly.

I had been trying to be strong for so long, it had only been a matter of time before my emotions overwhelmed me. I burst into tears and Michelangelo gathered me inside his strong arms. With my face buried against his chest, I allowed myself to have a long overdue cry. As I sobbed, he patted my back, caressed my hair, and murmured consolingly.

I hadn't realized how utterly lonely I was—how badly I craved affection until I looked up at his face and saw unmistakable desire burning in his eyes. He lowered his head and pressed his lips to mine, kissing me gently…cautiously, as if he expected to be pushed away. The sensible part of my brain was waving a red flag and screaming for me to pull away, to slap his face, and curse him out for taking such liberties with me.

But instead of upholding my dignity, I looped my arms around his neck and pulled him closer. Moaning, I parted my lips invitingly. He cupped my face as our tongues danced together. His lips then moved to my neck, making a path of kisses down to my chest, causing me to tremble.

It was a moment of madness where body ruled over mind. My heart knocked so loudly in my chest, I was mortified by the sound that seemed to announce how deprived I'd been of genuine affection.

I'd never stepped outside my marriage before. Not ever! Everything in me screamed for me to put a stop to this madness. But Michelangelo's kiss was so achingly sweet, I clung to him, drinking in the taste of him, and urgently kissing him back.

His hands roamed over my body, and the warmth of his touch caused me to squirm and moan softly.

Suddenly, the doorknob made a clinking sound, and I realized I hadn't locked it. Panic seized me. Michelangelo and I abruptly pulled away from each other as the door opened to a crack. I was incensed that someone had entered my dressing room without my express permission.

Self-consciously, I smoothed out the front of my rumpled dress and was completely stunned to discover that my panties had been lowered. They were hanging below my knees. How the fuck had that happened? I glowered at Michelangelo, close to slapping the shit out of him.

In the split-seconds before the door opened fully, I desperately tried to pull up my panties, but I wasn't quick enough.

Standing in the doorway with a hand over his mouth and his eyes bulging in astonishment was Ralphie.

"Haven't you ever heard of knocking? What the fuck do you want?" I yelled angrily as I yanked my panties over my hips. I couldn't believe that I—someone who'd always been super vigilant about preserving my good image—had been caught with my fucking panties down. I could have strangled that goddamn Ralphie for barging in on me.

Michelangelo sprang to his feet. Adjusting his clothing, he hurried toward the door. "I'll give you your privacy, Cori. I, uh, I'll talk to you later."

I didn't even bother to respond to Michelangelo. I wanted to stab him in the eyeballs repeatedly for causing the horrible dilemma I was in. If the sexy, fucking bastard hadn't used his magical fingers on me to stroke my flesh and slide my panties down, I wouldn't be in such a God-awful position.

"I…I…I'm sorry, Cori. But I need your help," Ralphie stammered. "They're tryna throw my mama off the show, and I wondered if you could put in a good word and do something to help her."

Not even God could save his disgraceful mother. But needing Ralphie's loyalty and silence, I decided to string him along.

"It won't be easy to get any sympathy for her after that stunt she pulled on set with cameras rolling. It was obscene."

"She had a slipup, but it wasn't her fault. One of the other moms—

Angus's mother—went out of her way to make my mom feel like an outcast. She turned her nose up at her and treated her like dirt. My mom is a super-nice person when you get to know her. But she was feeling insecure. That's why she started drinking backstage. She needed liquid courage to get through the taping."

Angus's mom had a fucking nerve turning her Nazi nose up at any damn body. But fuck that bitch and Trenell Carter, I had my own issues to deal with. I had to make sure that Ralphie didn't spread any malicious gossip about the uncompromising position he'd caught me in.

"Listen, Ralphie. I'm going to do everything I can to keep your mom on the show, but you have to promise me that you won't breathe a word about what you observed in here."

Ralphie frowned. "I don't know what you're talking about. When I came in here, you were taking a nap, and I apologize for disturbing you, Cori."

Giving me that toothy smile that I'd grown to like so much, Ralphie made it a point to lock my door from the inside before exiting my dressing room.

Thank God I could count on Ralphie to keep my secret safe, at least for now. He wasn't going to be a happy camper for long. I'd have to figure out a way to keep his mouth shut after his foster mother was sent packing.

CHAPTER 16

J osh made a last-minute decision to replace the contestants' mothers with celebrities, and then he cancelled filming for the rest of the day. After the terrible embarrassment of getting caught with my panties down, I couldn't wait to get out of the studio.

Boom. Boom. Boom. Someone was beating on my dressing room door like a war drum. The sound was loud and authoritative, jolting me out of my desk chair. The pounding matched the throbbing in my chest as my heart beat uncontrollably. *What now?*

I unlocked the door and wasn't surprised to find Josh standing there looking evil as hell.

"Ralphie has to go. There'll be no negotiating, Cori. After that fiasco with his foster mother, I want him gone!"

Too beaten down to protest, I simply held up my hands in surrender. Had Ralphie not caught me in a compromising position, I would have continued to fight for him to stay. But under the circumstances, I was also eager for him to leave the show.

"I'm glad you finally see things my way. If you'd listened to me sooner, we wouldn't be in this mess."

"You're right," I conceded. With no fight left, I closed the door after Josh left and then slumped down into the couch.

Poor Ralphie. He had a real chance of winning the prize, but his foster mom had blown it for him.

Once a contestant had been targeted, the judges were instructed to critique their food unfavorably no matter the complexity of their technique or how scrumptious the dish turned out to be. Although it saddened me that Ralphie would be treated unfairly, I was also a bit relieved that I wouldn't have to see him again after tomorrow. He was a reminder of my shameful behavior with Michelangelo.

How I had allowed myself to fall for that pretty boy's charm was beyond me. Michelangelo was wonderful eye candy, but he didn't have shit on my husband.

Negative thoughts began to flit around in my head. Suppose Ralphie became so upset about being eliminated that he wanted to get even with me? Suppose he decided to run his mouth about what he'd seen? No, he wouldn't do that…not after all I'd done for him. Or would he? I pushed the frightening possibilities out of my mind.

Letting out a sigh, I wearily ran a hand through my hair before clicking off the light. I couldn't get home soon enough.

After such an abdominally bad day, I wanted nothing more than to watch a movie and cuddle with my hubby. But Maverick was still upset with me for moving forward with the surrogate pregnancy.

I wondered what Grandma Eula Mae would advise me to do if she were still among the living. She believed that the combination of pussy, brains, and female cunning could reduce the strongest man to a blithering idiot. She'd probably be ashamed of the way I was squandering my power.

I thought about what she'd said about the value of pussy on one of her old tapes:

If more women realized they had a goldmine between their legs, they wouldn't give the goods away. I don't care if a gal has the face of a moose, or if she's knock-kneed, pigeon-toed, or slue-footed... if she knows the value of her pussy, she can make the meanest, most hardened criminal shed tears. You see, physical attractiveness is well and good if your goal is to get noticed, but in order to rein a man in, a woman needs more than a pretty face. There ain't a bitch on earth that can keep a man if she has piss-poor bedroom skills.

I'll give you an example. I once had a gal who went by the name of Sophronia. She was built like a brick shithouse and had the beautiful face of an angel. After applying her makeup, she used to draw a beauty mark just north of her mouth. Now, Sophronia was already the number one gal at my establishment, but that facial polka dot made her stand out even more from the rest of the girls. Other gals tried to copy her, hoping that a mole on their faces would help them attract more customers. But it was called a "beauty mark" for a reason, and it looked ridiculous on regular-looking gals.

I'm telling you, Sophronia had the men lined up waiting to get in the sack with her, and no amount of persuading could make her regulars try out any of my other gals. While waiting for Sophronia, the gentlemen callers would spend a few dollars to converse and drink with the other whores, but they were saving the big bucks to spend on Sophronia. On more occasions that I care to recall, a big spender left my premises with a wad of cash untouched and secured inside his pocket after growing tired of waiting for Sophronia.

Seeing money walk out the door was frustrating to me and my whores.

One night, Vincenzo Drucci, a local mobster known as Big Vinnie, stopped by, looking to have a good time with some sporting girls. He brought in a group of his Italian cronies and other well-to-do local men, such as bankers, law enforcement officials, lawyers, merchants, politicians, and such. Those men were corrupt in one way or another, and were in Drucci's pocket, so to speak.

My place was packed to the rafters that night and all the gals were turn-

ing tricks, regardless of any physical deficiency they may have possessed. Everybody was making money including a one-legged gal who called herself Deluxe. Ha-ha, that name tickled the hell out of me.

There was this gal named Ida—tall and gangly, and with an unattractive, big gap in her front teeth. I used to tease her and say that I could park my Coupe de Ville in that big space between her teeth. Ida didn't have much in the looks department, and she usually ended up with the bottom-of-the-barrel customers—the worst kinds of cheapskates. But that night, she lucked up and got herself chosen by a Jewish fella, Milton Wallach. Mr. Wallach owned a mom-and-pop corner store, but had recently been able to parlay his profits into the opening of a big ol' supermarket that was well-lit, with shiny tile flooring, handy shopping carts, self-serve aisles, and counters staffed by checkout girls.

It was the late 1940s, and at that point in time, only affluent whites were welcome to shop in those flashy new grocery stores. I was born and raised in Memphis, Tennessee, and I'd personally experienced the horrors of Jim Crow. The constant lynchings and cruelty to coloreds is what sent me up North in the first place. But let me tell you something, crackers up North are just as prejudiced as the rednecks down South. Only difference is that they're a little more polite about their bigoted ways.

In Philadelphia during the forties, Negroes weren't getting lynched but we had to abide by an unwritten law that upheld segregation. We better not had taken our black behinds from the colored side of town and tried to mingle with crackers on their side of the tracks. We weren't welcome in their neighborhoods unless we came to cook, clean, or do some kind of a service for them. Meanwhile, whitey was free to venture into our areas whenever he got good and damn ready. Hell, back then, the Jews and Italians owned all the corner stores in the colored neighborhoods. The mail carrier was white, the ice delivery man was white, the insurance man was white, the landlord was white, the milkman was white…everybody who earned a living off us was white. And those white men strutted into our neighborhoods and into our homes without the least bit of fear.

But I digress.

That gal, Ida with that big ol' gap in her teeth had legs as skinny as twigs, and they were crooked to boot. I heard she had rickets as a child, poor thing. She was skinny like Olive Oyl and built straight up and down with a flat chest, like a boy's. Ida was one homely whore. And her hair! Whoo, my Lord. It was a shame the way she would sweat out her nappy hair as soon as she finished with her first customer. That knotty-headed wench cost me an arm and a leg trying to keep her hair looking presentable. The beautician I paid to do the gals' hair always complained when Ida sat in the chair. She said Ida's hair was so coarse that even after applying globs of hair pomade and pulling a scorching-hot pressing comb through her naps, Ida's hair still looked dry and brittle and would hardly hold a curl.

Yet, with all those flaws, Ida managed to capture the heart of Mr. Wallach. All the gals were shocked. Then rumors started. My gals said that Ida had used an unnatural method to snag that rich Jewish man. But you can't believe the word of a bunch of jealous whores, now can you? Anyhoo, rumor had it that Mr. Wallach had a teeny-tiny, little peter about the size of my baby finger…some said it was smaller. They said he couldn't get any friction going inside the loose lining of Ida's big, overused pussy, and so Ida, being a resourceful ho, suggested that he fuck her in the mouth instead of her pussy.

Now, there wasn't anything new or unusual about mouth-fucking. All my gals gave head. Shit, most of my clientele came to my place for the sole purpose of getting a professional blowjob since their prissy wives either flat-out refused to blow them or did a piss-poor job of it when they made a feeble attempt.

On the subject of fellatio, I have to say that I profited very well off of certain kinds of blowjobs. I figured it only made sense to charge my customers twenty extra dollars to face-fuck the gals who were blessed with big, blubbery lips. The feeling of two fluffy pillows cushioned around their little pink peckers was something they could never get from those thin-lipped hussies they were married to.

But let me get back to Ida. Ida didn't have thick lips, but she had something that none of the other gals had. According to rumor, Mr. Wallach damn near lost his mind when Ida introduced him to sliding his dick in and out of that space between her teeth while she massaged the head with the tip of her tongue.

I'd seen and heard of some crazy goings-on in my lifetime, but I like to died laughing when I heard that bullshit.

Word got out, and suddenly white men were lining up for skinny Ida instead of beautiful Sophronia. They didn't give a damn that by insisting upon seeing Ida, they were admitting they weren't packing much of anything.

Mr. Wallach wasn't thrilled about sharing Ida with a gaggle of other men, and so he did something that was pretty damn farfetched in those days. Heck, what he did would be considered a radical move, even today. Mr. Wallach walked out on his wife and three kids. He left them in the nice, ranch-style home they'd lived in when he'd only owned the mom-and-pop operation, but he used his newfound wealth from the super-market to buy a sprawling mansion, which he and Ida moved into and set up housekeeping.

Mr. Wallach told folks that Ida was his maid, and the whites seemed to go for that bold-faced lie, but all the coloreds knew the real story. Heck, if Ida was the maid, then why was Tilda Fowler traveling ten miles by bus every day to clean that big ol' palace? The other domestics who rode the bus with Tilda got an earful of the goings-on in that mansion. That's how word spread through our community that Ida wasn't cleaning a damn thing in that house. She may have been polishing the head of Mr. Wallach's knob with her tongue, but that's about it.

So, while an ugly duckling whore was being treated like royalty and sitting around with her feet up all day, pretty-faced Sophronia was still spreading her legs for up to twelve or more tricks a day. Goes to show you that looks don't mean a damn thing. When it comes to hooking a man for good, a woman better have some superior bedroom skills. Good sex is the only thing that matters in this world. And you can quote me on that. As a former madam, I believe I know a thing or two about the bizarre yearnings of men.

Those old audio recordings Grandma Eula Mae had left behind were a roadmap on how to keep my man happy and satisfied, but I'd been too self-absorbed to realize it. Although I preferred to have a normal sex life without indulging too much freakiness into my bedroom, I could pretend to be a freak. I still refused to allow Maverick to mangle my flesh like a pit bull, but I'd think of something that was perverted enough to keep him content with being with me, only.

CHAPTER 17

I was dressed in a flowing Robert Cavalli silk caftan, but Maverick was downright sloppy in basketball shorts and a T-shirt. We paid a lot of money to have a chef prepare and serve our meals, and the least Maverick could have done was dress properly for dinner.

Usually, we sat closer to each other during our meals, but tonight, Maverick sat at one end of our formal dining table and I sat at the other. There was no conversation, only the sounds of clinking cutlery as we dined on nut roast.

The vegetarian nut roast was incredible. I could taste a variety of nuts, mushrooms, quinoa, squash, dried apricots and cranberries, heavy spices, and a hint of onion and garlic. Tamara served the nut roast with a spicy tomato sauce. Side dishes of braised mixed greens and grilled asparagus with an Indian spice mixture completed the meal. It was truly a feast to the eyes and palate.

I wanted to discuss the wonderful components of the meal with my husband, but he was being antisocial. I also would have liked to ask Tamara for her nut roast recipe, but it would have gone to her head for a chef of my caliber to inquire about one of her creations, so I merely commented that the meal was tasty as she poured our wine.

Head lowered while looking down at his tablet, Maverick only grunted his approval of the divine meal without bothering to look up.

Tamara cleared the table and soon after, she brought us dessert. The servings of strawberry shortcake that she placed before us were so artfully presented, they deserved to be photographed.

"Oh, this looks yummy, Tamara," I complimented.

"Thank you. Would you like coffee to go with your dessert?"

"No, I'm fine. What about you, Mav? Would you like a cup of coffee?" I asked sweetly, giving the impression that Maverick and I were on good terms.

"I'm good," he mumbled, slouched over, eyes still glued to the screen.

Unlike me, Maverick continued to be distant, proving there was trouble in paradise. He didn't have the decency to pretend that our marriage was as strong as ever. I found it embarrassing that Maverick was being so obnoxious in front of the help. Not wanting our chef to be privy to any other signs of marital strife in our home, I offered to clean up after dessert and dismissed her for the evening.

"Are you sure?" Tamara asked.

"Yes, absolutely," I responded with a strained smile.

As Tamara turned to leave, I caught a glimpse of her reflection in a mirror on the wall. There was a trace of a smirk on her face. Engaged or not, that bitch had the hots for my husband and she was jubilant that our marriage was falling apart. No doubt, Tamara would trade in her fiancé in a hot minute for a wealthy TV star like Maverick. She probably fantasized about her and Maverick double-dating with Kevin and his wife and attending red carpet events. Fuck if I would ever let that shit happen.

I suddenly got a wonderful idea that would throw Tamara off track about the state of my marriage. I also wanted to punish her for that smug smile and for lusting after my husband.

"Tamara!"

She turned around. "Yes, Cori?"

"I've had a change of heart. Sorry, but you won't be able to leave early after all. It suddenly occurred to me that I'd like a veggie omelet in the morning. Would you prepare one for me, please? Load it with an assortment of vegetables. Oh, yeah….put it in a microwavable container so I can reheat it in the morning."

Having in-house chefs at my disposal at the studio who could whip up an omelet for me at the snap of my fingers, I was merely fucking with Tamara for the hell of it. She was aware of it and shot a glance at Maverick. The look in her eyes beseeched him to intervene on her behalf.

I glared at him. The fury in my eyes told him I was about to black the fuck out if he as much as made eye contact with Tamara. As insufferable a bastard as he was, Maverick wasn't crazy enough to go against me and defend our chef.

Feeling triumphant, I said with chortling laughter, "Thanks, Tamara. I don't know what I'd do without such a dedicated servant like you."

Tamara flinched, visibly irritated at being called a servant. She referred to herself as a personal chef, but to me, she was nothing more than a glorified servant.

Maverick sent a reproachful glance in my direction, silently telling me that that I was being mean and petty.

I didn't care. Mean and petty was exactly what I was going for. Tamara would think twice about smirking in my presence in the future.

Maverick had to be nuts if he thought I was going to sit back and let a smirking bitch disrespect me in my own home, and he had to be even crazier if he thought I was going to quietly wait while our marriage imploded. I'd had quite enough of his sullenness and silent contempt, and I refused to take it for another fucking second.

Grandma Eula Mae had left far too much information on how

to deal with men for me to allow a lowdown Russian cunt like Katya or a lowly chef like Tamara to lure my sexual deviant husband away from me. That whore, Katya was only pretending that she liked getting bitten. No one in their right mind would derive pleasure in some shit like that. But those Russian hoes were about their money, and she was willing to endure all those bite marks as long as she got what she wanted. And what she wanted was my multimillion-dollar man. In Maverick Brown, Katya and whory bitches like her saw dollar signs and a glamorous lifestyle.

It would be over my dead body that I let any bitch steal my husband from me. I had a plan in mind and was about to put it in motion, but was distracted by the amount of noise Tamara was making as she rattled around in the kitchen. I supposed she was taking out her frustration on the pots and pans. I mentally blocked out the racket, gathered my thoughts, and then cleared my throat as I prepared to speak.

"Dinner was exceptionally good," I said in a contrived pleasant voice.

Maverick nodded.

"That nut loaf was awesome. It was a perfect meat substitute. I liked it so much, I think Tamara should start using packaged meat substitutes as the main course every now and then."

Maverick looked up at me; confusion clouded his face. "You're the one who made me aware that mock meat is full of preservatives. Why would you want to add something unhealthy to our diet?"

He put down the tablet and I was elated that I'd finally gotten the son of a bitch's undivided attention. "Tamara does a great job of keeping our menu flavorful and interesting; I don't miss eating meat at all. By the way, Cori, please don't invite me back to your show. That greasy food and the meat I put in my mouth and later spat out, had my stomach feeling queasy for days."

"You don't miss meat at all, Mav?"

"Not at all."

"I do," I said and then forked up a bite-size of strawberry short-cake and swished it around the sauce that Tamara had decoratively swirled on the plate.

"Mmm, this is good. Try it, Mav."

"In a moment. I'm checking out the stats of a young rookie I may want to interview."

Dismissing me, and not even glancing at his dessert, Maverick picked up the tablet and returned his attention to the screen. He crinkled his brows together as if trying to concentrate and also sending a message for me not to disturb him again.

Checking out sports stats, my ass. He was probably on a porn site, viewing some type of sexual debauchery. If he wasn't on a porn site, then he was perusing an escort site, selecting his next Russian fuck-mate. The next bitch would probably be named Mishka or some shit like that.

I stood, picked up my dessert plate and sauntered over to Maverick. He looked up at me and quickly clicked off his tablet, preventing me from seeing what was on the screen.

I wasn't worried about whatever his nasty ass had been looking at because I had something so freaky in mind, I'd make him totally forget about cybersex and skinny Russian whores.

Licking some of the whipped cream off my fork, I gave him a sultry look and said, "I wasn't being completely honest with you. I don't actually miss meat, and I don't want a meat substitute. I miss the taste of *your* meat, Mav. Can I have a taste of you?"

Thrown off guard, he uttered a sound of surprise. Without waiting for him to reply, I set the plate on the table and lowered myself down to my knees.

"Oh, shit," he groaned.

Although he was still upset with me over the surrogate situation, his dick obviously wasn't harboring any ill will toward me. It was bobbing up and down so excitedly inside his shorts, he quickly began tugging on the elastic waistband, lowering the nylon fabric, and freeing his eager, one-eyed beast.

He held it out for me, expecting me to immediately take it in my mouth and calm it down. But I had other ideas. I held it delicately in my hand, and then, using a cheese spreader knife, I gently smoothed whipped cream and strawberry sauce onto his swollen dick.

I slid the knife up and down, lightly caressing his dick with the edge, and creating an element of danger that had Maverick sucking in his breath.

"Ooo, shit, baby. What are you doing?"

"I'm adding extra sweetness to my meat before I tear it up."

"Eat it, baby," he said, taking ahold of his dick and guiding it to my lips.

Instead of pulling his strawberries-and-cream-covered dick inside my mouth, I slowly licked the sweetness off of him, causing him to softly groan and hump. "Stop playing, Cori. Eat the fucking meat."

I ignored his request and continued licking and murmuring, "Mmm. My husband has prime beef." After I licked him clean, I proceeded to use the tip of the knife to pick up strawberry slices and carefully lined them along his erection. I placed my lips around the head of his dick and sucked one strawberry slice after another into my mouth. As I chewed the strawberries, Maverick was groaning and writhing, his voice rising to a pitch that drew Tamara from the kitchen.

"Is everything all right?" she asked and then stopped dead in her tracks when she took in the erotic scene before her.

I pulled Maverick's burgeoning manhood out of my mouth and

casually said to Tamara, "Bring me the can of whipped cream from the fridge. And more of your strawberry sauce."

"We don't need that shit. Just suck my dick, Cori," Maverick insisted. Then, he softened his tone and whimpered. "Please, Cori... please suck my dick."

Overcome with desire, he was unconcerned that Tamara was witnessing us in a very private moment. He didn't care that our chef was privy to him grunting and groaning as he tried to stuff my mouth with penile meat.

"Go get the whipped cream and strawberry sauce, Tamara," I repeated sharply.

"Uh, the whipped cream didn't come from a can. It's homemade," Tamara explained in a shaky voice, and I enjoyed her discomfort.

"Can't you see this is an emergency? Go get whatever home-made shit you whipped up and hurry back with it!"

Tamara dashed out of the dining room like an ER nurse running to get first aid essentials. Alone with my horny husband, I made sure he remained out of his mind and deliriously horny by nibbling the remnants of strawberries off his erection and telling him that he had the best dick meat any woman had ever been privileged to taste.

I had been well aware of his weakness for Brazilian women and I realized how much he enjoyed our annual ménage à trois, but it was insane that I hadn't understood what a twisted degenerate I was married to until recently. He was weak for any version of immoral, smutty sex, and now that I knew exactly what I was deal-ing with, I was confident I could keep my husband satisfied.

I planned to replay Grandma Eula Mae's tapes and learn all the tricks of the trade. I intended to reenact all the decadent fuckery that went on in her whorehouse back in the day.

Tamara returned with two bowls, which she quickly set on the table and then tried to haul-ass out of the dining room. But I wasn't having that. Since she had the gall to smirk and was probably flirting with Maverick behind my back, I expected her to pitch in and help me satisfy him.

"Hand me the bowl of strawberry sauce," I said to Tamara.

Looking uncomfortable, she passed the bowl to me. Delirious with lust, Maverick was half on the chair and half off. "Help me with him," I barked at Tamara.

"I don't think—"

"Do you want to keep your high-paying position with my husband and me?"

"Yes, but—"

"But, nothing! Get over here and hold his dick while I put strawberry sauce on it."

Despite being half out of his mind, Maverick understood that I was giving Tamara permission to touch his privates, and the knowledge caused him to wind his waist and groan with desire. Then he began to thrust so wildly, he toppled himself out of the chair.

With his shorts gathered around his legs, he was on the floor looking like he was having a seizure. I placed the bowls on the floor and beckoned Tamara to join me. She crouched down and gently grasped Maverick's dick as if she were a nurse, tenderly caring for a patient in critical condition.

As Tamara held Maverick's throbbing dick in place, I spread on the strawberry sauce.

"Baby, no! I don't want any more of that shit on me. Just suck on it…or let me fuck you," Maverick pleaded. Of course, I ignored his pleas. I topped the sauce off with the sliced strawberries I picked from his untouched dessert, and then smoothed on the homemade whipped cream. His long brown dick was decorated to perfection and I had to have a picture of it.

While Tamara held his dick firmly in her hand, I picked up my phone and began snapping pictures that would be mementos for Maverick and me to enjoy while snuggled in bed, reminiscing about the kinky good time we had tonight.

Tamara gazed at the tasty treat in her hands and licked her lips. "Since you're watching your weight, Cori, I can eat the dessert off Maverick if you want." Tamara's voice held a desperate ring. I glanced at her and she looked like she was ready to pounce on my husband's dick and suck the shit out of it.

I'd allowed too many bitches to suck my husband's dick, and I wasn't going down that road again. "No, that's okay, Tamara. I got this."

"Come on, babe. Let her suck it," Maverick interjected pitifully.

"No, I got it."

Maverick made a whiny sound of protest and Tamara gnawed at her bottom lip as if pondering a way to get his dick inside her mouth.

"Just hold it steady for me, Tamara. I'll do the rest."

Tamara deliberately put a flimsy grasp on his dick.

To mess with her head, I flicked my tongue against her strawberries and cream-coated fingers. She let out a soft moan as she slid her hand up and down Maverick's shaft.

I had both those motherfuckers—Maverick and Tamara—whimpering and writhing like two dogs in heat. As she gave my husband a handjob, I lifted up my caftan and then squatted over the gooey dick she was holding. I had pushed down only halfway when Maverick started twitching in a familiar way that told me he was already busting a nut.

After he finished coming, I eased off Maverick and lay with my legs gapped open. I beckoned Tamara.

At first she seemed resistant to eating my pussy, but then she came crawling over to me. Maverick's dick sprang back to life as he watched Tamara slurping on my pussy.

I sat up a little, stroking Tamara's hair as I watched her devour my pussy. I wondered if her fiancé was aware that he was engaged to a big freak. Probably not.

And though Tamara loved to run her mouth and gossip with her ex-chef friend about what went on in my household, I doubted if she'd divulge that her job description had changed from chef to in-house pussy eater.

CHAPTER 18

After Tamara cleaned up and left, Maverick and I lay cuddled together in bed, talking about our fun night and gazing at the dick pictures I'd taken. It felt good to have my man back. He didn't mention anything about wanting me to make an appointment for him with the escort service, and I was careful not to bring up the subject of Sophia and our unborn child

We were deliriously happy, and in order to keep us that way, I'd have to get some more freaky ideas from Grandma Eula Mae's tapes. Once I started throwing some old school-style whore-fucking on him, I'd be able to change Maverick's adverse feelings about the way our child was being brought into the world.

Hell, by the time I finished fucking him every which way, he'd be ecstatic over the idea that I had a functioning pussy that wouldn't have to be benched for the duration of a pregnancy.

I had a fleeting thought of my unfortunate incident with Michelangelo and quickly dismissed it from my mind. He had caught me in a weak moment. It was my husband that I truly loved.

To ensure that what had gone on in our dining room remained private, I had reminded Tamara of the confidentiality agreement she had signed when she began working with us. She was so embarrassed about eating strawberries and cum-cream out of my pussy that she readily agreed to keep quiet on the subject.

Finally, my marriage was back on track and all was right with my world.

Well, almost everything was right in my world. I still had to contend with the bullshit that was going on with Ralphie. I dreaded his reaction after he was eliminated from the show tomorrow, but I'd deal with that when the time came.

Even though Maverick and I had already fucked three times tonight, I wanted to make sure that he had no energy left for extra-marital affairs. So, when he was about to doze off, I shook him awake and handed him my phone. "Scroll through the pictures," I whispered. As I expected, the images of his dessert-decorated dick aroused him. I climbed on top of him and fucked him once again.

While we were going at it, he mumbled that we should raise Tamara's pay even higher for the inconvenience of her gaining a few extra pounds from constantly eating sugary desserts out of my pussy.

Oh, so this motherfucker wants Tamara involved in our sex life on a regular basis. I hoped I hadn't created another monster, but as long as Tamara kept her tongue in me and off my husband, I could deal with her joining us in bed. Or more accurately, joining us on the dining room floor.

It was a fucking zoo on the set. The D-list celebrities that were hired as guest-judges to replace the piece that featured the con-testants' mothers were not working out very well. We'd known in advance that they wouldn't have the slightest idea of how to describe food, and so they were provided with a list of key phrases. Apparently, they were all too lazy and egotistical to prepare for the camera by studying. They were winging it, and ruining the segment.

This one bitch, a former model that looked like a cat woman from too much plastic surgery, kept saying every dish tasted divine. Josh corrected her over and over, explaining that every dish couldn't possibly taste divine. He urged her to give a more in-depth critique and to speak in food language.

While the contestants were off-set, the director coached her. "It's loaded with salt and has too much garlic. Though I appreciate your effort, this is an overly ambitious attempt to recreate one of Cori's most famous signature dishes," the director said, giving the idiot former model a word-for-word description of the preacher's dish. He practiced the spiel with her for over thirty minutes.

But when the cat-faced model returned to the judges' table, she smiled for the cameras and simply said in a breathy voice, "This dish is divine, darling!"

For once, Josh and I were in agreement. We shared a look of mutual disgust.

When the model got to Michelangelo's dish, she said, "This plate of food is not only divine; it's also sexy, like the man who prepared it." Then she batted her lashes flirtatiously and tried to flash the bright smile that she'd been known for back in the eighties. Problem was, her skin was pulled too tight to replicate that famous grin and what she produced looked more like a grotesque grimace than an alluring smile.

Her behavior was embarrassing, causing me to cringe. What a disaster! *Cookin' with Cori* was turning into a freak show right before my eyes.

Fortunately, some of the other celebrity judges were more willing to follow the script that had been written for them, but they often strayed, adding their own personal remarks and impromptu entertainment segments.

For instance, a burned-out country singer followed the script when he described Becca's terrible food, but at the conclusion of his critique, he began to ham it up by suddenly bursting into a country song. The nutcase singer serenaded us with an inappropriate little ditty about spaghetti and cheese. The song had nothing whatsoever to do with the soul food he'd sampled. I suppose it had been so long since the washed-up bastard had had an opportunity to sing to an audience, he couldn't resist using my show with its millions of viewers as a vehicle to try and revive his dead career.

Of course the song could be edited out, but still…the nerve of him.

Were all the celebrities we'd hired suffering from some type of brain disorder? The lack of professionalism they displayed was almost as bad as the crude behavior of Ralphie's foster mother. Maybe if Josh hadn't cut corners and had spent money on big-name celebrities instead of hiring a group of has-beens, we wouldn't have had to suffer through multiple takes.

Sadly, it seemed that my chances of winning an Emmy this year were dwindling swiftly. All because I'd been kind enough to step in and prevent Ralphie from being unfairly eliminated. Nice guys finish last, I thought with a defeated sigh.

At last, we were down to the eliminations and Ralphie appeared distraught when he found himself standing next to Becca, who had actually done a horrible job. One side of her fried pork chop had been burned to a crisp and the other side was barely cooked.

Ralphie's meal, on the other hand, had been cooked to perfection. I felt so guilty, it was hard to look at him.

After I rattled off all the criticisms the judges had with Becca's food, I turned to Ralphie and gave an Oscar-worthy speech. "Ralphie, after being a front-runner throughout this competition, you really dropped the ball tonight. We asked you to prepare one of my signature dishes with a twist and you gave us chicken and dumplings that was so greasy, it was barely edible. Slimy chicken skin floated in your broth. Your carrots weren't cooked long enough and were hard and inedible. Your dumplings were like clumps of unseasoned flour that stuck in the judges' throats." I shook my head solemnly. "I don't know what went wrong, but your meal was a disaster."

I was lying through my teeth. Ralphie's flavorful food had been switched with some crap the behind-the-scenes chefs had concocted.

Ralphie dropped his head in contrition as I falsely accused him of a number of culinary sins.

"I don't know what went wrong, Cori. I tasted my dish and it seemed, uh, well, to me it tasted perfect."

"Sadly, your dish was far from perfect," I replied. Then I looked from Ralphie to Becca, as if trying to decide whom to send home. Finally, after a lengthy amount of time had passed, I said the fateful words… "Becca, by a wing and a prayer, you're safe tonight. And that means, Ralphie, it's time for you to turn off your burners and exit Cori's Kitchen."

Ralphie's knees visibly buckled and he made a pitiful croaking sound as if his life had just come to an end. Barely able to stand, he would have never made it back to his workstation. Fortunately, the segment where he was supposed to walk back to his station and turn off the flames of his stove had been prerecorded at the beginning of the competition. All he had to do was turn around and walk off set.

Sensitive soul that he was, he shook like a leaf and sobbed into his hands. Stumbling as if he were punch-drunk, Ralphie became the first contestant on Cori's Kitchen that required assistance during his walk of shame.

Ralphie's exit was so emotional that the celebrity judges and a few of the remaining contestants were wiping tears from their eyes.

I felt bad for him, too, but I also had a ray of hope regarding the Emmys. With Ralphie's tear-jerking performance, maybe my show would get nominated after all.

CHAPTER 19

Being a madam was not easy work. I didn't have to lie on my back to earn a living, but keeping a bunch of whores in line taxed my nerves. On the days that I had to whip their asses, my physical strength was sapped. I didn't play with those bitches; I would beat the hell out of them when they acted up. I had to. Otherwise, they would have run all over me.

Out of all of the lowdown things that some of those gals did, I have to say that there's nothing worse than a thieving whore. It's bad for business when customers can't trust that a hooker isn't going to run through their pockets and help herself to money she didn't earn.

I'll never forget the day the police commissioner himself, Paddy O'Grady, came barreling out of one of the rooms, face red with fury and wearing only his boxers. He was gripping the arm of the newest member of my stable, a Spanish gal who went by the name of Margarita.

"I caught myself a thief," O'Grady bellowed, yanking Margarita forward.

Naked as a jaybird and eyes popping out with fear, Margarita shook her head vigorously, denying that she was a thief. She kept up her protest in rambling Spanish. None of us knew what the hell she was saying. She fought to break loose from O'Grady's grip, but she couldn't get away. His hold on her was as secure as a handcuff.

He was a big, burly Irish fella with as much tangled red hair on his broad chest as he had on his head. Even more unruly red hair covered his upper lip. His wild mustache added to his threatening look. He reminded me of a big, red-colored grizzly bear. He acted like one, too. None of the gals liked him. Not only because he was a mean ol' cuss, but also due to the unnatural favors he demanded from the gals.

No one wanted to turn a trick for free, so I could understand why Margarita felt she deserved to be compensated, but it boggled my mind why she thought she could pull one over on the police commissioner when he was trained to catch thieves.

"What are you going to do about this pickpocket, Eula Mae?" O'Grady hollered, slamming Margarita against a wall and smacking her across one cheek and then the other. He was heavy-handed and her face turned colors and puffed up right away. I didn't like seeing my merchandise getting damaged with visible marks, and so I told the commissioner to simmer down and let me handle the situation.

"How do you plan to handle it?"

"I'm gonna whip her tail with my razor strap."

I sent my best gal, Sophronia, to go get my razor strap. I noticed excitement gleaming in her eyes when she raced off to get it. Margarita was Sophronia's biggest competition, and Sophronia was eager for her to get knocked down a peg or two.

Infuriated that Margarita had given the commissioner a reason to raise hell, I grabbed her by her long black hair and tugged her over to my business office, which was nothing more than a small room behind the kitchen of the whorehouse.

Being that I was handling the situation, I expected O'Grady to go back to the bedroom, get dressed, and leave the premises. But he was eager to see the show and followed behind Margarita and me.

"Don't worry, Commissioner. I'm gonna light fire to this whore's ass," I assured him.

"I want to see how you deal with that thief with my own eyes," he replied stubbornly.

I'd always whipped my gals in private and on my own terms. I wasn't comfortable with the idea of O'Grady standing around eyeballing a

*personal moment between me and a whore. Most Johns who had problems
with any of my gals trusted that I'd dispense punishment accordingly.
But not O'Grady.*

*If I would have asked the commissioner to give me some privacy, he
would have shut down my business and locked up me and my gals.*

*Sophronia returned with the strap and O'Grady ordered her to go
fetch his clothes. "Fetch" was his exact word. Being the most favored gal
at my establishment, Sophronia wasn't accustomed to being treated like
a puppy. Sulking, she left my office and went to retrieve the commissioner's clothes.*

*While I was whooping Margarita's ass, O'Grady pulled out his peter,
which was a decent size for a peckerwood.*

*"Teach that bitch a lesson. Burn that ass up," he jeered, jerking on his
dick as I wailed on Margarita. Margarita wriggled and screamed while
O'Grady grunted and panted like an animal. He was fist-fucking himself so vigorously, his ruddy face was slick with perspiration.*

*I was growing tired, but realized I couldn't finish off the ass whipping
until O'Grady had finished whacking off. I took a deep breath and lit
into Margarita so hard that blood began to trickle down her butt cheeks.*

*Sophronia slipped into my office, gawking at Margarita's bloody ass
as she held O'Grady's neatly folded clothing.*

*Never in a million years would I have thought that that would be the
moment when Sophronia would fall from grace, but life is full of surprises.*

*"Lick the blood, lick it all up," O'Grady shouted, manhandling his
privates at a frantic pace.*

*I briefly stopped beating on Margarita and stared at the commissioner
in confusion.*

"Don't stop! Beat the skin off that bitch," he ordered me.

*I quickly raised the strap again and let it cut into Margarita's ass,
causing more blood to trail down the back of her thighs.*

"Nigga bitch, I told you to lick it up, goddamn it!"

Lick what up? I wondered as I froze, holding my strap midair. I had a vague idea of what the crazy son of a bitch was telling me to do and the thought made my stomach turn.

With spittle gathered in the corners of his mouth, he looked like a madman as he pointed at Sophronia and then at Margarita's bloody ass. Suddenly enlightened, I nearly collapsed as relief rushed through me with a violent force.

O'Grady wanted Sophronia to lick the blood off Margarita's hind parts.

While Margarita was hunched over and crying her little heart out, I noticed Sophronia trying to inch her way over to the door.

"Where do you think you're going, Sophronia? If you don't do what the commissioner told you to, he's gonna lock your ass up." I hated putting my best gal in such an awful predicament, but I didn't have a choice.

Margarita was so weak from the beating, she could hardly stand up straight. I had to physically bend her into the right position for Sophronia to work on her.

It was terrible. I had two distressed whores on my hand. Margarita was crying from the pain I'd inflicted upon her and Sophronia was bawling her eyes out over the unnatural deed she was being forced to do.

Fortunately, the disgusting blood licking didn't last too long. O'Grady quickly shot off a load that spilled over his beefy hand.

O'Grady dismissed both Sophronia and Margarita. Sophronia burst out of my office with blood stains around her mouth and down the sides of her face, scaring the dickens out of my other gals.

Despite her inability to speak English, Margarita was able to convey to the gals that Sophronia had sucked the blood out of the cuts on her ass. Back in those days, folks were funny about anyone suspected of dealing in dark arts. Being labeled a bloodsucker didn't go over very well with Sophronia's regulars or with the other whores. Folks were afraid of her and none of the gentlemen callers wanted to be behind closed doors with her, anymore.

Sophronia went from being my number one gal to being dead last.

After a while, she started messing with heroin. When she lost her looks, I had to let her go. She begged me to keep her on, but I couldn't. Her haggard face and tarnished reputation was bad for business.

I'd wasted my valuable time listening to Grandma Eula Mae talk about that police commissioner, O'Grady and the two prostitutes. Licking and sucking on blood was not the kind of thing I cared to introduce into my bedroom. Disgusted, I turned off the recording. True, I'd been getting some juicy information from Grandma Eula Mae, but I hadn't discovered a damn thing that I could put to use from that particular part of her whore stories. Blood licking—ugh! How revolting!

After talking about the freaky police commissioner, she went on to vent about police corruption and local politics back in the old days. She talked about a bunch of shit I wasn't interested in. I fast-forwarded for five minutes, and when I hit "Play," she was still going on and on about crooked politicians and dirty cops.

I glanced at the clock and sighed. I wished I could find something juicy to add to my sex repertoire, but I didn't have time to pore through the tapes. Maverick was a presenter at the ESPY Awards ceremony and my glam squad would be arriving at our apartment at any moment to get me ready for the red carpet.

Maverick no longer used the services of the escort agency. With Tamara playing the role of our sex toy, and allowing Maverick to bite her ass, titties, and pussy, he no longer needed Katya. After he finished biting on Tamara, I was right there with a wet pussy for him to bust a load in.

My husband and I were good, again. Our marriage was stronger than ever, and I intended to do everything in my power to keep it that way.

CHAPTER 20

Last night's ESPY Awards and the after-parties had been thrilling, but now, my tired ass was paying for all the fun I'd had. I could barely keep my eyes open as Clayton applied my makeup. We were both sipping cups of Pu-erh tea, a fine blend of dried and fermented leaves that came from the Chinese Yunnan region next to the Tibet border. I didn't always share my luxury tea, but I'd had such a good time last night, I was feeling charitable.

Clayton took a long sip of tea. "Mmm. This tea is delicious, but I have to say, you are making me earn my pay, today."

"What do you mean?"

"You look exhausted, and I'm doing everything I can to make you look wide awake, but hiding these bags under your eyes is not easy."

"Work your usual magic with concealer."

"I'm trying, but you overpacked, baby. I've never seen you carrying this much luggage," he quipped.

"Ha-ha, you got jokes, but it's too early in the morning for me to laugh."

"I'm serious. Concealer isn't working, so let's try an ice pack to get down the puffiness and then I'll reapply the concealer." He wiped the concealer from under my eyes and then pulled his phone from his pocket.

He called one of the college interns who was working on the show as production assistants, but were basically, gophers. "Bring a bowl of ice to Cori's dressing room, pronto!" Clayton enjoyed exerting power.

"What about Preparation H? Isn't that quicker?" I asked.

"Chile, that's an urban myth. You can go blind if any of that shit gets in your eyes. You better keep it up your ass and away from your eyes."

"Thankfully, my ass is just fine. No Preparation H for me."

Clayton gawked at me.

"Why are you looking at me like that?"

"Because you're lying."

"Why would I lie about that?"

"Are you telling me that you don't suffer from even a minor case of hemorrhoids?"

"Hell, no! Why would I? I never pushed out a baby. And back when I was a child, my grandmother would have a fit if my cousins or I sat on a hard surface. She said it would give us 'the piles,'" I said, chuckling at the memory.

"Umph."

"Umph, what? Speak your mind."

"I'm not trying to get all up in your business, Cori, but if you don't ever have to dab on a little bit of Preparation H, then you must not be handling yourself in the bedroom—if you know what I mean." Clayton winked in an overly confident way that suggested he knew more about how to cater to a man in a bedroom than I did, which I found offensive.

"No disrespect, Clayton. I don't mean to be offensive because you know I'm not homophobic, but—"

"Here we go," he said, rolling his eyes. "Let me brace myself for all the disrespect that's about to come out of your mouth."

"No, seriously. I'm all for gay rights, marriages, and everything, and you're completely aware of that. But being a gay man, what would you know about sex between a heterosexual, married couple?"

"Oh, I know plenty," he said smugly. "Every one of my lovers has been a so-called heterosexual man—and quite a few have been married."

"Ew. I'm not talking about the fruity, down-low brothers. I mean, real, heterosexual men."

"There's no such thing as a real heterosexual man. All men either want their salad tossed or they want to toss someone else's. Or both. But I'm a true-blue bottom; I don't toss salads. I have a problem when a man wants me to pump dick into his ass. I'll let him suck my privates, if he's into that, but I won't fuck my man in the ass."

"That's way too much information, Clayton. And it's too early in the morning for me to be listening to the sordid details of your sex life. What kind of masculine man would want to suck a gay man's dick?"

"Girl, plenty of 'em."

The intern arrived with an oversized bowl of ice, and Clayton and I went silent. It seemed to take her longer than necessary to situate the bowl on the table beside me. Trying to make room for the large bowl of ice, she fiddled around with our teacups and the array of makeup that was spread out, rearranging the setup. Once she'd finally left and closed the door behind her, we resumed our conversation.

"Why do you think anal sex is sordid? It's as normal as vaginal sex," Clayton said, all up in his feelings, and sounding defensive.

"To each his own, but come on, Clayton. Be realistic. God gave women pussies for men to insert their dicks and procreate. It's as simple as that. Now, I'm not knocking your lifestyle or anything, but you know damn well that the Lord gave you an ass to shit out of and He didn't intend for you to turn it into a fuck-vessel."

Clayton scrunched up his lips. "I can't believe you're such a narrow-minded, ignorant bitch. No disrespect," he said snidely, mimicking the words I'd spoken earlier.

"You are seriously overstepping your boundaries, you Fruit Loop motherfucker," I spat, lashing out at him for calling me a bitch.

He applauded theatrically. "Nice to know how you feel about gay people. Thanks for letting your true colors show."

"I apologize for calling you a Fruit Loop, but you shouldn't have called me out of my name, either."

"True. I'll give you a pass…this time. Truce?"

I nodded.

"All I'm saying is expand your mind. Sex isn't supposed to simply be a way to procreate; it was also intended as an expression of love and a way to give and receive pleasure. You're a prime example of that. No shade," he quickly added. "You fuck your husband regularly, don't you?"

"Yeah, and…?"

"Well, you two haven't made any babies, yet. So you're obviously not smashing to procreate. Look, you're the one who tweeted about hiring a surrogate, so it's not like I'm making a false statement."

"Okay, you're aware that I can't have kids, aren't you?"

"Yeah, I read something about it in the blogs."

"I would carry Mav's baby if I could," I lied. "Under normal circumstances, a man and a woman are supposed to breed. But two men can't do anything except play the roles of poop chute packers. No shade."

"The male G-Spot is the prostate gland, which women don't possess. Why would God give men such an intense pleasure center if we're not supposed to use it? Wanna know what I think? I think men and women were supposed to procreate and make the Earth plentiful, but the purpose of two male lovers is to provide each other with the kind of extreme sexual pleasure that a woman could never give."

"That's bullshit."

"Have you ever directly touched Maverick's prostate?"

I scrunched up my face. "Hell, no!"

"Don't knock it unless you've tried it. Believe me, he'll thank you for it." Again, Clayton winked, acting as if he knew something I didn't know.

"I'm confused. If all men love getting dick rammed up their asses, and you claim to be a true-blue bottom, then how does your man get satisfied?"

"First of all, no pussy in the world can compete with a tight asshole, and secondly, I don't have anything against giving my man a little tongue action, if you know what I mean."

"Ew. You lick assholes?" I grabbed my cup of tea and covered the top with the palm of my hand. "I hope that intern didn't mistakenly rearrange our teacups because I'm scared to drink after your nasty ass, now."

"Girl, ain't nothing wrong with my mouth."

"So you say." I contorted my face as I moved my cup far from Clayton's reach.

Being overly sensitive, Clayton snatched up both cups of tea and stormed over to the washroom and poured out my super-expensive Pu-erh tea. I could hear him rinsing both cups out, swishing water around vigorously. He came out of the bathroom, drying one of the cups with a paper towel.

"Now, you don't have to worry about catching anything from me. Would you like me to make you a fresh cup of tea in your sterile cup, your highness, or are you afraid you might catch something from my hands?"

"You're being ridiculous."

He put a hand on his hip. "Maybe you want to hire a new make-up artist, too. Someone you won't be likely to catch any kind of diseases from." His voice cracked, and I realized how badly I'd hurt and offended him.

"I'm sorry, Clayton. I took it too far."

"You sure did, bitch," he replied with a hint of a smile.

"Well, I'll be careful to watch what I say around your sensitive ass from now on."

"Since I keep my ass lubed up real good, it's far from being sensitive, honey." He gestured flamboyantly and burst out laughing, demonstrating that our little tiff was over.

With the competition narrowed down to only four contestants, I had much more free time than usual. I had finished taping my segment where I explained the next task to the contestants super early and had the rest of the day to myself.

Today the kids were participating in New York's campaign against hunger and were cooking tasty meals at a community soup kitchen in the Bedford-Stuyvesant section of the city. Their task was to prepare my recipes in a heart-healthy and diabetes-friendly way, using only a fraction of the fat, sugar, and calories found in my classic Southern cuisine.

Their judges would be the impoverished souls who depended on the soup kitchen for sustenance. Azaria and Norris would be on hand to count the votes and declare which contestant had garnered the most votes. Lucky them! Azaria was always trying to outshine me and I wished her luck preening for the camera while inhaling the stench of the homeless. It wouldn't be an easy feat.

I didn't have to appear on camera again until tomorrow when another contestant would be sent packing. That someone was supposed to be Becca, but I didn't think our female viewers (who were the majority) would appreciate seeing Becca kicked off the show. I needed to talk to Josh about keeping Becca around until the final two. I felt we needed to make it seem like our remaining female contestant at least stood a fighting chance.

Clearly, it was time for Angus, the racist skinhead to go home. I had no doubt that I could persuade Josh to agree to get rid of him next, instead of Becca.

For the finale, Josh wanted the pretty boy and the preacher to duke it out. He believed that Yancy's quirky personality and Michelangelo's dreamy looks would keep the viewers riveted. And that was probably true, but I had a personal vendetta against Michelangelo. How dare he jeopardize my unblemished reputation by pulling down my damn drawers while I was in an emotionally weakened state?

He had to go. If by some fluke, he ended up winning the competition, I would have to make appearances with him, promoting his ventures as well as promoting the show. I didn't want to be tempted into any more intimate situations with that smooth-operating panty-peeler. I had enough problems in my life and couldn't risk being accused of fooling around with a contestant.

I'd already made sure that Ralphie would keep his mouth shut by flying Ellie to Chicago to personally pay him off with cash. Ellie reported back that she had to twist his arm to get him to take the money. He didn't feel that I owed him anything and said he was grateful for everything I'd already done for him.

It was a great relief to learn that he didn't hold a grudge against me for allowing him to be sent home. I truly appreciated his loyalty.

CHAPTER 21

I thought about using my leisure time to shop for baby clothes or maybe meet up with an interior designer to discuss concepts for the baby's nursery. But the fabulous evening Maverick and I had spent at the ESPY Awards had robbed me of sleep, and what I needed more than anything was a long nap. I told my driver to take me home. Usually, I'd communicate with Ellie, check emails, or make calls during the ride home, but today I simply I wanted to close my eyes and enjoy the peace.

My peacefulness was short-lived when my thoughts flashed to the conversation I'd had with Clayton early this morning. According to Clayton, there was no such a thing as a heterosexual man. He'd said all men wanted to suck dicks and get fucked in the ass, but I found that statement to be ludicrous. If there were such vast numbers of men who were sexually attracted to other men, then why did Clayton have such a tumultuous and sad love life? He was constantly bitching about being done wrong by one of the many unidentified men he was known to refer to as his fiancé. Every month he had a new fiancé. No ring on his finger, but he was constantly engaged to some anonymous man.

On further thought, why was he always kicking it with his queen friends on special holidays instead of being booed up with one of his future husbands? I should have asked him that during our discussion. Hindsight sucked.

A real man like Maverick, who loved the female anatomy, would never be interested in plugging the butthole of a hairy ol' man. He certainly didn't want a dick or anything else being shoved up his ass. And if a motherfucker with a swinging dick tried to stick an erection anywhere near Maverick's mouth, that gay-fish would get a beat down he'd never forget.

Coming to the conclusion that Clayton was delusional, I drifted off to sleep. When we reached my apartment, the driver woke me by gently calling my name. That short nap gave me a second wind, and instead of going up to my apartment and getting in bed as I'd planned, I waved goodbye to my driver and then walked around the block to the garage where I kept my whip parked.

With dark shades hiding my face, I drove to Babeland, a sex entertainment boutique. This was the kind of shopping excursion that I would normally have had Ellie handle for me, but it was a sudden decision and she was taking care of other business on my behalf.

Hastily, I snatched up three different types of anal sex toys: a shaft ring with an attached anal arm, a beaded butt probe, and a very small butt plug for beginners. If Maverick enjoyed the tiny butt plug, we'd work our way up to the other devices.

The idea of sticking objects in Maverick's asshole was repugnant to me, but the Mavcor brand was potentially a billion-dollar business, and if I had to go as far as to strap on a damn dildo and fuck my husband's brains out, then that's what I'd do to keep our marriage intact.

After I got home and emptied the contents from Babeland on the bed, I had second thoughts about trying to introduce Maverick to anal sex. The objects looked intimidating and dangerous, like they'd rip him a new asshole.

The idea of tampering with Maverick's ass was gross, and doing something that could possibly cause the smell of shit to drift around my bedroom was out of the question. Repulsed, I dumped all the anal devices down the trash shoot. Rethinking the situation, I decided to introduce Maverick's ass to something small and gentle—like the soothing tip of a tongue. But not *my* tongue. Fuck that!

I wondered if Tamara would be amenable to tongue-fucking Maverick. She was definitely a thirsty bitch who would probably do most anything to attain the status of mistress to my successful, wealthy husband. Maybe I should string her along and make her think that Mav was looking for a discreet side bitch.

I'd sweet-talk her into eating Maverick's ass, but after that, I'd have to give the slut her walking papers. I couldn't have a shit-licker cooking for me.

Bringing up the subject of Tamara licking my husband's ass was going to be really awkward. I had no idea how to broach the subject. Hopefully, after brainstorming, I'd be able to come up with a clever idea.

I checked the time and was surprised it was only half past noon. Tamara wasn't scheduled to start preparing our dinner until five, giving me ample time to come up with a devious way to convince her to cooperate.

Meanwhile, my second wind was over. My eyes were getting heavy. I threw back the covers and slid into bed. I also clicked on my grandmother's recording, allowing myself to be lulled to sleep by the sound of her voice and the infinite wisdom she imparted.

It pissed me off when the newspapers referred to my business as a house of ill repute. That description gave the impression of a ramshackle place in need of repairs and a good scrubbing down.

My brothel looked as good as most rich folks' homes. It was decked out with plush carpeting, expensive furniture, and original art that I got from this intellectual fella named Albert Banner. Mr. Banner had traveled all over Europe buying paintings from artists who were new on the scene. He was a regular at my place and also gave me stacks and stacks of books to line the walls of the main room. It tickled me the way he would pick out a book of poetry he'd donated from the library and then take the book up to the room with him and his chosen gal.

My whores called him the "Poetry Man" based on the fact that he recited long passages of Yeats, Tennyson, Longfellow, or Wordsworth while slowly undressing the gals. The only reason I know the names of those poetry fellas is due to Mr. Banner bringing the new additions for the library straight to my office before placing them on the shelves. Thank the Lord he didn't read me any poetry, but he sure made me suffer through listening to the life story of each and every one of the poets he admired. I only put up with that crap because Mr. Banner was one of the kindest and most generous men I'd ever met.

Lots of men came to my place to socialize as much as they came to screw the whores. My place was more than a whorehouse; it was a sort of gentlemen's club where the upper-crust folks could sit around drinking good liquor while playing backgammon and card games. If they wanted solitude while waiting for their favorite gal, they'd sit and quietly read a book from the library that Mr. Banner had donated.

I made a shitload of money by doubling and tripling the price of the booze I sold. And I charged a pretty penny for my famous dinners, also. White folks loved my cooking. They couldn't get the kind of food I served at home. My Southern-style cooking was as foreign and exotic to those Northern crackers as were my colored and Spanish whores. I charged my clients extra for damn near everything, and it occurred to me to put a price on the books they selected from my library, but I didn't. I figured charging folks to sit and read would be downright tacky. And there wasn't anything tacky about Eula Mae.

Every so often, folks wanted to rent out my place for exclusive, all-night parties and that's when I really raked in the dough.

Of course, O'Grady always got his cut. His bribes and kickbacks were already costing me a fortune, but when his greedy behind started demanding an even higher percentage of my exclusive parties, I had to draw the line. It was to the point where O'Grady was making damn near as much as I was without investing one red cent into the business.

So, I finally stood up to him, which was a big mistake on my part. That ornery son of a bitch sent two paddy wagons and three squad cars to my place. Those coppers didn't merely kick the door in—no, sir, they showed me they meant business by tearing down the door with axes and sledgehammers.

I would have opened the door for them, but that would have deprived them of the fun of raiding the place. Oh, how those boys enjoyed causing a ruckus: blowing on their whistles, kicking over furniture, and smashing lamps with their billy clubs. Whores were running naked through the place, screaming and stampeding toward the back door. The tricks, holding shoes and a pile of clothing in their arms, were climbing out windows and huddling together on the rooftop.

Those coppers loved creating mayhem. Grinning with malicious delight, they collected the fleeing whores and chained us all together as they hauled us off to the county jail.

Believe me when I tell you that jail is not a place for a woman to be.

Mr. Banner tried to use his money and influence to get me out, but those honkies made me do a fourteen-day stint before they gave me bail. Though some may think two weeks isn't a lot of time, it was too goddamn long for me. I'll tell you something: when my court date came around, I was scared shitless that the judge was going to send me upstate and make me do some hard prison time. I was nervous, but I didn't let it show. I pulled up at the courthouse in my Cadillac. I was glamorous as a movie star when I strutted inside the courtroom wearing dark sunglasses and wrapped up in a full-length mink coat. Pictures of me were splattered on the front pages of all the Negro newspapers in and around the Philadelphia area. I was notorious, honey!

It turned out the judge was a regular at my place, and I got off with only a slap on the wrist. But in order to continue running my establishment, I had to give in to O'Grady's demands. Lord, how I despised that man. My hatred festered inside me to the point where all I could think about was getting revenge on him.

First of all, he had ruined the life of my best girl, Sophronia. It hurt when I had to run her off my property when she was hiding behind bushes, trying to secretly solicit my customers as they entered and exited the premises. According to gossip, she was offering to suck a dick for fifty cents and would suck off an entire party of men for two measly dollars.

My heart went out to Sophronia, but I was a businesswoman, and I couldn't have her skulking about my property, harassing customers while looking like death warmed over. It didn't take much to run Sophronia off. All I had to do was threaten to come outside and whoop the living daylights out of her. But there were times when that heroin habit of hers had her feeling brave. At those times she'd get right stubborn and ornery, and would refuse to carry her ass off my property. Whenever she got out of hand and refused to skedaddle, I was forced to come outside and scald her with a bucket of hot water. I didn't like treating Sophronia so harshly, but it was the only way to get rid of her junkie ass.

Besides Sophronia getting on my nerves, there was O'Grady. That man was a monster and it seemed he lived and breathed to make my life miserable. When he started raiding my place on a weekly basis, he left me no choice but to find a way to get rid of him.

If I had to hear my grandmother admit to committing a heinous murder, I was sure I wouldn't be able to sleep peacefully, so I turned off the recording. Before I knew it, I was in dreamland.

"What are you doing home so early, baby?" Maverick's deep voice entered my dream and gently pulled me out. I yawned and stretched and then sat up and smiled at him.

"I had a short day at the studio," I said, inhaling a whiff of something that smelled wonderfully spicy. "Is Tamara here already?"

"Yeah, she's been here for over an hour."

I glanced at the clock. It was after six, and I was surprised I'd slept for so long. I was also disappointed that I hadn't gotten an opportunity to talk to Tamara in private before Maverick came home.

"Listening to your grandma's tapes?" he asked, gesturing toward the old-fashioned tape player on the nightstand.

"Yes. I miss her and listening to her voice, hearing her talk about the good old days makes it seem like she's still here."

Maverick nodded in understanding. He had no idea that Grandma Eula Mae had been a notorious madam in her heyday. He was only aware of her culinary skills and how she'd cook for and hosted numerous civil rights activists at her restaurant and put them up in the hotel she ran for colored travelers in need of lodging.

"Listen, babe. I, uh…" Maverick hesitated as a slow smile crept across his face.

"What's the smile for?" He looked so cute and kissable, I couldn't help from smiling, too.

"Tamara brought an assistant with her tonight."

Instantly pissed, I scowled and folded my arms across my chest. "That's presumptuous of her. Fuck if we're paying for a goddamn assistant. No one gave her permission to bring extra help."

"Calm down; it was my idea. I was joking around with Kevin Berenbaum at the station today and he mentioned that back when his wife was his chef, she used to bring a helper with her from time to time."

"But it's not as if we're having a big dinner party. Why does Tamara require a sous chef to cook a simple dinner for two people?"

Maverick and I had been more than generous with Tamara, and it annoyed me that she was trying to squeeze more money out of us.

"Before you blow up, let me explain." Maverick spoke in a calm tone as if I were a loose cannon, apt to explode at any moment.

Matching his calm tone, I said, "Okay, explain."

"Kevin's wife and her kitchen helper used to put on a novelty act during the meal...if you catch my drift." He raised his brows twice, suggesting that the novelty act was something salacious.

I'd had an idea of my own—a novelty act that I wanted Tamara to perform—but Maverick looked so excited about whatever our chef and the kitchen helper had plotted, I supposed I could put my plan on the back burner for now.

"I hope Tamara's helper is discreet. The last thing we need is for someone to sneak and take pics of us and post them on Instagram. Did you confiscate the bitch's phone?"

Maverick looked appalled by the suggestion. "No, I didn't take her phone. What do I look like, the head of security for Drake or Chris Brown? I printed a copy of our confidentiality clause and she signed it."

"Okay, but can you give me an idea of what the novelty act consists of?"

"I'm not sure, but you should put on something comfortable—and no panties." He winked at me as if a mere hint of a naughty surprise should have excited me.

I wasn't excited in the least. Having my cooch eaten by a woman was more of an annoyance than a turn-on. I spread my legs for bitches purely for Maverick's enjoyment. Sure, my body reacted when a carpet muncher was trying to suck a nut out of me, but as far as my emotional needs went, I preferred feeling my husband's strong arms gripping my shoulders while forcefully plunging dick into me.

After Maverick left the bedroom, I turned on the shower. In no rush for the novelty act, I deliberately took my time, letting the water jets pummel my shoulders and back while I closed my eyes and imagined my favorite fantasy: me standing on the stage, wiping away tears as I accepted my Emmy.

CHAPTER 22

I entered the dining room, wearing a black-and-white Givenchy dress that had an ethnic look about it. I felt like an African queen about to hold court.

Maverick sat at his place at the dining room table, and I took a seat at the opposite end. Tamara emerged from the kitchen, pushing a serving cart. Behind her was the most ratchet-looking bitch I'd ever seen. The little thot was carrying a silver tray with a bottle of wine and two monogrammed crystal wineglasses. She was rocking a sparkly bustier and a super-short, tight skirt. Her seven-inch heels were leopard-print and had fringes dangling around the ankles. I frowned at her fingernails that were shaped like sharp daggers with multiple colors and designs.

Unbelievably tacky, she had to be a stripper. She looked like she'd been yanked straight off the pole of one of the sleaziest strip clubs in town. Her ass was so humongous, there was no way it was real. Her nasty-looking ass had to be the result of butt implants or ass injections. I would bet money that the ho was all over YouTube grinning at the camera while twerking and throwing that big ass around in complete circles.

My eyes scrolled up to her weave and I blinked in revulsion. Her hair, a pale shade of green with lavender, pink, and gold streaks running through it, was an assault to my eyes. She looked vile and unclean, like she was full of STDs. She looked like the kind of girl whose pussy smelled like ass.

"Hey, y'all! We up in this bitch with the food and wine," the stripper announced, bouncing her shoulders, and wiggling her ass like she was the featured entertainment at a bachelors' party.

It was embarrassing to imagine this gutter slut entering my exclusive apartment building and announcing that she'd come to visit Maverick and me. I shuddered to think about how offended our concierge must have been by our skanky guest.

I shot Maverick a murderous look. He returned my look with a dumb expression, like he didn't understand what my problem was.

Astounded that Maverick and Tamara would think it was okay to invite such ghetto-trash into a fine and decent home, I swiveled and gawked at both of them.

But neither met my gaze; both pretended that it was perfectly normal for Tamara to have an assistant that looked like she missed the cut for *Love & Hip Hop.*

Tamara cleared her throat. "Cori, this is Heavenly."

I groaned inwardly. Of course, she would have a stripper name. I felt appalled and annoyed and personally violated that someone named Heavenly was in my presence and was actually standing in the dining room of my sumptuous apartment.

"Hi, Cori," Heavenly said, grinning. From her confident smile and the way she dragged out the word, "hi," I could tell that Heavenly thought she was the shit.

I didn't bother to return her greeting. Instead, I addressed my husband. "Did Heavenly sign her stripper name or did she use her government name on the confidentiality agreement?"

"She used her real name," Maverick responded. Embarrassed by my sarcasm, his eyes darted downward.

Taking me totally off guard, Heavenly shot across the dining room and slammed the silver tray on the table. The crystal glasses clattered loudly against the wine bottle. Startled, my body involuntarily jerked in alarm.

"Yo, bitch, don't be talking trash about me and acting like I ain't even standing here. If you got a question about me, then ask me. I don't need your husband or no-fucking-body else to speak for me."

The nasally tone of her voice grated on my nerves, not to mention her grammar. "She's a novelty act, indeed," I said, speaking pointedly to Maverick. "I want this tacky chick out of here!"

"Who you calling 'tacky'? Fuck you, you dumb bitch, acting like you better than somebody. Bitch, please," Heavenly squawked in her annoying voice.

I gawked at Maverick and Tamara. "Are either of you going to do something?"

"You're overreacting, Cori," Maverick said with a stupid smile that I wanted to slap off his face. "You and Heavenly got off on the wrong foot, that's all."

I couldn't believe that my husband was actually taking up for a ho that was disrespecting me in my own home. I was about to curse him out when Heavenly suddenly moved into my personal space. She bent over, positioning herself so that her face was only inches from mine.

"Don't start with me, bitch. I don't appreciate being called out of my name. Just because you on TV, shit don't make you better than me." Looking around the room, she smirked and said, "You got ahead in life when you lucked up and sucked the right athlete's dick."

Appalled, I gasped. "You better get the fuck out of my face!" I pushed my chair back, putting a little distance between us.

"And you better watch that smart-ass mouth of yours...don't be talking shit about me," Heavenly clapped back.

"I want her off the premises this instant," I yelled at the top of my lungs.

"Cori! Babe, calm down," Maverick said.

"No, I'm not calming down. I want this clown bitch out of my home." At that point I stood up and to my utter shock, Heavenly pushed me back down.

"We about to have a problem, you bougie bitch. Even though this is your crib, you can't insult me and expect to get a pass." Heavenly dug her sharpened nails into my shoulder.

"Ow!" I tried to squirm out of her clutch, but she was clawing me with her dagger nails, holding me in place. It was a natural reaction to swing my fist at her in defense.

To my horror, she reacted by grabbing the wine bottle from the table and wielded it like a weapon. "I told you not to start with me, bitch. Put your hands on me again and I'ma crack you in the face."

Maverick wasn't doing a damn thing. He was sitting there gawking as if mesmerized. To get Heavenly off me, I picked up the glass of ice water from in front of me and tossed the water in her face. The shock of the cold water caused her to loosen her grip. I jumped out of my chair and rushed her, going for the weave and trying my best to yank that rainbow-colored bullshit clean out of her head.

The pain of her tracks being ripped out of her scalp disabled her. I was about to beat that bitch's ass when Maverick decided to jump into the fray. Somehow he managed to get her weave out of my fists. Tamara grabbed Heavenly, holding her back, while Maverick held me.

Heavenly struggled to break Tamara's hold. "Get off me, Tamara. Let me go. I'ma beat that bum-bitch's ass."

Being called a bum-bitch by a broke-ass trick caused me to flinch, but I recovered quickly. "Try to beat my ass! You're not going to do shit, you thirsty bitch." I had come down to her level, and I didn't care. "I can't believe I'm breathing the same air as a disgusting prostitute like you," I shouted with my face twisted in disgust.

"It's true. I be out here chasing dick to pay the rent. I do what I gotta do to pay my bills, but you need to look at your own damn self, before pointing a finger at me. I was invited here to get in a situation with your husband, so tell me…what does that say about you? I wouldn't even be up in this piece if it wasn't for your dry-ass pussy with no walls and no type of grip."

Her accusations about my cooch were a goddamn lie, and I reacted with a straight face—I didn't bat an eye. "Listen, stank ho…I'm asking you nicely to please leave the premises. Go twerk that fake ass on some other man because you are not touching my husband!"

Heavenly let out a bitter laugh. "Everybody got a little ho in 'em, so don't act like you don't. I bet you hoeing for the network to get ratings for your corny show. I wonder who you had to smash to get your face on TV."

"Be quiet, Heavenly," Tamara said, giving her a hard yank. "I think we should leave."

"You think?" I shouted mockingly. "You no longer work for us, Tamara, so take your hooker friend with you and get the fuck out!"

"It's not Tamara's fault," Maverick said, still holding me.

"I don't care. Her employment is terminated as of right the fuck now!"

"I ain't going nowhere 'til I get my coins," Heavenly yelled in a high screechy voice. "If y'all want me to roll, then somebody better pay me for my time."

With every fiber of my being, I wanted to fight that bitch, but I had to walk away from this one. It wasn't worth it. I had a show to tape and couldn't risk turning up at work with my face scratched up. Clayton would have fainted on the spot if he were tasked with the job of having to patch up my clawed face with makeup.

"Pay that whore and get her out of here," I told Maverick, and then jerked away from him. With all the dignity I could muster, I held my head high, and exited the dining room.

I sat on a chair in the bedroom, seething. Being married to a sexual deviant wasn't easy, but I'd done my best to keep my husband happy, but this time, Maverick had pushed me to my limit. Maverick and his whoring ways were going to be the ruination of the wholesome image I'd carefully crafted for us.

I glanced at the time and felt myself growing angrier. Why was it taking him so long to pay the bitch and get rid of her? I stood up, intending to find out why that stank ho was still on the premises. But I only managed a few steps toward the door before Maverick entered the bedroom, looking guilty. I wondered if he'd tried to get his money's worth by getting a quickie before the bitch bounced.

"Has Tamara and the stripper left, yet?"

He nodded.

"How much did you pay the ho?"

"Five hundred."

"Some novelty act," I said snidely, shaking my head as I repeated his terminology.

"We were supposed to have a good time. I had no idea she would go from zero to a hundred so fast."

"That's how those crack babies act. What were you thinking when you invited that trash to our residence? Don't you realize that hood rats like her don't care anything about a confidentiality agreement? She'll post a picture up on Instagram without a second thought. What does she have to lose? If you were to sue her, what would you get? Nothing except a bunch of bad press. We can't afford a scandal, Mav. I can't understand why you'd flirt with disaster."

"She won't say anything, babe." He rubbed my arm, trying to placate me.

"How do you know?"

"She was recommended by Tawny."

"Who the hell is Tawny?" I asked with my face scrunched up.

"That's Kevin Berenbaum's wife."

"I thought his wife was an ex-chef, not an ex-stripper."

"Tawny was never a stripper."

"Well, you could have fooled me with a name like *Tawny*. How does Kevin's wife who travels in a private jet and was given a small island as a wedding present even know a lowlife like Heavenly?" I said the stripper's name like there was shit was on my tongue.

"They've used her services before and Kevin sort of put me in touch with her."

"He *sort* of put you in touch? What does that mean? And why would you tell Kevin Berenbaum about our sex life?" I felt instantly humiliated that Maverick would share such sensitive information with someone of Kevin Berenbaum's status. It wasn't as if he and Kevin were best buds or anything. Their relationship was clearly defined as boss and employee.

Maverick took a deep breath. "I rarely even see Kevin or speak to him on the phone. But…apparently Tamara talks to Tawny and—"

"Tamara signed a confidentiality agreement with us."

"She probably thinks it's okay to confide in a close friend."

I rolled my eyes. "So, who told you to hire Heavenly?"

"Kevin texted me. He said something like, 'I hear you have a naughty chef. Add on to the fun with Heavenly. Talk to Tawny.' Next, he texted his wife's number. It seemed like a direct order, so I called her. You don't ignore the big guy when he makes a request."

"I don't get it. First, he forces us to keep Tamara when I wanted to fire her and now he's telling us who to bring into our bedroom. He can kiss my ass. I'll be goddamned if Kevin Berenbaum or anyone else is going to control my life."

"It's not like that, Cori. You're blowing things out of proportion. Kevin never told me that I couldn't fire Tamara, but I had sense enough to know that since she and Tawny were friends, it wouldn't be a good idea to piss Tawny off before I signed the deal."

"Yeah, well, the deal has been signed for weeks. So what's your excuse for letting him talk you into inviting filthy trash to our home?"

"Let it go, Cori. Let's have dinner and try to forget that tonight ever happened."

"I don't have much of an appetite after being accosted in my own home. And I'm not eating anything that Heavenly touched."

"Suit yourself," Maverick said with a shrug.

He turned to leave, and I blurted, "Did Heavenly suck your dick while I was confined to our bedroom?"

"No."

"You're lying, Mav."

"All right, she gave me some head…it wasn't a big deal."

"Unbelievable! A woman attacks your wife and you feel it's okay to stick your dick in her mouth."

"But I was thinking about you the whole time, Cori."

I made a sound of disgust.

"For real. I never saw you go at a chick like that before. Watching that cat fight got my dick hard as steel."

"Our marriage is so fucking pathetic," I said quietly, feeling hopeless and lost. "What was Tamara doing while Heavenly gave you head?"

"Uh…she wasn't doing anything."

"Be honest, please."

"Okay, Tamara licked my balls."

All I could do was let out a long, weary sigh. No matter how much I gave in to Maverick's sexual whims, none of my sacrifices were enough for him. With his out-of-control, male-ho behavior, I was getting the impression that I would never be enough to completely satisfy him.

Not only did I have to worry about Brazilian bitches and Russian whores, apparently, I also had to keep an eye on hoes from the 'hood. What was the use in trying to protect our reputation if Maverick was going to continue to get blowjobs, bite on asses, and dick-down anything that moved?

"I sincerely hope that girl didn't have her phone out, sneakily filming the blowjob she gave you. Low-caliber hoes like her have no shame. They proudly post their sexual conquests with celebrities online, simply to get more Instagram followers."

"She wouldn't do that."

"You don't know what that bitch is capable of."

Maverick's face clouded over, revealing his dark side—a side of him that I was keenly aware of, but his adoring fans had never seen. "Trust, she wouldn't want to make an enemy out of me."

CHAPTER 23

Expecting the white supremacist to act the fool after he got the ax, Josh had plenty of extra security on hand. Angus didn't disappoint. His exit was ugly.

With an evil expression that looked satanic, he gave the remaining contestants a roving middle finger, and called Azaria Fierro a spic-cunt as he groped his privates threateningly—like he intended to rape her.

As two security men were hustling him off set, he fixed his mean, blue eyes on me. I shuddered, and then braced myself for an explosion of ethnic slurs.

"What are you looking at, Kizzy? You chitlins-loving, Aunt Jemima-bitch," Angus spat.

Though I was braced for the worst, I still cringed as he continued his verbal attack. "I bet your great-grandmother loved opening her funky thighs for her slavemaster. 'Fuck me, Massah! Fuck me good and hard with that lily white cock of yours,'" Angus taunted in his version of slave dialect.

His vile words ripped into me like an onslaught of knives, piercing my very soul. I was speechless. I thought I could handle a racist attack, but being the recipient of such impassioned hatred had stolen my breath away.

Once Angus had finished terrorizing me, he released a demonic burst of laughter before directing his hateful rant at Josh.

Referring to the injustices inflicted upon Holocaust victims, he taunted Josh by yelling that Josh's relatives had been turned into soap and that he had lamp shades in every room of his house that were made from the human flesh of stinking Jews.

Josh turned such a deep red, his face looked purple. He let out a cry of anguish and actually swooned. He went down in slow motion, like in the movies. As malicious as Josh could be at times, there was obviously another side to him that was extremely fragile.

His assistant and several college interns tried to revive him by patting his face, fanning him with a clipboard, and calling his name.

Being that there wasn't a stretcher on hand, members of the crew had to half-carry and half-drag Josh back to his office.

Meanwhile, escorted off the premises by security, Angus yelled racial epithets throughout the journey from the cooking area to the back door. Of course, TV viewers would never see or hear about Angus's meltdown. The televised version of his exit from the show had been prerecorded. But still...what a mess!

I'd never developed a taste for hard liquor, but when I closed the door to my dressing room, I grabbed a bottle of whiskey from my mini bar and tossed back a shot with no chaser. It had been a terrible, terrible week and my nerves were shot to hell.

I was about to have another shot when there was a beep from my phone. It was a text from Josh's assistant informing me that the set would be closed tomorrow.

Tomorrow was Friday and that meant our final three contestants would be locked away in their hotel rooms for an extra-long time. Better them than me—I would go stir-crazy.

Having extra time on my hands, it occurred to me that Maverick and I should probably spend some time quality time with Sophia. The agency stressed that couples should stay in close contact with their surrogate. But I wasn't in the mood for the tension that would more than likely exist between Maverick and Sophia. She definitely was not a fan of his after he'd chomped on her thighs.

I wasn't in the mood to placate Sophia. Maverick and I needed some couple time, and I wondered if he'd be amenable to a weekend getaway. Football season hadn't started yet, and though he'd been doing a few sports interviews for his new show, he wasn't that busy, yet. I wasn't sure if his show was going to succeed. It seemed kind of boring to me. Last week he taped an interview with a disgraced jockey from New Zealand who had been disqualified from riding horses for seven years for throwing a race so that he could profit from a bet he'd made.

A show about a sleazy New Zealand jockey didn't seem exciting enough to draw a large audience, but Maverick seemed to believe that his Sunday show was his ticket to garnering the same level of respect as Bryant Gumbel. With his new contract, he was earning more than Bryant Gumbel, but Maverick also wanted to be perceived as a respected sports journalist.

Maverick knew everything there was to know about football and was a great sportscaster, but he was no television journalist. Loving him the way that I did, I would never bruise his ego by telling him that he couldn't hold a candle to Bryant Gumbel when it came to hosting an investigative sports series.

I smiled as I envisioned Maverick and me getting away from the city for the weekend, cuddled up together in a cabin in the woods— somewhere upstate or maybe Connecticut. *On second thought, scratch that.* Neither of us could deal with insects and we'd both run for the hills if a raccoon, snake, or any kind of forest creature came near our front door.

We needed quality time together in a tropical environment. Somewhere close—like the Bahamas. Our marriage had become so tainted and dirty, it no longer remotely resembled the relationship of two people who were lovingly committed to each other.

Our marriage needed to be rejuvenated, and we needed to take the time to reflect on what was good about our marriage.

As I envisioned us gazing at the stars in the moonlit sky and holding hands during walks on the beach, a sudden thrill went through me. I imagined the beautiful photos of Mav and me that would pop up on the blogs during our romantic getaway.

Of course I would alert the paparazzi as to our whereabouts. Stargazing wouldn't mean a thing if our fans couldn't vicariously enjoy the moment with us.

I smiled as I phoned Maverick at the station. Expecting him to be busy taping or going over interview questions with his producer, I was prepared to leave a message. Surprisingly, he picked up. "Hey, Cori. What's going on; is everything okay?"

"Everything is fine. I don't have to be on set tomorrow and was wondering if you were free to get away…maybe to Miami or the Bahamas?"

"Aw, I wish I could, babe, but something came up."

I was instantly deflated. "What?"

"I got an assignment to go to Brazil for a week."

"Brazil? Why? It's not Carnival season." Maverick went to Rio every year for Carnival and sometimes returned with rare and defiant STDs that were a challenge for his doctor to treat. He used condoms with prostitutes in the States, but for some reason he liked to fuck those Brazilian whores bareback.

Feeling faint, like all the life was being sucked out of me, I went silent.

"Are you there, babe?"

"I'm here." My voice was barely a whisper.

"I know what you're thinking…"

"The last time you went to Brazil you fucked eleven different whores during the trip. And you didn't bother to put on a damn condom, even once."

"I'm not going there for fun. I have an exclusive interview lined up for the show."

"An interview with whom—a bitch named Alessandra or Tereza?"

Maverick chuckled. "No, it's not like that. I promise you, my trip is all about work."

"Right."

"Remember that soccer referee from Brazil who was in the news last year?"

"No, I don't," I said sullenly.

"Yes, you do. We laughed about it when we watched the video. The dude who pulled a handgun out on the managers and the players in the middle of an amateur soccer match."

"Okay, I remember. But it was amateur soccer. Why would your network be interested in someone associated with an amateur sport? Furthermore, your people usually fly the guests to New York. Why do you have to travel all the way to Brazil?"

"The ref is afraid of flying."

"Wow," I said sarcastically and then went quiet again. I hoped my silence would make my husband realize how much he was upsetting me.

"Listen, Cori, I have to go. Do you want to go out to dinner tonight? I figured we'd eat out since we don't have a chef anymore."

"A nice restaurant isn't the answer to our problems, Maverick. Every time you go to Brazil, you lose your damn mind. I'm not trying to mess around and catch AIDS because you won't strap up."

"I'm not going there for personal pleasure, I swear. But if I do get into anything while I'm there, I promise I'll wear a condom. Okay? Feel better?"

"Not really. I feel—"

"We'll have to talk about your feelings when I get home. Love you, Cori. Bye."

Before I could utter another word, he hung up.

Our relationship was a disaster, and I was a pathetic human being to be involved in such a sick and twisted marriage. Sadly, I didn't know how to get out of it.

I was convinced that as soon as we had our son, Maverick would be inspired to change his ways and become a decent role model.

But who was I trying to fool? In my heart, I was well aware that the unborn child I was forcing upon Maverick was not the solution to our problems.

In deep despair, I began to cry. Afterward, I felt purged. Shedding tears had been cathartic, but now I wanted revenge. If Maverick thought he was the only one in the marriage who could fuck around, he was sadly mistaken. Fuck him! He could have his Brazilian whores, and I hoped that this time he got hit with a disease so severe it caused his dick to shrivel up and fall off.

I decided to make plans of my own. Plans that included the kind of man who would appreciate spending time with me.

I nibbled on my fingernail as I thought hard, trying to figure out a way to accomplish an undercover hookup with Michelangelo.

CHAPTER 24

Maverick had gotten up early to catch his flight to Rio de Janeiro and I was up, too. I fixed him coffee and made a cup of green tea for myself. Drinking my morning pick-me-up, I went through his luggage, making sure he'd packed enough clothes for a week.

He was so accustomed to me playing the role of the long-suffering wife who took all kinds of shit off him, it wasn't surprising to him that I was up early helping him get ready to fly out of the country to go fuck a bunch of whores.

I checked his bag one last time before zipping it. "Honey, you didn't pack any condoms." I spoke warmly, keeping any hint of the animosity I was feeling out of my tone.

"I don't need any. I told you this trip is about business."

I thought about those exotic STDs he was apt to get and groaned inwardly. "Pack the condoms, sweetheart. Just in case you need them," I said, giving him the kind of smile that an overly permissive parent gives to a spoiled brat kid that she adores but can't do a damn thing with.

"You're right, Cori. You never know what will happen in Brazil. Those women…whew! They can turn a saint into a sinner." Laughing, he went inside his closet and came out with a jumbo-sized box of condoms.

"Really, Mav? You need all of those?"

"Better safe than sorry," he quipped, and I smiled at his stupid humor.

If my fans only knew that the woman they admired was having a discussion with her husband about taking precautions against catching a venereal disease from whores, they'd lose all respect for me.

Maverick's phone jangled a melody and he peeked at the screen. "It's my ride to the airport." He kissed me on the forehead and grabbed his luggage.

I stood in the doorway, watching him walk jauntily toward the elevator. "Call me and let me know you arrived safely."

"I will," he replied without bothering to turn around.

I stood there until he stepped inside the elevator and the doors slid closed. Then I shut the door to our apartment and engaged the digital lock. I checked the time and frowned. It was only six forty-five. Much too early to start putting my plan in motion.

I began pacing. It probably would have been best to wait until nightfall before trying to sneak Michelangelo out of his hotel room, but Maverick had tried my patience, and I couldn't wait that long.

It wasn't that I was in dire need of sex, I wanted to get even with Maverick for all of his man-whoring over the years.

I was so amped up with adrenaline, I burned off a lot of energy by popping in an *Insanity* DVD and working out like crazy. After showering, I browsed through my closet, selecting the clothes and jewelry I would wear during the long, romantic weekend with Michelangelo.

By ten o' clock, I was ready to get in touch with him. Contacting him was a risky endeavor, and it was the risk factor that made the adventure even more exciting. Now that we were down to the final three, each of the contestants had the luxury of their own private room. Problem was their cell phones had been confiscated and the hotel phones had been removed from the rooms.

In order to reach him, I had no choice but to call the suite where they were allowed to hang out as a group. The rules of the competition allowed them to venture down to the lobby but prohibited them from leaving the hotel premises. They were supposed to use their free time preparing themselves for the next challenge by studying the recipes in my cookbooks and DVDs.

I called the suite and crossed my fingers, hoping Michelangelo would pick up.

"Yello!" said a man with a Southern drawl.

Fuck, fuck, fuck. It was the fucking preacher!

Though disappointed, I didn't miss a beat. I instantly went to my backup plan. "Hey there, Yancy. It's Cori Brown. How are you?"

"I'm fine as of now, but I won't be for long if you're calling to give us some bad news. I hope you're not gonna tell me that our leisure time is over and you have some kind of atrocious challenge for us to do," Yancy said with a groan.

"No, not at all. I was only calling to remind you guys to study and to wish you all luck. Are you all together in the suite?"

"Becca and I are playing cards and losing our minds from boredom. Michelangelo hasn't come out of his room today."

"He's probably studying. A word to the wise…your time would be best spent if you were studying, too. The competition is going to get even more difficult, Yancy."

"I'm sure the three of us have studied your recipes so much, we know them up and down, in and out, and sideways." He laughed loud and heartily at his corny joke. I chuckled politely.

"Okay, well, congrats on making it to the final three. Good luck on Monday. Now, I'd like to speak to Becca, please." I didn't actually want to speak to Becca, but I had to make it look good.

He put Becca on the phone and I repeated the spiel about studying. Her slurred responses let me know that she had been drinking—and it was only a little after ten in the morning. I'd heard from

LaTasha that Becca was a lush, but now I realized it with certainty. It was a good thing she didn't stand a prayer of winning. We couldn't send an unreliable drunkard on a press junket, nor could she be trusted to represent my brand.

I pretended not to notice that Becca was tipsy. After wishing her luck, I told her that I needed Yancy to get Michelangelo.

"I'll get him," she offered.

I considered her offer, but declined. "No, Yancy can do it."

"Okay." She sounded disappointed.

I didn't give a fuck about her disappointment. She struck me as the kind of drunk who became flirtatious and sexually uninhibited. I didn't want to risk her going to Michelangelo's room and then worming her way into his bed while I was waiting on the phone.

Becca relayed my message to Yancy, and I heard the preacher say, "Okay, be right back."

Nervousness set in as I waited to speak with Michelangelo. I was playing with fire and the mixture of fear and excitement was so exhilarating, my heart began to pound.

It took less than five minutes for Michelangelo to pick up the phone. "Hey, Cori. What's good?"

Ah, that voice. So smooth and sensual. I was immediately catapulted back to our make-out session in my dressing room. His hands gliding over my body, gently squeezing my breasts, and then meandering between my thighs and stroking my clit through my panties, and bringing it to rigidness. Thinking back, the clit action was probably when I became entranced and was unaware that he had pulled my panties down. I wondered if he'd slid a finger inside me while he was playing with my cooch. Did I hump his finger and moan? I wondered.

Suddenly, I was aroused and was eager to finish what we'd started in my dressing room. "Listen, carefully, Michelangelo. Don't let on that we're having a personal conversation."

"Okay."

"I've been avoiding you, but after what happened with Ralphie walking in on us, I'm sure you can understand the position I was in."

"Yeah, I understand."

"But today I'm willing to take a risk. I want to kidnap you for the day. But, for obvious reasons, Becca and Yancy can't know. So, play along with me, all right?"

"Sure."

"Do you want to be kidnapped?"

"Oh, yeah," he said in a voice that didn't betray any emotion. His response was so lackluster, I wasn't sure if he wanted to spend a day with me or not, but I pressed onward.

"Have you been studying my recipes?"

"I was watching one of your DVDs when Yancy knocked on the door."

"Oh, very good. I'm glad you're staying on top of your game."

"I'm trying."

"Well, I want to wish you luck for the next competition."

"Thanks, Cori."

"Also, I want you to figure out a way to slip out of the hotel, undetected. Meet me at Pinkberry at the end of the block at noon."

"Will do. See you later."

I hung up and broke into a smile. For the first time in my marriage, I was actually going to step out on my husband and fuck another man. I so desperately wanted to pay Maverick back, I would have chosen the first swinging dick that passed my way, and so I felt extremely lucky that the man I was going to cheat with was easy on the eyes.

If that fine-ass Michelangelo was as good at his fuck game as he was with those long, magical fingers of his, I was in for a hella good ride.

CHAPTER 25

Not having access to the driver the network provided, I had to drive myself to meet Michelangelo. Miscalculating traffic, I arrived twenty-five minutes earlier than I should have. With time to kill, I gazed at the cheerful-looking menu and ordered a Pink Bubbly, which was described as being a light and sweet, champagne-like, nonalcoholic beverage.

Incognito, I had on a floppy straw hat and huge sunglasses. I sat in the back and sipped on the drink, which tasted pretty good. I checked to see if Maverick had left a text or voicemail to let me know he'd arrived safely. Of course, he hadn't. He'd probably gone straight to a brothel after checking into his hotel.

Fuck you, Maverick; I have a side piece of my own to spend the weekend with!

I'd never been this infuriated over Maverick's man-ho ways. I supposed it was the idea that he was willing to risk diseases to be with the women he once referred to as being the most beautiful in the world. He acted like he lost his mind when it came to Brazilian women.

Azaria Fierro was from Brazil, yet he hadn't given her the time of day when he was a guest on my show. At least not to my knowledge. I supposed she was too Americanized for his taste.

I glanced up and was surprised to see Michelangelo sauntering inside the frozen yogurt shop. On the sly, I checked out his confident stride, and decided that I definitely liked his swagger.

When he noticed me, he flashed a big, gorgeous smile. There was something about the delight in his eyes that made me feel girlish and pretty—and desired, and I hadn't felt that way in quite a while.

Don't get me wrong; my husband and I had amazing sex, but Maverick hadn't broken into a big grin at the sight of me since the early years of our marriage.

Michelangelo began making long strides toward me. The eagerness in his walk made me fear that he might greet me by picking me up and swinging me around. Younger men could be overly enthusiastic, which would be fine if we were behind closed doors. One never knew where the paparazzi were lurking.

I stood up and firmly held up a palm.

Taking heed, he stopped walking, and I pranced right past him and went out the door. I headed for the parking garage two blocks away, and he trailed slowly behind me. We remained silent when we got off the elevator and were approaching my Porsche Cayenne.

I opened the cargo door so he could put his backpack inside.

"Nice ride," he said and then closed the door.

"Thanks."

Inside the privacy of the SUV, our eyes locked and I suddenly couldn't wait for him to stretch my cooch out. The waves of heat radiating from his body told me he was feeling the same way.

I pressed the button that turned on the ignition, and put the air on full blast.

The next thing I knew, he was leaning close and speaking softly. "Is this really happening? Am I really here with you?"

Blushing, I dropped my eyes.

He moved closer, so close I could feel his warm breath against my cheek. The touch of his hand against my neck put chills all over my heated flesh. There was a whirl of sensations inside me that I couldn't control. Any moment now, I would be getting down and dirty in a parking garage with a contestant. God, if the media knew about this…

I shivered with desire when Michelangelo dipped his head lower, his mouth aiming for mine. He crushed his lips against mine with a passion that Maverick hadn't shown for far too long. Sure, Mav's fuck game had not diminished. He could still make me cum loud and hard. But there was no more romance. He kissed me like I was his sister or a cousin.

Michelangelo's mouth was hot over mine, his tongue wild as it parted my lips and stroked inside. My hands went up to push him away, simply so I could take a moment to catch my breath and think rationally. But instead of pushing him away, my arms ended up wound around his neck, and my fingers became tangled in his thick mass of hair.

Close to him, I couldn't identify a particular brand of cologne. His fragrance had an earthiness about it, reminding me of leather and rosewood and sweet memories of love.

"I need you," he whispered against my lips and then began kissing me with heated energy, letting out a soft groan as his hands became reacquainted with my body, fondling my breasts, rubbing the lush globes of my ass, and squeezing my hips.

His desperation seemed to match mine and I was assured that we both wanted the same thing: steamy sex in the parking garage.

I should have worn a dress, but I didn't let the inconvenience of having on pants deter me. I yanked the pants past my hips and then over my sandals, and Michelangelo began to furiously work on his belt buckle. While he struggled with his zipper, I leaned over the gear shift that separated us and kissed his face, his neck, and his ears.

I was so worked up, it took a tremendous amount of willpower not to lick him all over like he was a delicious treat.

With a hungry look in my eyes, I glimpsed him taking his dick out. My mouth watered at the sight of his throbbing erection. I didn't know what to do first: bend over and suck him or perch my-self on top of him and fuck his brains out.

Unable to stop myself from at least touching it, I wrapped my hand around the length and cradled his balls in my other hand. I stroked him slowly and sensually until his head dropped back against the headrest in surrender. Droplets of creamy moisture beads dribbled out of the slit and I licked my lips in anticipation. The sensation of his dick, so hot and heavy in my hands, had my pussy clenched up painfully. I was in such a quandary. My mouth was watering with the desire to slurp on his dick, while at the same time, my cooch muscles were clenching and convulsing.

"I need that pussy," Michelangelo murmured in a husky voice. Taking away my options, he reclined the passenger seat as far as it would go and then tugged on my arm until I was straddling him.

"Damn, you're beautiful," he said, studying my body. He kissed his way down my neck, and then went lower, taking a rigid nipple into his mouth. He sucked it gently before laving it with his tongue.

Moaning, I groped for his dick and whimpered his name. I grasped a handful of juicy dick and then guided the head to my silky opening.

"Um, the condoms are in my bag in the trunk," he uttered.

"Fuck a condom!" My pussy was drooling with urgency. It was so wet, it made a loud gushy sound when he penetrated me. I pushed downward, impaling myself on his rock-hard appendage, making sure that I took in every thick inch. Each dick thrust caused pussy juice to splash and splatter. My pussy was so boisterous, it seemed to be shouting out in unabashed appreciation.

"Damn, you're juicy," he moaned, clenching my waist as he stroked inside me. He was giving it to me hard, and I was giving it back, slamming my pussy down his lengthy pole.

We were fucking the shit out of each other, but at one point, he took control. He gripped my side with one hand and grabbed ahold of the overhead handle with the other and commenced to pounding me so hard, I needed an anchor. I wrapped my arms around his neck, held on tight, preparing to be fucked into unconsciousness.

The dick was so exceptionally good, it had me babbling nonsensically. I was getting so loud, I had to bite my lip to contain the noise. Not wanting to draw attention to our illicit tryst in the parking garage, I went from lip biting to gritting my teeth in an effort to hold back a scream. But my attempts failed me and uncontrollable shrieks slipped out. Afraid that a passerby would think I was being murdered in my SUV, I had to quiet down. I accomplished that by biting into the headrest, fucking up the buttery leather interior with deep teeth marks.

When Michelangelo let go of the overhead handle and began to increase his speed of fucking, it was clear what was about to happen.

"Don't cum, yet!" I said sharply.

"I can't hold it, baby," he grunted. He came with a roaring sound and I looked around apprehensively. I was certain that some do-gooder was going to run up on us and bang on the window in an effort to stop a crime in progress. Fortunately, no one bothered us.

I was disappointed that he'd come so quickly, but was placated by the knowledge that he had all day to make it up to me. I remained in position, caressing him, and kissing his neck while he panted and struggled to catch his breath.

As I rubbed his muscular back, I glanced around the vehicle. Strange things occurred when lust took over. We had used my ride like it was a mini hotel room with wheels, and now the windows were steamed, one sandal was in the driver's seat and the other had landed on the floor in the back. One leg of my pants dangled from the steering wheel and the other was draped over the console. My Birkin bag had toppled off the backseat and was wedged beneath the driver's seat. Behind Michelangelo, the headrest was chewed up like a vicious animal had attacked it.

He opened his eyes. "What the fuck?" he said, noticing the mayhem.

"I have no idea." Shaking my head, I lifted off his lap and began gathering my things.

"I'm sorry about that," he said as I fished around in my handbag, searching for some tissues. Trying to clean his cum out of my pussy with him sitting right next to me was awkward, but there was no way I could drive all the way back to my apartment with semen dribbling down my legs.

"You're sorry about what?"

"For not being able to hold my shit. That's not even like me to cum that quick. It must have been my excitement over being with you."

"It's okay, you can make it up to me when we get to my place."

He frowned. "Is that where you're taking me—to your crib?"

"Mm-hmm."

"What about your husband?"

"What about him?" I said sassily.

He gave me a look.

I laughed. "Don't worry; he's out of town."

"Yeah, but that's not cool for me to be up in that man's house. Wouldn't it be more respectful to go to a hotel?"

"It's equally disrespectful to fuck another man's wife—in or out of his residence," I countered.

"Yeah, but—"

"He's out of the country. There's no chance of us getting caught."

Michelangelo didn't look convinced. But I didn't care. I knew beyond a shadow of a doubt that my whory husband was somewhere in Brazil, most likely sucking on a big, fake titty at that very moment.

CHAPTER 26

I felt bold and didn't make any attempts at being discreet when I entered my building with another man by my side. The concierge did a double-take as Michelangelo and I strolled past the front desk. He actually gawked at us as if he expected me to provide him with the identity of my companion. With no intention of satisfying his curiosity, I waved hello and kept moving.

God only knew how many women the concierge had seen Maverick bring home over the years while I was away, and now I was seizing the opportunity to sully what should have been the most sacred place in our home—the bedroom my husband and I shared.

I couldn't wait to feast my eyes on Michelangelo's entire naked body. Sucking dick wasn't my favorite sex act, yet a twinge of desire spiraled through me as I imagined myself on my knees, being face-fucked. For some unknown reason, I wanted to have raunchy sex with him. I wanted to be the whore that my husband had been throughout our marriage.

I got hot merely thinking about the welcome-home gift I had in mind for Maverick: hardened cum stains on his side of the bed. What could he say after he'd been hoeing all over Brazil?

From now on, I was going to give Maverick a tit for a tat. I thanked God that I had such a delectable piece of eye candy to conspire with me.

Inside my apartment, Michelangelo looked around at the lavish décor and made a number of compliments. He paused in front of the long sectional couch, as if planning to take a seat.

"Don't bother to sit down; we're going straight to the bedroom."

He looked surprised.

"I hope you don't feel offended that I want to use you for your body," I said playfully.

"I don't mind. Go right ahead and use me."

Getting permission to treat a man as an instrument of sexual pleasure felt empowering. Thrilled with my shiny new plaything, I guided Michelangelo along the hallway that led to the bedroom.

I wasted no time coming out of my clothes. He owed me big time and I was ready to collect. I rarely felt like a seductress around Maverick. Our lovemaking was usually initiated by him. With Michelangelo, I was in charge.

When I noticed he hadn't removed one stitch of clothing, I quickly went from feeling like a sex goddess to feeling stupid. He was fully dressed and giving me a weird look.

"Is something wrong?" I had an urge to grab the duvet off the bed and cover myself.

"Nothing's wrong," he answered, unmoving, standing in the same spot.

"You're being weird." I felt a little frantic, wondering if there was something about my body that turned him off. Maybe I wasn't as seductive as I'd thought.

But he put my doubtful thoughts to rest when he walked up to me and dropped to his knees. His large hands grasped my hips and I glanced down at the sight of him brushing his lips against my baby-smooth cooch.

Although I had wiped his cum out with tissues in the Porsche, I wasn't sure if there was a lingering scent. I would have jumped in the shower had I known he was going to stick his face between my legs and nuzzle my pussy like it smelled as fresh as morning rain.

I wriggled uncomfortably. "Maybe I should take a quick shower."

"No. I love the way you smell." He removed a hand from my hip and his fingers lightly touched the damp petals of my folds. "Are you always this wet or is your pussy dripping for me?"

"It's all for you."

He made a soft grunt before his tongue began to delicately lick at my silky folds. He didn't try to penetrate my walls with his tongue. He proceeded to drive me insane by softly licking the outside of my cooch, and my body jerked like it was being zapped by a stun gun.

His style of eating pussy wasn't anything like my husband's. Don't get me wrong; Maverick was good at oral sex. He dove right in and didn't bother with any of the gentle-licking that Michelangelo was doing.

He had me squirming around so much, it's a wonder I didn't topple over. "That's enough," I whispered, but he kept at it, alternating between licking my folds and then closing his mouth around my clit as his tongue flicked against it rapidly.

Ready for Michelangelo to stop torturing my clit, I went into a semi-squat position—a nonverbal way of saying, *"Get up in this this pussy, please!"*

The way he was eating out my box was so electrifying, my legs started shaking. Desperate for deep penetration, I went into a variation of a Sumo Squat with my legs wide apart and my feet turned outward. My pussy was wide open and ready for him.

A quick study, Michelangelo got up and pulled me toward the bed. He nudged me to sit down, and then he resumed his position between my legs. At some point I wrapped my legs around his neck. He gripped me at the waist and then stood up, continuing to eat my pussy while walking around my vast bedroom. He cupped my ass and sucked my pussy like he was slurping raw clams out of the shell. The sound effects he was making with all the slurping and sucking was causing my cooch to run like a raging river.

He laid me down on the bed and stretched my legs into a V, splaying me wide open. Hovering over me, he devoured me with his eyes as he observed my most intimate body part. In response, my pussy wept with joy.

He splayed me even wider as he embedded his tongue as deeply as it would go, tongue-fucking my cooch until I was writhing around and begging for mercy.

After giving me the best head I'd ever had, Michelangelo puckered his lips around my clit and began tugging on it while teasing the tiny head with the tip of his tongue. He was a master of oral sex, and although I was in heaven, I was ready for some dick.

I sat up a little and struggled to get his belt unfastened. But he kept eating pussy, digging his tongue into my sloppy wet hole and then darting up to my clit and swishing across it. Each tongue stroke felt like an electric shock. The way he was toying with my clit should have been illegal. He had me scooting around on the bed and yelping like a wounded animal.

Somehow, I ended up with my head and torso hanging over the edge of the bed, while my lower region bucked and writhed against his face as his tongue delved into me deeply. On the edge of sanity, I cried out, "Fuck me, Michelangelo! Please, baby, please." My voice was so loud and urgent, he finally realized I wasn't playing with his ass anymore.

At last, he began to unbuckle his belt. I pulled myself up and busily tried to help him. He removed his pants, and then tore off his shirt, displaying the most beautiful washboard abs I'd ever seen. I couldn't help from reaching out and running my hands over his eight-pack. From head to toe, Michelangelo was a work of art. So deliciously handsome, he looked edible—like an exquisite piece of high-priced gourmet man-candy.

He kissed me and slipped in his tongue, which was coated with my nectar. I sucked on his tongue, enjoying the spicy-sweet flavor.

Pulling me to my knees, he positioned me for doggy style. He slid a finger inside of me and then joined it with a second, thick finger. Seizing my ass in both hands, he fucked me from behind. Sizzling hot and creamy, my pussy opened up easily, enabling his dick to slide in without a struggle. I spread my knees wider apart, inviting him to fuck me as deeply as possible.

Doggy style was a good way to start off, but I couldn't cum in that position. Pulling away from him, I flopped on my back, and urgently reached for him.

He got on top and I guided him to my hot spot. Once inside, he changed his pace, switching to a slow, winding movement that stroked against every inch of my satiny walls.

"This is what I've wanted since the day we began shooting. Never thought I'd get it, though. You feel so good, I'd fuck this pussy every day if you let me, Cori."

I nodded, unable to participate in a verbal conversation during such an intense moment.

"I go crazy whenever you're on set. Do you have any idea how hard it is to compete in a cookoff when your dick is hard?"

I murmured a sound, but I actually had no idea that he'd been harboring such intense feelings for me. But we'd have to discuss his erections on the set at another time. All I wanted to do in that moment was focus on getting satisfied.

In sync with me, Michelangelo pushed his dick in to the hilt and moved extra slowly while my inner muscles gently grasped, rhythmically massaged, and then clutched his shaft possessively.

"Give me more. Harder! Oh, go deep!" Mindless words escaped my lips as I rode him. "Does this dick belong to me?" I asked in a throaty whisper.

"It's all yours, baby. Every fucking inch," he responded in a growl and then pushed his entire length into my body, locating my G-spot and stroking it masterfully.

On the cusp of an explosion, my pussy tightened around his shaft like a vise. My body became wracked with tremors and pulsed in ecstasy. Heat gathered in the pit of my stomach and tingles corkscrewed up and down my spine. Cries of passion erupted from me and seemed to echo off the walls. A kaleidoscope of vibrant colors danced behind my closed lids as an orgasm tore through me. Then I went limp and collapsed with my breasts pressed against his chest, the sweat from our bodies comingling while our hearts pounded together.

Michelangelo had amazing energy. We made love over and over. I couldn't get enough of him and he couldn't get enough of me. I was lying in his arms, and gearing up for the next round when he shifted his position and sat up lazily, stealing a peek at the clock on the nightstand.

He peered down at me. "It's getting close to dinnertime. I should probably be getting back to the hotel."

"Don't worry about food. If you're hungry, I can fix us something or we could cook together. Wouldn't that be fun?"

"I'd love that, but I can't stay."

"Why not?"

"The contestants always eat dinner together in the suite. Becca and Yancy will be looking for me. They'll bang on my door if I don't show up."

"Oh, damn." I'd completely forgotten that we needed to be careful about arousing the suspicions of his fellow contestants.

"I don't want to leave, yet, baby. But I don't want to give people a reason to gossip, either."

"You're right." I nodded as if I was in total agreement. In reality, my mind was spinning, trying to come up with a way to keep him in bed with me.

He bent over and kissed me softly on the lips, and then threw the covers back and got out of bed. Panic set in as I watched him gathering his scattered clothing from the floor.

"I have an idea," I blurted.

He cocked his head to the side, waiting to hear what I had to say.

"Why don't you take a taxi back to the hotel, have dinner with Becca and Yancy, and then pretend that you've decided to go to bed early…or you could tell them that you want to go back to your room and Facetime with your girlfriend. I'm sure you can think of a way to excuse yourself."

"I like the Facetime idea."

My heart dropped. "Wait. Hold up. Do you have a girlfriend?"

"Yeah."

I felt like I'd been punched. Being married and all, I shouldn't have felt betrayed, but I did. "Is your relationship serious?"

"I'd like it to be."

"Well, damn. If it's like that, why'd you even agree to meet up with me?"

"Because…"

"Because what?" Angry, I spoke in a sharper tone than I had intended.

"Because in my dreams, my girlfriend is you."

Totally, disarmed, I felt myself turning red. "Don't tease me like that," I said, attempting to give him a gentle elbow to the ribs, which he deflected and then put a wrestler's move on me, pinning me down and covering my face with sloppy, wet kisses.

"Ew. Get off me. Stop!" I said, laughing.

"Nope. You tried to crack my ribs and now you have to pay." He held my wrists together with one hand and began tickling me in the armpit with his free hand. I couldn't recall the last time I'd been tickled—but I recalled that it was something that Grandma Eula Mae used to do. She chased my cousins and me around the house when we were little kids, and whomever she caught, got tickled unmercifully.

Laughing and wiggling under Michelangelo's tickling assault, I felt like a little kid again.

I wondered what was happening here. Michelangelo and I were laughing and playing around like a pair of lovebirds. Maverick and I rarely laughed together. We mimicked the sounds, but we seldom truly laughed and we most definitely were never playful with each other anymore.

I cut an eye at Michelangelo and wondered if I was developing feelings for him. That would be crazy and totally out of character for a woman like me who was usually all about business. My main focus in life was to continue building the Mavcor brand.

Maverick and I were bound together for forever, and I accepted that. All I was doing with Michelangelo was indulging in revenge sex and having fun in the process.

I couldn't wait for Maverick to discover that he wasn't the only one who could reap the benefits of being in an open marriage.

Hugged up together, Michelangelo and I walked through the living room and stood at the door.

"Promise me you won't linger around, bullshitting with Yancy and Becca. Promise me you'll get back here as soon as you can," I said, caressing his arm.

"As soon as I finish eating, I'm gonna stand up and announce that I have to Facetime with my girl. But it won't be a lie because I'm going to hop in a cab, and tell the driver to step on it so that I can do some real face time between those luscious thighs."

He'd caught me off guard with that remark and had me blushing and giggling, again. Before he walked out of the door, I pulled him to me and gave him a lingering kiss. "Seriously, hurry back because I miss you already," I admitted.

"I'll be right back," he promised, and then he was gone.

I wanted to stand in the corridor and watch him walk to the elevator, but that kind of behavior would make me appear to be overanxious and juvenile. Forcing myself to get a grip, I went inside, closed the door and leaned against it.

My body was still warm from Michelangelo's heat and I could still feel his touch. With a deep inhale, I wrapped my arms around myself as my lips curved upward into a smile.

CHAPTER 27

I hadn't eaten all day and I wasn't hungry. I was too excited to sit down and eat a full meal. With time to kill while waiting for Michelangelo to return, I munched on a bag of kale chips, and turned on Grandma Eula Mae's recording.

People thought that all I did was sit around counting money. They spoke of me as if I had ice water running through my veins. But truth be told, I had a gentler side that I couldn't afford to let others see. My gals would have tried to walk all over me and my enemies would have known exactly how to hurt me if they knew my Achilles' heel.

After O'Grady had me and my girls locked up for the umpteenth time, he took over, marching around my establishment like he owned the place. Man, oh, man. I wanted to put a bullet in his ass for strutting around like a barnyard peacock and bossing me around like he was the true owner of my brothel.

According to the gossip mill, I was romantically involved with Mr. Banner, but there was no truth to that rumor. Mr. Banner enjoyed my whores and he valued our friendship. We had mutual respect for each other, but that was as far as it went.

Through my friendship with Mr. Banner, I met a Negro physician who was also a lover of art. This physician, a fine-looking and dignified man, had introduced Mr. Banner to a local artist. A colored fella named

Horace Pippin, who was untrained and whose work was considered crude by art lovers. His paintings looked like crap to me, too, and I didn't have a trained eye. But Mr. Banner bought up the man's entire collection and added it to his gallery. White folks fell in love with Horace Pippin's folk art and pretty soon, he was getting commissioned to paint for folks from Europe and other faroff places around the world.

I have one of his paintings. It's up in the attic somewhere. Heard his work is worth a fortune now, but I haven't had the energy to go digging around up in the attic to find the dusty painting. If any of my descendants ever bother to listen to this recording, you need to get your butt up in the attic, find the painting, and get it appraised.

Okay, what was I talking about? Lord, that quick, I lost my train of thought. I hate the way my memories come and go. Oh, I remember. I was talking about the Negro physician who became very, very important in my life. His name was Dr. Felder Bradwell.

When Mr. Banner caught the clap from one of my gals, he convinced Dr. Bradwell to start treating all my gals, behind the scenes, of course. Not only did he treat their various womanly ailments, but he also gave them regular checkups to make sure their privates stayed in good working condition. Before long, the white customers secretly began getting treated by Dr. Bradwell—after hours, also. None of them would have been caught dead paying a visit to a Negro doctor during daytime hours. They'd rather slink to his office in the dead of night than put themselves through the embarrassment of facing their regular family physicians with yellow puss leaking out of their peckers.

With Dr. Bradwell in my corner, I didn't have to rely on ol' Hattie Baker and her risky coat hanger method of getting rid of pesky pregnancies. Dr. Bradwell did the abortions safely, and no one bled to death from a punctured uterus or got infected from a rusted wire hanger.

He was a handsome man with wavy hair that he wore brushed backward, showing off his chiseled facial features. He had beautiful dark *eyes and wore a thin, neatly trimmed mustache. Although the round spectacles he wore gave him an intellectual look, those eye glasses couldn't hide the doctor's good looks.*

I would venture to say that when I was first introduced to Dr. Bradwell, it was a case of love at first sight. For both of us. There we were, two people from very different worlds, and yet we both recognized something familiar in the other.

Felder, as I referred to him behind closed doors, was a married man. He was married to a high-society gal named Daffodil, and it took two years of hell before he came to realize that Daffodil was crazy as a bedbug. When she started showing up at his practice wearing a wrinkled slip covered by a terrycloth robe that was encrusted with oatmeal and egg yolk, he had no choice but to put her away in a mental institution. Back then, folks didn't divorce their spouses the way they do today. You married for better or for worse and stuck by those vows

In the eyes of the law, I was carrying on an illicit affair with a married man, but Felder and I were so much in love, our bond was surely sanctioned by the Lord.

We were both masters at keeping secrets, and no one, not even Mr. Banner, was aware of the fiery passion that burned between us.

Felder despised Commissioner O'Grady for continually locking me up. He hated the man as much as I did, maybe more so. It bruised his ego something terrible that he couldn't protect me from O'Grady, and his desire for revenge was starting to eat at him.

I'm ashamed that we had to sacrifice an innocent woman to get to O'Grady, but in times of warfare, there's always collateral damage.

I had this new whore named Baby Cakes, a cute little petite thing, with the deepest dimples and big, round eyes. She looked childlike and adorable, and the men went wild for Baby Cakes. She was so tiny that even the puniest customer could feel like a he-man when he picked her up and carried her up the flight of stairs.

I was fit to be tied when during her very first week of employment, one of those dirty bastards gave her the clap—not only in her pussy, but also in her throat.

It burned me up having to lose money due to Baby Cakes being out of commission for a while. If it were up to me, she would have been back sucking and fucking as soon as Felder gave her the shot of penicillin. But Felder always insisted that the gals he treated lay low and refrain from sexual activity for at least two weeks.

Felder shocked me when he decided to hold off giving Baby Cakes a dose of penicillin. He confided that he planned for her to infect the commissioner when the ol' brute made his regular Wednesday night visit.

There was no doubt that O'Grady would want a toss in the hay with Baby Cakes. He made it a point to try out all the new meat, free of charge, of course.

"If giving O'Grady the clap is your idea of punishment, I don't think it's severe enough," I complained to Felder.

"You have to trust that I know what I'm doing, Eula Mae," Felder responded. "When O'Grady comes slithering to the back door of my medical office looking for a shot of penicillin, I'm going to hit him with a dose of something much, much stronger."

"Something that'll land him in the hospital?"

"Or worse," Felder replied in a grim tone.

But neither Felder nor I could have predicted how O'Grady would react to discovering that he'd gotten the clap from Baby Cakes.

He was so furious, he didn't take the time to gather his men with their axes and sledgehammers to ransack the place and shut it down. He came thundering through the front door, with fire in his eyes. "Where's that whore, Baby Cakes?" he shouted.

"What could that sweet little Baby Cakes have done to you, Commissioner?" I asked in an innocent tone. As I tried to calm him down, I secretly mouthed to one of my gals to hurry to the parlor where Baby

Cakes was playing cards with a gentleman and tell her to run and hide.

"That bitch burned me!" O'Grady bellowed.

"Dr. Bradwell will fix you up, Commissioner," I whispered discreetly.

"Yeah, and in the meantime, I'm going to put some hot lead in that dirty whore's ass. I wonder how she's gonna like whoring around in hell." He pulled out his gun and all the girls scattered. The gal I had told to warn Baby Cakes that the commissioner was coming for her, abandoned her duty and ran screaming in the opposite direction of the parlor.

With the commissioner on the warpath, waving his gun in the air, whores were hollering as they ducked behind furniture. Johns ran out both the back and front doors, carrying their clothes and other belongings bundled up in their arms. Uncaring that they were stripped down to their underwear, those tricks got the hell out of the whorehouse before any bullets started flying.

To this day, when I think about what the commissioner did to Baby Cakes, I have to hang my head in shame. But neither Felder nor I could have predicted that O'Grady would have taken that kind rage out on such a sweet, little, defenseless gal. No one is ever happy about catching the clap, but when it happens, the average man gets his shot and goes on about his business.

If Satan ever had a brother, his name had to be O'Grady. That ruthless bastard pulled off his belt and wrapped it around Baby Cakes's neck and dragged her around the parlor long enough for her to nearly choke to death. While she was at death's door, he pistol-whipped her back to life, cracking her jaw, busting her lips, and knocking out teeth in the process.

It was a horror to observe and while all the other gals were hiding, I was right there in the parlor, crying and begging O'Grady to have mercy on poor little Baby Cakes.

I recall noticing that Baby Cakes's blood had splattered on some of the leather-bound books in the library and also some of the paintings that Mr. Banner had bequeathed us.

The one thing that gives me a little peace of mind is the fact that Baby Cakes was out cold by the time O'Grady stuck his revolver all the way up her vagina and pulled the trigger.

After killing her, he adjusted his clothing, put his belt back on and returned his weapon to its holster. Then he strolled on out the door, leaving me to contend with the ravaged, bloody body of a dead whore.

I never asked Felder what he put in that needle he injected O'Grady with. There was no reason to inquire. Having no medical training, the contents he used wouldn't have meant a thing to me, anyway. What did matter is that O'Grady suffered terribly.

Whatever Felder shot him up with had him in and out of the hospital with mini seizures that kept occurring every week or so. The man would think he was free and clear, health-wise, but the next thing you know, he'd wind up on the floor, kicking like he was being electrocuted.

All those seizures took a toll and after a while, he lost his ability to speak, became wheelchair bound, and was drooling so badly, he had to wear a bib around his neck.

His wife, Mrs. O'Grady, thought it was her Christian duty to bring him out to community events like the annual policemen's softball game. Everyone was there, including me. And I made it a point to get in line with the rest of the community and pay my respects to O'Grady. When my turn came, I told his wife what a fine police commissioner her husband had been and when she turned her attention to the ballgame, I bent down and whispered in his ear: "Payback's a bitch, muthafucka. That was a helluva injection the good Negro doctor gave you, don't you think? You bragged about sending Baby Cakes to hell. Welp, she's not living in misery like you are. I bet you'd give damn near anything to end your miserable life and join her. But you have to keep on living—shitting your pants and being fed like a baby. A pretty woman like your wife probably has a couple gentlemen callers to take care of her needs. After all, with you being a pissy-pants invalid, you can't do anything for her."

I spoke those words with a sweet smile on my face while O'Grady grimaced and twisted in his wheelchair. He'd understood every word I'd spoken, but there wasn't a damned thing he could do except grunt and drool.

Grandma Eula Mae's story had gotten real juicy, and I reluctantly clicked off the tape. I wanted to take a leisurely bubble bath so I'd be refreshed and smelling good when my boo returned.

As I grabbed a towel, my thoughts returned to my grandmother. *Wow! Grandma Eula Mae and her doctor friend were G's. They handled that O'Grady dude—assigned him a fate worse than death. And he deserved it.*

I had no idea that she'd ever been in love with a doctor, though. Hearing the way her voice had gone all soft and sugary when she described him revealed a side of her I had never known. I wondered what had happened between her and Dr. Felder Bradwell that caused her to leave him for the man she eventually married and had two daughters with.

But I forgot all about Grandma Eula Mae's love life when my phone pinged and the concierge announced that I had a guest. "Send him right up," I said, twirling my hair and smiling in anticipation of more earth-shattering orgasms.

CHAPTER 28

I t was the best weekend I'd had in a long time. Blissful and sensual, yet wild and raunchy at the same time. My only regret was that Maverick wouldn't get an opportunity to witness the cum-stained sheets. I'd changed them twice over the course of the weekend because sleeping on crisp, clean sheets was an absolute must for me.

Michelangelo and I fucked all over the apartment, and I felt vindicated in the knowledge that our naked asses had not only desecrated my marital bed, but had also christened the kitchen counter, the dining room table, the sunken bathtub, the shower, and the balcony.

Unabashed lust came at a cost, however. My cooch had been fucked raw and felt like it required bedrest for a week.

Monday morning rolled around, and both Michelangelo's and my presence were required at the studio. He slipped out of bed at four in the morning. I could hear him tiptoeing around, trying not to wake me as he got dressed. He was so considerate, I couldn't help comparing him to Maverick, who never let me sleep in peace whenever he got up first. Maverick would shake me awake and ask me if I'd picked up his black Givenchy suit from the dry cleaner, or he'd rouse me from sleep, using my cooch as a cum bucket during rushed, pre-dawn sex that didn't remotely resemble lovemaking.

My sweet Michelangelo was the complete opposite of my selfish husband, and I appreciated his thoughtfulness.

During the ride to work, I checked my messages and wasn't surprised that Maverick still hadn't gotten in touch with me. And for once, I didn't care. Having good side dick cured me of all my jealousy and insecurities over Brazilians and Russian bitches. Never again would I lose a wink of sleep over Maverick's whorishness.

At the studio, I was all smiles and my squad noticed the difference in me.

"Girl, you don't need any bronzer this morning; you have your own natural glow," Clayton complimented. In the midst of him dabbing on foundation, there were two sharp raps on the door. Josh's authoritative, signature knock. Clayton and I shared a disgusted look.

"It's open," Clayton called out.

Josh entered, looking frazzled and harried as usual. Raking his fingers through his hair, he said, "Would you mind excusing us, Clayton. I need to speak to Cori privately."

"Not a problem." Clayton sounded agreeable but his scowling expression told a different story. He put down his makeup brush, twisted his lips in annoyance, and pranced toward the door.

"What's his problem?" Josh asked after Clayton had left.

"You know how he gets when it's that time of the month."

Instead of laughing at my attempt at a joke, Josh looked at me with a serious expression. "Cori, there's been a big change in the direction of the show."

"What kind of change? We agreed that Becca's going home, right?" I searched his face, but he refused to make eye contact with me.

"As you know the majority of our viewers are women and we don't want to alienate that demographic. We decided to keep Becca around for the final two. She won't win, of course, but feminists won't be able to say that we've been discriminatory."

"Okay, so who's going home...Yancy?"

"Of course not. We've already tapped Yancy to win this thing. Southern Baptist preacher...it makes sense."

I blinked in incomprehension. "What are you saying? You're sending the one and only remaining African American contestant packing. Oh, hell no, Josh. Fuck that! You and your cronies better put your heads back together and make a decision on either Becca or Yancy because you're not sending the lone black man home. He needs to be in the final two and you know it!"

"Oh, Cori. It's so cliché to keep a black person around as a mere token."

"A token? That man can cook circles around Becca and Yancy put together."

"But it's not about who can cook and who can't. It's about the audience's reaction to the contestants."

"We won't know how the audience reacts to any of them until the show airs in the fall. I can guarantee you that our female viewers will be creaming their panties over Michelangelo."

"True, I don't doubt that he has sex appeal, but when we used a test audience, they reacted more favorably to Becca than Michelangelo."

"That's bullshit."

"It's true. As dippy as Becca is, the test audience loved it when she whispered chants over her food and used weird hand gestures as if casting spells over the dishes she prepared."

I rolled my eyes. "This is an outrage, Josh. I am the only black woman who has a prime-time cooking competition show, and it was bad enough that there were only three black contestants on my show to begin with. Now you want to get rid of the last black person who also happens to be the strongest player in the competition. Michelangelo is articulate and handsome, and he can cook. He deserves a shot at success. I can't believe that you and those other fucked-up producers prefer to keep a drunken, hocus-pocus bitch and an asshole country preacher over someone as genuinely talented as he is."

"You always try to make everything about race, but I promise you, Cori, in this instance, that isn't the case. We want to keep the people that we believe will increase viewership."

"Oh, so you're saying that a flawlessly beautiful black man who's in phenomenal physical shape will cause viewers to switch the channel, but a chunky, grizzly-faced, redneck preacher can keep them glued to the screen?" I got out of my seat and started pointing a finger at Josh. "You're talking so much shit, it's a wonder this room isn't reeking from the stench."

Josh flinched and turned red when I called bullshit on his racist spiel.

I got all up in his space, frowning and snarling. "After that hateful rant from Angus on Friday about blacks, Jews, and Hispanics, I'd think that you of all people would be over your racist ways, but clearly you still hate and fear the black man."

"That's not true."

"Fuck if it isn't. You're singling Michelangelo out, racially profiling him exactly the way cops do when they encounter a young brother."

"But some of my best friends—"

I waved him off. "Oh, kiss my ass. I'm not trying to hear that tired line of bullshit."

My vile language caused Josh to wince. Seeing his visceral reaction inspired me to tell him off in a way that would rival Grandma Eula Mae's profanity-laced tirades during her final days.

"First of all, you need to fuckin' admit that you're a goddamn bigot. If it's too hard to tell me the truth, then you need to start being honest with your own goddamn self. Personally, I think a racially intolerant person like you does more harm than a hate-monger like Angus. At least I know where the hell I stand with a racist bastard that's ranting and raving about his white superiority. But I can't stand a sneaky bitch-ass like you who tiptoes around, starting a bunch of bullshit behind the scenes. If I can't have a black man in the final two, then all of you discriminatory dickheads can kiss my black ass. In fact, talk to my lawyer because as of right the fuck now, I'm officially out of here."

"What are you saying?"

"I quit!"

"No, Cori, please. Don't leave. You need to cool down and think about all the gossip and the bad press the show will receive."

"America has a right to know what's going on here," I retorted with a neck twist that I threw in for good measure.

"I heard every word, and you gave me a lot to think about. I agree that Michelangelo is a much better choice than either Becca or Yancy." Josh began to inch backward toward the door. "I'm going to call another meeting with the producers and see if we can come to a different conclusion. I'm sure I can persuade them to look at the situation from your perspective. I want to thank you for your honesty, Cori. Thanks a lot."

When he pulled the door open, Clayton, Robin, and Gina, who'd obviously been ear hustling, all toppled inside the room. Annoyed with them, Josh sucked his teeth and slammed the door behind him.

The four of us were silent as we listened to the sound of Josh's retreating footsteps. As soon as we were certain he was out of ear-shot, Clayton cried out, "Power to the people!" Robin and Gina raised their balled fists.

"You read his slimy ass," Gina remarked.

"Mm-hmm," Robin agreed. "You went in, Cori. You cussed him out and called him every name in the book."

Clayton nodded his head. "I agree that Michelangelo should win. He's fine enough to host his own show or at the very least, he could be the sidekick to another celebrity chef. I'd volunteer to be his makeup man, free of charge. Ooo, I'd love to powder his nose and apply some long lush tongue licks to that tight anus." Clayton flicked out his tongue, and it undulated in a disturbing snake-like manner.

I gave Clayton a curious look. "Do you get a gay vibe from Michelangelo?"

"Not at all, I'm sorry to say. But a man can dream."

Relief flooded through me.

Becca forgot to add the turnip greens component to my famous, Southern crab cakes. She also substituted turmeric for curry powder, which gave the dish an unpleasant bitter taste that the judges and I found offensive. Her crab cakes were undercooked in some areas and burned to a crisp in others. Her macaroni salad was bland and tasteless. Overall, her dishes were a disaster, and it was out of the question for her to advance further.

She accepted her loss graciously and with humor. With her supposed spell casting and weird chanting, our Wiccan contestant would be quite memorable. Viewers would definitely respond to her madcap character, and I appreciated the zaniness she brought to the show. However, it was time to get serious and select a winner.

Tomorrow Yancy and Michelangelo would compete against each other. Unlike other cooking competitions, we wouldn't be bringing back the losing contestants to help them prepare their final meal. They would be assisted by Azaria Fierro and Norris Buckley, and I would be the sole judge of their dishes. Still, the whole thing was a farce since it had been predetermined that Yancy would win.

I was on my way to Josh's office when I noticed Azaria huddled up with Michelangelo in the contestants' break room, supposedly discussing their strategy. I wasn't surprised that she'd angled a way to be paired with him, but what I found disturbing was her body language. She was sitting extremely close to him—so close her boobs grazed his arm. Clearly, she was trying to seduce my man!

I felt rage simmering inside me, but fought to keep it contained. Instinctively, I wanted to charge forward and scratch her eyes out, but I had to behave professionally and be mindful of keeping my side dude a secret.

Getting their attention, I cleared my throat. Azaria looked up and tossed me a fake smile. When Michelangelo gazed at me, I saw earnest eyes filled with something that was hard to define. Was it lust that I saw reflected in his eyes? Was he thinking about our long weekend together and how we'd fucked in every sex position of the Kamasutra? I wondered if like me, he was anxious to get together, again.

"Azaria and I were discussing strategy," Michelangelo explained. "She thinks we should go with your fried catfish and grilled corn on the cob recipes, but—"

I held up a palm. "Don't tell me. If you divulge your strategy, I may not be as unbiased as I need to be."

"Aw, damn, I blew it!" Michelangelo grumbled.

"It's okay," Azaria soothed, patting his hand. "We'll start from scratch and come up with another winning idea."

I noticed that her hand lingered on his caressingly. I didn't like it, but somehow I managed to keep my composure.

Sensing that I was getting upset, Michelangelo eased his hand from beneath hers.

"Well, I'll leave you two to continue strategizing," I said, satisfied that Michelangelo wouldn't allow himself to be seduced by slutty Azaria.

CHAPTER 29

After a long day on the set, I was too tired to keep listening to Sophia's voice. It was after ten at night and I'd been on the phone with her for forty-five minutes. She was running her mouth nonstop and I was waiting for a lull in the conversation so I could politely get off the phone.

"I feel abandoned. It's like you've forgotten I exist. With my husband deployed in Afghanistan and my son spending the summer at the military academy, I feel totally isolated—I'm all alone," Sophia complained. "I'm nauseous all the time and lately I've been having dizzy spells. Oh, and did I mention that I suddenly have varicose veins? My legs look horrible and they hurt like hell."

Oh, Lord, help me. I can't take much more of this torture.

Ever since I'd begun my whirlwind fling with Michelangelo, I hadn't given Sophia or the baby a moment's thought. Now that she had my attention, she was milking it. Handholding a needy individual was not my strong suit, and my first impulse was to pawn her off on Ellie. But there was no polite way of saying, "Excuse me, I don't have time to listen to you whine. Please call my assistant if you want someone to listen to you gripe about your pregnancy."

I took a deep breath. "I've read that green tea has medicinal qualities that help with morning sickness." I'd heard no such thing, but it sounded good. "Do you have any green tea, Sophia?"

"Hmm. I never heard that, but I'll check and see if I have any green tea."

I could hear her footsteps as she padded to the kitchen. I heard cabinets open and close. I rolled my eyes, regretting I had picked up the phone and accepted her call.

"Okay, it looks like I have chamomile, oolong, Lemon Zinger, Orange Mandarin and…um, I'm trying to see if there's any more packs of tea in the back of the cabinet."

Oh my fucking God, this bitch is trying to hold me hostage on the phone while she checks every teabag in her fucking cabinet.

"Sophia." I spoke her name through clenched teeth. "Why don't you make a quick run to a convenience store and buy some green tea."

"I would, but with the vertigo I've been experiencing…" She paused and allowed a moment of ominous silence. "I don't think it's wise for me to go out alone."

This needy ho had already been paid good money for her services, and if she thought she was going to guilt-trip me into ripping and running all over creation to keep her stocked in tea, pickles, and ice cream or any other food craving, then she was sadly mistaken.

"Why don't you try the oolong tea? I'm sure it will help with the nausea," I said, running out of patience, but somehow managing to monitor my tone.

"What about the vertigo? I never experienced dizzy spells when I was pregnant with my son. My doctor says that vertigo is normal in the first trimester, but I know my body, and it's not normal for me. I don't feel comfortable being alone; can you come over and sit with me for a while?"

She had to be kidding. I almost burst out laughing at such a ludicrous request. This bitch was really pushing her luck.

"Sophia, I have to prepare for an interview with the food editor of *Food and Travel* magazine, first thing in the morning," I lied. "Why don't you call me back tomorrow evening?"

"Okay," she said in a pathetic voice.

I ended the call and let out a long breath. *That bitch gotta be crazy if she thinks I'm at her beck and call.* Free from Sophia's needy clutches, I made a mental note not to pick up her calls for the next several months. As far as I knew, I had not signed up to provide emotional support all hours of the day and night. If she wanted a sympathetic ear, then she needed to call her husband in Iraq…Iran…or wherever the hell he was deployed.

Thirty minutes later, my phone rang. The screen read: *UN-AVAILABLE.* Suspecting that Sophia had blocked her number, trying to trick me into picking up, I ignored the call. A few moments later, my phone rang again.

Oh, hell. I'd be guilt ridden for life if something was really wrong with Sophia and I ignored her, so I reluctantly picked up.

"Yes?" I said in an aggravated tone.

"Are you upset with me, baby?"

It was Michelangelo, and hearing his voice gave me butterflies. "No, I'm not upset with you. Why would I be?"

"I could see it in your eyes that you didn't appreciate finding me in a cozy situation with Azaria. I know how it looked, but I want you to know that I wasn't doing anything wrong. I was keeping it strictly professional."

"You're free and single to do whatever you want. I can't control you," I teased.

"But I wasn't doing anything. She was the one sitting close and who kept finding reasons to rub on my hand."

"I know what a flirt Azaria is. I was only playing with you."

"Oh, you enjoy playing with my heart?"

Although he was being playful, I could tell by his voice that he was getting as emotionally attached as I was.

"*UNAVAILABLE* came up on my screen—where are you?"

"I'm at a pay phone. I expected it to be hard to find one, but I lucked up and only had to walk a few blocks from the hotel."

"I'm touched that you went out of your way to contact me, but it was a risky move. With only two days left until the finale, Josh's minions will probably be checking on you guys pretty regularly. "

"True, but I wanted to hear your voice. I miss you. Believe it or not, I couldn't care less about winning the competition. At this point, the only thing I want to win is your heart."

Touched by his sweet words, my hand went to my chest. "I miss you, too," I admitted. "But there's nowhere for this relationship to go, and you and I need to keep things in perspective."

There was a lengthy silence while Michelangelo absorbed what I'd said.

"Okay. I only called to verbalize my feelings, and now that I have, I'll say, goodnight. Pleasant dreams, Cori."

"Goodnight," I responded. I was about to hang up when I surprised myself by suddenly blurting, "Wait! I need to see you. Can you get a taxi and come over?"

"I'm on my way," he said with a chuckle.

I was playing with fire, again. I could only pray that my life didn't go up in flames. I had no guilt over cheating on Maverick, but it wasn't wise for me to get emotionally involved with Michelangelo or any other man. Having a friend with benefits was all I had wanted, but apparently neither of us had control over our emotions. And that was frightening.

Financially, I was locked-in with my husband. We were a team. As wealthy as we were, we still had yet to reach the pinnacle of success. We needed to stay together, even if we had to pretend to be happy. Sacrificing was necessary to reach the great heights we'd both dreamed of.

It would be foolish for me to fuck up what I had with Maverick. Undoubtedly, the public would be much more tolerant of Maverick's adulterous ways than mine. If Maverick got caught with one of his whores, there'd be gossip, but it would die down eventually. But if the public discovered that I was having a lurid affair with a contestant, all hell would break loose. The double standard would always exist, and if word got out that I was fucking around with Michelangelo, I could kiss goodbye everything I'd worked so hard for.

I'd always been level-headed with a clear vision of what it would take to achieve my dreams. So, why was I tempting fate? Revenge was the easy answer, but it was more than that. Michelangelo brought out a side of me that hadn't emerged since college. I felt happy and alive around him, and it was time to accept that I'd been holding on for dear life to a marriage that was nothing more than a business arrangement.

Sadly, I wasn't going anywhere and neither was Maverick. Michelangelo would return to Ohio in a few days, and I prayed that I'd be able to get him out of my system after he was gone.

CHAPTER 30

Depending on traffic and Michelangelo's skill at hailing a cab in New York, I had an hour's wait at the minimum.

My phone rang and I feared that Michelangelo had second thoughts and was calling to cancel, but when I saw Sophia's name displayed on the screen, I quickly hit the "Ignore" button. While waiting for my boo to arrive, I'd much rather fill the time listening to my grandmother's wild tales than have Sophia hold me captive with her pregnancy complaints.

It was irrational thinking, but a part of me believed that there was a personal message for me, hidden somewhere in Grandma Eula Mae's recorded memoir. I believed she was providing me with wisdom from the grave that would help me to navigate through life's challenges.

After plotting together and turning O'Grady into a slobbering idiot, Felder and I grew closer than ever. We had an extraordinary love for one another, but we didn't flaunt our feelings out in the open. As a respected physician, Felder had a reputation to uphold and it wouldn't have looked right for him to be gallivanting around town with another woman while his wife was locked up in the crazy house. And it would have been particularly scandalous if word got out that he was cavorting with the madam of a notorious cathouse.

Even with all my furs, fine jewelry, and flashy cars, the members of Negro society turned their noses up at me. But I didn't give a damn. I had everything a woman could ask for, including the love of my life.

But things between us changed drastically when Daffodil got ahold of some medication in the crazy house and died of an overdose. Suddenly, Felder was an eligible bachelor and everyone from young debutantes to wealthy widows had their eye on him. He was getting invitations to all kinds of charity balls and cocktail parties, which he turned down, of course because he wasn't interested in any woman except me.

I had always thought that out relationship would remain the same for the rest of our lives. Who would have thought a physically healthy woman like Daffodil would end up dying so young? Suddenly, Felder started pressuring me about squaring up and settling down. He said he wanted to turn me into a respectable wife. He realized I wouldn't ever be accepted in Philadelphia, where I was well known from being on the front page of colored newspapers every time my place was raided.

He was willing to close down his practice and begin again on the West Coast where no one had ever heard of me.

The average woman would have been thrilled, but I wasn't ready for marriage. It was all too sudden for me. There had been a certain thrill in sneaking around and being involved in an illicit love affair.

At twenty-eight years old, I was footloose and fancy free. I didn't want to give up my freedom yet. There was no way that I was going to start popping out babies and having nothing to look forward to except making beds and cooking meals for a family. The square's life seemed more like a punishment than something to strive for.

So, Felder and I had a big fallout over my refusal to get hitched. He accused me of toying with his emotions. Said he'd been willing to give up his practice and relocate while I was unwilling to make any compromises. Then he threw in my face that he'd been willing to kill for me and had risked a long prison sentence when he'd shot up O'Grady with that poisonous concoction.

I'll never forget the pained look in Felder's eyes when he told me our affair was over. Eventually, he remarried a young social worker named Gertrude. She had a rich daddy who desired that his daughter be out of the work force and suitably married.

When pictures of Felder and Gertrude's lavish wedding made it to the society section of Jet *magazine, I felt sick to my stomach with envy. I could have been the bride wearing a white dress if I hadn't been so foolish-minded. I told myself that there was no way he preferred that candy-faced social worker over me. And I set out to prove it.*

I waited until about six months after their wedding before I showed up at his medical practice, after hours. One look at his handsome face and I realized I'd been a damn fool to allow the great love we'd shared to fall by the wayside.

"You'll always be the love of my life, Eula Mae," Felder told me as we made passionate love on the examination table. "I can't go on without you. You must come back to me. Without you, I feel as if I'm dying inside. Say you'll come back, Eula Mae—please," he pleaded.

In that moment, I realized that Felder's love was too precious to give up, and it wasn't likely that I'd find that kind of deep love, ever again.

It had been stupid to choose running a whorehouse over true love. My brothel could be shut down at a moment's notice if the new police commissioner decided he didn't want my place blemishing the town.

It turned out that by getting rid of O'Grady, I had jumped from the frying pan into the fire. The new commissioner was a pious and religious man who despised whores. In the short time he'd held O'Grady's old position, he'd already raided my place five times. There aren't but so many times a woman can get carted off to jail—even if it's only for a week or so at a time—before she breaks from the mistreatment and degradation.

Suddenly, there was nothing that I wanted more than to become Mrs. Felder Bradwell. "I'm ready, Felder. We can run off to the West Coast and start a new life, like you wanted."

"What are you saying?" he asked, gazing at me with a shocked expression on his face.

"I'm ready to be your wife. I know it'll be scandalous for you to ask Gertrude for a divorce, especially so early in the marriage, but there's no other way around it."

He stared at me speechless.

"It may take Gertrude awhile to sign the divorce papers," I rattled on. "But we shouldn't let that stop us from leaving town. We could live as a common-law couple while she's dragging her feet and stubbornly holding up the process."

"Eula Mae, I can't marry you." There was anguish in his voice.

I gasped, but it felt more like a scream. "Why not? Don't you love me anymore?"

"Of course I love you. I never stopped. But I can't marry you. Gertrude is pregnant. What kind of man would I be if I left my wife at a time like this?"

"But you said out of your own mouth that you wanted me to come back to you."

"I do…with all my heart. I figured you were still opposed to marriage and preferred a secret romance like we had before Daffodil passed away."

Tears filled my eyes. "I've changed, Felder. That's not what I want anymore."

"But it's all I can offer you. I would never knowingly hurt you, and I'm so sorry, Eula Mae. You made it clear that you'd never give up your independence for me and I was willing to accept that."

He took me in his arms and held me comfortingly as I cried. Then I pulled myself together and walked out of his life—forever.

The new commissioner finally shut me down for good. Locked me up and tried to throw away the key. I was incarcerated in a women's prison when I discovered I was pregnant—with twins, no less. When I was released a year later, I had a heck of a time getting my baby girls out of foster care. *The court system would not release them to me as long as I was single.*

So, I married Reginald Boyd, a plumber who'd done work at my place from time to time. He was a big ol' country boy who'd always been sweet on me. Reginald adopted my girls and gave them his last name. He never asked who their real father was and I never volunteered the information. My daughters never knew that Reggie wasn't their natural daddy. And I never told Felder that he was the father of my twins. What would have been the point?

Putting my ambition first had cost me the love of my life and forced me into a loveless marriage. My daughters grew up without a man around because I divorced Reginald after five years of misery. They say you live and learn, and I learned the hard way that my idea of success was a fleeting and foolish thing. There's nothing as lasting or as powerful as true love. It saddens me that both my daughters took after me and are married to their careers. They're both successful women, but neither one could keep a husband for very long. One day they're gonna realize that their highfalutin jobs can't keep them warm at night.

Hopefully, at least one of my granddaughters will get her priorities straight and put true love before career success. But I don't want any of my grandbabies to marry the wrong man, either. If a man doesn't place you on a pedestal and treat you with the utmost respect, if he isn't willing to sacrifice his career and even his personal freedom for you, then he's the wrong one.

Take it from me, I had a great love once, but I selfishly threw it away. Although I had many other lovers, I never found that kind of pure devotion I got from Felder, not ever again in life.

What the hell? Was Grandma Eula Mae speaking directly to me from the grave? Was she telling me that Maverick was a disrespectful, selfish son of a bitch and Michelangelo was my knight in shining armor? If so, I found her advice to be ridiculous. I barely knew Michelangelo, and from what I'd learned about him, he didn't even have a job. His only possible role in my life could be that of a temporary plaything. Maverick, on the other hand, was a sports icon with numerous lucrative endorsement deals. He was also a well-paid sports analyst. Being hitched to his wagon had opened many doors to me that wouldn't have normally been open. Sure, he was a selfish bastard with kinky sexual predilections, but no one was perfect.

Furthermore, Maverick was the father of my unborn son. Becoming parents guaranteed that we'd be joined at the hip for life.

My grandmother's idea of the characteristics of a good man was outdated and sounded like an unrealistic fairytale. I didn't require anyone to kill or maim for me. I didn't have the kind of issues she'd had in life.

Michelangelo filled a certain void, but I'd be a fool to even consider leaving Maverick for him. Grandma Eula Mae couldn't relate to the problems of career women in the millennium when she was stuck in the forties and fifties.

t took over two hours for Michelangelo to arrive at my apartment. When I opened the door for him, he wrapped me in an embrace so tight, you would have thought we'd been separated for months.

"Sorry it took me so long to get here, but it's hell for a black man to get a cab in New York. I couldn't even get an Uber."

"Aw, I'm sorry you had to go through that. Instead of asking you to come to me, I should have picked you up."

"No, I'm good; I'm not complaining. I was so happy for the invitation, I was on the verge of jacking somebody's car if one more cab had whizzed past me." He laughed, displaying his pretty white teeth. "You look pretty," he added in a soft voice, his eyes bright with appreciation as he admired me in my sheer black negligee.

Thinking back to the beginning of the competition, I recalled how I thought Michelangelo was an egotistical, aspiring actor, using my show for exposure. Now that I knew him on a more personal level, I realized I couldn't have been more wrong about him.

It was a shame that Yancy was going to win, despite the fact that Michelangelo was the better cook. I wondered if it would be kinder to warn him in advance so that he would be emotionally prepared for the loss. I was about to tell him, but suddenly changed my mind. There was no point in giving him the sort of bad news that could potentially ruin the decadent evening I had planned for us.

Ready to get our night started, I moved my mouth over his, catching his bottom lip and gently sucking on it. I felt him growing hard and my nipples tightened with anticipation. The tingling sensation between my thighs prompted me to slide my hands around his waist, pressing my body closer as I rocked against his erection. His head went back and a low groan escaped his throat.

"Let me love you, baby." His voice was husky with longing, and I wasn't sure if he was asking if he could fuck me in the foyer or if he was literally asking me to accept his love.

Revved up, I yearned to taste him. I ran my tongue against the corded muscles of his neck. He tasted lightly of salt and male musk. He lowered his head and his teeth scraped my rigid nipple, sending an electrical charge through me.

His hands slipped under the hem of my short nighty, rubbing my thighs and then sliding around to my ass. "I need you," he murmured.

"Not yet. I have a treat for you," I said, slowly sinking down to my knees.

He caught me by the wrist and pulled me upright. "Wait. Cori. There's something I need to know."

"Yes?"

"What are we doing? Is this real? Are you feeling me the way I'm feeling you...or are you just having fun?"

"We're both having fun, aren't we?"

"Wow. It's like that? Okay, I get it." He had such a devastated look on his face, my gaze strayed toward the floor.

"You were well aware that I was a married woman when we started messing around. What else did you expect from me besides a good time?" My voice was verging on shrill.

"I don't know. I figured your marriage was falling apart...or something."

"Why would you think that?"

He shrugged. "People in stable marriages usually don't cheat on their spouses. And the way you were crying that day in your dressing room, I thought…" He paused and shook his head. "Look, what do I know? Forgive me for thinking we had something a little deeper than fun."

"I'm sorry," I mumbled, unable to look him in the eyes.

He tucked his finger under my chin, gently urging me to look at him. "Listen, I'm not trying to be rude or anything, but I should go."

"Don't leave, Michelangelo. Stay with me, please."

"I can't. "

"Why can't you?"

"First of all, I'm dead wrong for being in another man's home."

"It's okay."

He gave me a look.

"Really. It's okay. I didn't mention it before, but you should know that my husband and I have an open marriage. We don't publicize our arrangement, but I'm confiding in you because I want you to feel comfortable about being here."

He shook his head. "I don't feel comfortable, and I really want to leave. I got the reality check I needed, and now that everything's in perspective, it's best for me to go back to the hotel and get some rest. Tomorrow's the finale—that's what I need to be focused on." He gave me a weak smile and then kissed me on the cheek.

I couldn't believe he kissed me on the fucking cheek. He turned to leave, and I felt a sudden rush of desperation. I grabbed the back of his shirt, pulling him back to me.

"Let me go, Cori. It's for the best." He wrenched himself free, opened the door and left.

What the fuck just happened? I looked around in bewilderment and caught a glimpse of myself in the full-length, art-deco mirror.

I felt ridiculous. I was dressed in heels and sexy attire, yet my man had walked out on me. I furiously kicked off the stilettos and stomped to the kitchen.

Yanking open the fridge, I grabbed a chilled bottle of organic wine that I had planned on pouring for the two of us. I filled a wineglass and guzzled it down and then quickly poured another. I tried to sip more slowly, but ended up emptying the second glass in only a few gulps.

I was feeling all alone and slightly intoxicated when I heard my phone ringing from the living room. Thinking it was Michelangelo, my mood instantly elevated and I raced out of the kitchen. When I reached the living room and glanced at the screen, my spirit sank when I saw my husband's name.

I started to ignore his ass since he'd taken his good sweet time to contact me. But curiosity got the best of me and I picked up. There was loud music and the sound of a crowd.

"Maverick?"

No response.

"Mav, are you there?"

"Hey. Uh, is this Cori?"

"Of course, it's Cori. Who do you think it is? You called me—and I must say that it's about time."

"Oh, I think I butt-dialed you by mistake."

I ignored the fact that he hadn't intended to call and forged ahead with a conversation. "How's the interview going with the soccer dude?"

"Fine. We still have to get some footage of some of the locals giving their opinions of that crazy mishap, and then we'll wrap up shortly afterward."

"I'm glad to hear that everything's going great, sweetheart. So, you'll be home Friday?"

"Hello? Hello? Cori, I can barely hear you. I'm at a club…um… working. We're in the middle of a shot that portrays the wild way the Brazilians celebrate after a soccer game."

"Oh, okay." I was about to say something sweet like, "Hurry home; I miss you," when I heard a female voice in the background.

"You're always on the phone, Maverick. Hang up so you can dance with me, baby," said a bitch with a Portuguese accent.

"Uh, that's my tour guide; I have to go, babe."

The line went dead and I was once again, all alone while my husband was out there slinging dick and having the time of his life.

Attempting to drown my sorrow, I poured more wine and then padded off to the bedroom with my wineglass filled to the brim.

I needed advice. Needed to hear words of wisdom. I clicked on Grandma Eula Mae's recording. But her conversation was focused on running her restaurant and the motel she owned. I fast-forwarded, hoping to get to some more juicy stories about her love life, but all she talked about was her businesses and the high cost of sending her twins to private school.

Searching for guidance, I popped in another cassette, and sped to the middle of the tape. I heard my grandmother telling anecdotes about the civil rights leaders she'd hosted when they visited Philadelphia. Stories I'd heard a million times before.

Exasperated, I groaned and turned off the tape player.

My fans viewed me as someone who had her shit together. Someone who was fortunate enough to be the adored wife of a dashingly handsome, world-renowned sports figure. And I, a celebrated television personality, was considered a success story in my own right. But the Mavcor image was bullshit. The clock was ticking on my relationship with my husband. He clearly was no longer interested in even keeping up the pretense of living in wedded bliss. If the new baby failed to make a difference, then I was going to have to make a decision about whether or not to continue keeping our failing marriage on life support.

En route to the studio, I read an email from Josh, informing me that he wanted to get in front of all the promotion that was required of the winner. The TV appearances on all the major morning shows couldn't be done until after the finale aired and the winner was publicly announced. But he wanted to get started on the print promo right away. The media campaign, he said, would be more successful if I were featured alongside the winner, giving the impression that I was personally mentoring him and guiding him in a direction that would ensure his emergence as a culinary giant.

Bullshit.

Near the end of the long email, he wrote that it wouldn't be a good look for the show if our latest cooking champion succumbed to the fate of others before him, and ended up doing nothing more than posting recipes on his blog and demonstrating how to prepare a dish on YouTube.

Ugh. I had an instant headache after reading Josh's email. The idea of being linked with the Baptist preacher was sickening. Poor Michelangelo had no clue that he didn't stand a chance of winning. Hopefully, his uncanny good looks would get him noticed by food show producers at other networks. He deserved to show off his cooking skills. Perhaps he'd end up becoming more famous than Yancy. It wasn't out of the question for the runner-up to outshine the winner of a competition show.

CHAPTER 32

We were back at the old warehouse to film the finale, and despite the bleak environment of the makeshift dressing room, my beauty team had me looking amazing.

My makeup was flawless. Clayton had done his thing, giving me smoky eyes and eyebrows so snatched they looked sculpted by the gods. He switched up my usual neutral-colored lipstick with a combination of burgundy lip liner and bold dark-plum lipstick that screamed, *"Kiss me!"*

My hair was laid! With her flat-iron wizardry, Gina gave me a coiffure that was light and airy, yet substantive with lots of body. I looked extra pretty with ever so subtle gold highlights in my dark hair. Viewers would be trying to guess what was different about me, but they'd never figure it out. All they'd know was that I looked extra gorgeous at the finale.

Robin dressed me in a blue Carolina Herrera pants suit and platinum heels. The ruffle at the hem of the jacket added a hint of whimsy that was a change in my usual look.

Michelangelo should have been busy prepping his meal, but I looked so good, he couldn't stop stealing glances at me as I filmed my intro.

With the cameras pointed at me, I said, "Tonight our two finalists are going to draw from their own repertoire of delicious Southern cuisine and create a three-course meal that will be judged by me alone. They'll get help from our very own Azaria Fierro and Norris Buckley, but they'll only have ninety minutes to work their magic, and the clock has already started ticking."

I waved my hand toward the kitchen stations where the two finalists, Azaria, and Norris were frantically prepping their food. "As you can see, Michelangelo, Yancy, and our celebrity judges are hard at work. The winning chef will be featured in *Bon Appétit* magazine. But that's not all. He'll also be featured in a starring role in my next *Cookin' with Cori* DVD release. That's right, the lucky winner will join me in my kitchen, but there's a twist," I said with eyes widened with theatrical mystery. "During the first part of the DVD, viewers will be receiving step-by-step instructions in preparing good home-style food from me. But in the second part, I'll become the student and learn some of the cooking techniques used by tonight's champion. Now, isn't that exciting?"

The cameras zoomed in on me for a close-up, and then followed as I moseyed over to Yancy's station. He and Norris were both working up a sweat as they bumped into each other, dropped kitchen equipment, and basically seemed out of sync.

"So what are you whipping up for us tonight, Yancy?" I asked, keeping a safe distance from the abundance of male perspiration that sprinkled the air as the two men raced around the kitchen. I wasn't sure if sweat had dripped onto his ingredients, and I told myself to be extra-careful and taste only an itty-bitty portion of Yancy's sweat-tainted food.

"Well, Cori, I'm starting off with Fried Chicken Livers Wrapped in Bacon, and then for the main course, I'm fixing Braised Ox Tails over Dirty Rice."

"That sounds awesome, and what's for dessert?"

"For dessert, I'll be treating you to Grandma's Summertime Peach Ice Cream!" Yancy rubbed his big belly and licked his lips.

"Is that peach ice cream a dish that your own grandmother actually made?"

"Yes, indeed; it's a family secret. The ice cream has been a cherished recipe in my family for many generations. But I'll be happy to share it with you, Cori, after I win this here contest," he said, giving me a knowing wink.

"No one can say that you don't possess confidence," I said with my fake TV smile plastered on my face.

"Well, I'm a man of faith, and my faith got me to the finale, and I'm sure it will see me through to victory."

"Lots of luck to you, Yancy," I said although I didn't mean it.

"Yep," he responded with his chest poked out as if he'd already been declared the winner. Yancy was more smug than usual. He sounded so fucking sure of himself, I wondered if Josh had pulled him aside and told him that he'd already been selected as the winner.

"Okay, let's find out what Michelangelo is up to," I said to the cameras as I made my way to Michelangelo's station.

Azaria and Michelangelo were working at a less frantic pace and were perfectly coordinated as they chopped, peeled, sliced, and diced.

Bent over an onion that he was chopping, Michelangelo looked up at me with one eye squinted after getting squirted with onion juice. With a narrowed eye, he looked even more handsome…if that was possible. He dabbed at his face with the sleeve of his chef's jacket and sent a warm smile in my direction. If he was carrying a grudge from last night, it didn't show.

"What's on the menu, Michelangelo?"

"I decided on a seafood theme. For an appetizer, I'm making Crab Bisque soup. My entrée will be Blackened Shrimp and Cheese Grits with Sautéed Mustard Greens. For dessert, I'll be serving Key Lime Pie with Almond Crumb Crust."

"Mmm. That sounds fantastic, but it seems pretty ambitious considering the time crunch." I looked at the red digital clock on the wall. "Time is ticking; do you think you'll have all of your dishes completed in time?"

"The shrimp and grits won't take long at all. It's the Key Lime Pie that's a big risk for me."

"Well, as they say, no risk no gain. Good luck, Michelangelo," I chortled, giving the cameras my most winning smile.

"Thanks, Cori," he replied as he quickly sharpened a knife and resumed chopping an onion.

The energy level was high and the lights seemed extra bright. The combination of anxiety and bright lights were giving me a headache and causing my makeup to run. It was almost time to taste the appetizers, and the moment the director called, "Cut," I rushed to my dressing room to rest for a moment and take something for my headache.

My team followed behind me. Inside my designated dressing room, as Gina began fussing with my hair, my phone pinged. I glanced at the screen and frowned when I saw an email from Josh with an attachment.

Robin told me to stand still as she steamed wrinkles out of my slacks. While Clayton touched up my face, I tried to review the notes Josh had emailed me regarding my critique of the finalists.

"Do you think the bigwigs are gonna let Michelangelo win?" Robin asked me.

"I don't know. I doubt it," I said, glancing at the notes.

"Well, I believe in miracles and my money is on our boy," Robin said as she smoothed out my jacket.

"My money's on Yancy," Gina remarked. "You heard what Josh said the other day. He thinks the preacher will resonate more with the viewers."

"Although I can't stand Yancy, I'm not trying to throw good money away. I'm betting on the preacher because I don't trust that Josh is gonna do the right thing," Clayton remarked.

I looked up from my phone. "I can't believe you guys are betting on the winner of the show. You may need to think about getting help for your gambling addiction."

"We're not the only ones with a gambling problem. A lot of people bet on the winner," Gina informed.

"Who else is involved?" I inquired.

Gina shrugged. "Everyone who works here."

"Who's everyone?"

"The entire crew, the producer's assistants, interns, the chefs who work behind the scenes, the cleaning people, secretaries, pretty much everybody. Except you and Josh…and the other big dogs," Clayton informed.

"Interesting," I said, returning to my notes.

"Give us a hint, Cori," Clayton pressed. "What did Josh say in those notes? Is Yancy still tapped to win?"

"I won't know until I taste the food."

Clayton wore a knowing smile. "Come on, Cori. You can tell us. We know the show is rigged."

I smiled mysteriously and resumed reading. According to my notes, I was supposed to heap praises on Michelangelo's Crab Bisque appetizer, telling him it was super creamy with perfect density. Surprisingly, Josh wanted me to complain that Yancy's chicken livers were overcooked and drenched in greasy bacon fat, making them tough and greasy.

Hmm. I wondered if the producers had had a change of heart and were going with Michelangelo, after all. But as I continued reading, I realized they hadn't changed their minds. After Yancy's appetizer critique, I was instructed to speak in complimentary terms regarding his entrée and dessert. Josh wanted me to tell Yancy that his ox tails were well-seasoned and that the broth was flavorful. His ice cream was to be described as a mouthful of yumminess that was beautifully presented and pleasing to the eyes. *Oh, what a crock of shit!*

As far as my critique of Michelangelo's entrée, I was expected to go in! Josh wanted me to speak to him in a scolding tone when I informed him of how disappointed I was in his presentation. I was instructed to make a face when I tasted his blackened shrimp and tell him that he went overboard with seasoning and should have streamlined the flavor profile. I was also supposed to complain that his cheese grits were mushy and heap on more criticism by telling him that the least successful thing on his plate was the mustard greens, which were overpowered by the onions and garlic.

I continued reading the note and came to the conclusion that Josh was the cruelest and most sadistic fucking bitch I'd ever known. He didn't simply want Michelangelo to be defeated; he wanted to annihilate the guy. I shook my head as I read his remarks regarding Michelangelo's Key Lime Pie dessert: Say something about the overwhelming acidity of the limes and mention that the crust lacked crunch.

For God's sake! It was an outrage that the critique was written without the benefit of me or anyone else tasting either finalist's food. It was downright criminal, yet I was helpless to do anything about it.

But after this season, which was bound to be a huge success with all the drama that went down with some of the wacky contestants, I planned to renegotiate my contract and demand producer credit. Whether the show was nominated for an Emmy or not, I wanted full producer credit and lots more money. I didn't want to be placated with a mere vanity credit, either. I planned to be an actively involved producer with my hands in everything from casting to selecting recipes.

In the meantime, I had to suck it up and do as I was told. I observed my reflection in the mirror and then thanked my beauty team. I told them I needed a few moments of privacy before I went back on set.

After Clayton, Robin, and Gina gathered their tools and left the dressing room, I looked in the mirror again and sighed. I was ashamed of the woman I had become. In a matter of minutes, I was going to look Michelangelo in the eyes and tell him that his delicious food sucked. If he believed me, my words had the potential of destroying his confidence and ruining his future in the culinary field.

What price fame? I couldn't stoop any lower in my marriage, and now I was throwing away any semblance of self-respect and pride I had in my career. If my mother and I were close, which we weren't, I would ask her for advice. Being the success-driven woman that she was, she'd probably tell me to suck it up and do what I had to do to get ahead.

Then I thought about Grandma Eula Mae. If she were still here, what would she think about my career decisions? There was no doubt in my mind that my grandmother, after taking all that shit off the police commissioner for so long, would tell me to stand up for myself and to protect the integrity of my show.

Sorry, Grandma Eula Mae, but I don't have your gumption, and I don't have a choice in the matter.

I popped an Advil. Chin up and determined to persevere, I walked out of the dressing room of the warehouse and returned to the lion's den.

CHAPTER 33

Presented with Yancy's appetizer, I took a very small bite. I chewed briefly and then quickly swallowed it down. Being a vegetarian, ingesting too much meat could cause me to hurl.

I rattled off my rehearsed critique, telling him that his dish didn't cut it. Yancy disagreed with my negative comments and didn't mind telling me so. *What a holier-than-thou creep!*

Michelangelo came forward and I took a spoonful of his Crab Bisque. "This is awesome. So creamy and smooth," I raved.

"Thank you, Cori. Thanks so much," he said graciously.

The entrées were next, and when I tasted Yancy's dish, I couldn't help making faces and going off script with disparaging comments. I hadn't planned on busting on his dish, but his ox tails had too much heat and the broth was oily and unbearably salty.

Although I didn't have the guts to literally poison the arrogant son of a bitch in the manner in which Grandma Eula Mae had done away with her enemy, I damn sure could cut Yancy down a peg or two with my poisonous tongue.

Once again, Yancy didn't take my criticism well. He made excuses and bickered with me. His ungracious behavior was not a good look for him.

When Michelangelo stepped forward and I took a forkful of his food, my taste buds did the happy dance.

"The shrimp is perfectly cooked. This dish is very well composed.

I love the balance of the cheese and grits—the texture is spot on. And the sautéed mustard greens, oh my God, so good—what is that tangy note I'm getting?"

"It's apple cider vinegar," he replied with a shy smile.

His humbleness was such a stark contrast to the obnoxious preacher. There was no doubt in my mind that when the show aired, Michelangelo would be a fan favorite.

From the corner of my eye, I could see Josh lurking in the shadows. I could feel him glaring at me, and I wasn't surprised when the director yelled, "Cut."

"A word, Cori," Josh hissed, and then hustled me off set. "What do you think you're doing?"

"Telling the truth about Yancy's food," I replied sassily.

"Are you nuts? Everything is in place for Yancy to win. You can't take it upon yourself to change the plans."

"I don't know how they choose winners on other cooking competitions, but I'm going to use integrity when I make my selection."

"You don't make decisions. You do as you're told."

"Not anymore. This is my show, bitch. So kiss my ass and deal with it!"

"Do not fuck with me, Cori. I'll have this show cancelled before I allow you to destroy a program that I created."

"Do what you gotta do, motherfucker, but I'm calling the shots at this finale. I'm going to rely on my palate and not your stupid notes to critique the food that I taste. So, go fuck yourself and get out of my way," I hissed, giving him a hard shove.

As I threw my head up and strutted away, I could feel Grandma Eula Mae smiling down on me.

The dessert segment was next and Yancy's peach ice cream was the bomb. Keeping it real, I told him it was the most delicious ice cream ever created on the show.

But as tasty as his ice cream was, it couldn't begin to compete with Michelangelo's Key Lime Pie with little flecks of fresh lime mixed throughout the pie filling.

Finally, it was time to announce the winner, and despite what was written on the card inside the envelope, I proclaimed on national TV that Michelangelo was the winner and no one could dispute my word!

I could see Josh holed up in a corner, looking like he wanted to choke me out. I imagined that he was telepathically hurling all sorts of derogatory remarks at me.

I laughed inwardly. *To thine own self be true.* Whatever the consequences of my actions, at least I'd be able to look in the mirror and say that I'd upheld my convictions.

Confetti and balloons floated from the ceiling and the finalists' family members seemingly came out of nowhere. Michelangelo's mother and his two sisters ran out on the stage and engulfed him in a hug.

Yancy had a devastated look on his face while his wife and children stood in the background sulking.

Next, all the losing contestants, minus Angus, charged the stage, clapping enthusiastically and congratulating Michelangelo. I had no idea where they'd been hidden. Their presence was a big surprise to me.

Ralphie was among them. Even though I'd secretly paid him off, my guilt over the way he'd been forced off the show prevented me from making eye contact with him.

Since the network had the responsibility of keeping the name of the winner a secret until the show aired on TV, the celebration that followed was held within the confines of the studio. A DJ materialized and began setting up his equipment. The food was catered by the behind-the-scenes chefs and there was plenty of liquor to ensure a good time.

I made my obligatory rounds, shaking hands with Michelangelo's family, and I chatted briefly with Yancy's wife and kids.

I noticed that Josh and his cronies didn't bother to hang around. They'd left right after the taping, and I didn't intend to linger around, either. Leaving the festive atmosphere, I strode to my dressing room, intending to pack up and slip out the rear door. There was no point in expecting my driver to be waiting for me in the front of the building. Being on Josh's hit list, I was certain he'd already canceled that amenity. I wondered in what other ways he planned to retaliate. He'd probably stop footing the bill for my assistant's salary and expect me to pay Ellie out of pocket from now on.

The show had wrapped, but instead of feeling jubilant, I felt off center. I'd jeopardized my career over my convictions, and now I had to face the consequences. I bit my lower lip, terrified of what the future held for me. Then I had a sudden epiphany. The show was called, *Cookin' with Cori*, so how the hell could Josh replace me?

The answer to that question quickly flashed in my mind, and I realized that I was doomed. Josh was such a vindictive little twit, he'd figure out a way to get rid of me while keeping the show running with a series of guest-hosts. Even worse, he'd probably stick that thirsty Azaria Fierro in my place. He was so far up her ass, I had the impression that he wanted to *be* her.

My agent had his work cut out for him in finding me suitable work. I'd turned down being the brand ambassador of an up-and-coming knife company, but now I was reconsidering that decision. If I didn't secure a number of endorsement deals, I could end having to earn a living by holding cooking classes at a community center. Oh, the shame!

At least my husband's career was secure, I told myself as I lethargically threw a few of my personal items in a tote bag. Ellie could pick up the rest of my belongings at the Chelsea studio tomorrow.

The moment I picked up my phone and called a car service, it seemed that the wrap party got extremely loud and the noise filtered into my dressing room. The music was pumping so loud and their voices were so boisterous, I could barely hear the person I was speaking to at the car service, and she could hardly hear me. I had to practically scream out the address of the warehouse as well as my instructions to have the car pick me up at the rear entrance.

I was stressed and my head started pounding, again. I took another Advil, but it didn't alleviate the pain. I had an hour to wait for the car, but unable to deal with the noise from the party, I decided to go outside and get some fresh air.

I slipped out the back door and heard it lock behind me. *Damn!* Locked out, I looked around my environment. The rear area was more rundown than the front and there was nowhere to sit except for a few stray cinder blocks. I considered leaning against the structure, but it looked filthy, and would surely stain my pants suit.

I thought about pounding on the door to get back inside but realized it would be a waste of time—no one would hear me. As if my life wasn't fucked enough, I was forced to stand in heels for an hour.

Suddenly, I heard the doorknob jangle, and I whirled around. To my surprise, Michelangelo was standing in the doorway, looking like a winner.

"Hey, congrats, again," I said, breaking into a genuine smile.

"Thanks. It doesn't seem real, yet." He looked at me oddly. "What are you doing out here in the dark? Are you okay?"

"I'm fine—waiting for my ride."

"I needed to get away from the noise for a moment. Mind if I join you while you wait?"

"Sure, I love your company," I said sincerely.

He unlocked the door from the inside, making sure he didn't get locked out, and then stood next to me.

"You look troubled. Are you sure everything's all right?"

"Couldn't be better. But enough about me, what are you going to do with the prize money…open a restaurant?" I asked, merely making small talk.

"I had planned to use the money to open a restaurant in my dad's honor, but now that it's a reality, I realize that a hundred thousand won't go very far in the restaurant world. To do what I intended, I'd need more backing. Maybe a partner. I may use the money to travel. Learn the food culture in places like Africa, Asia, and Spain. That kind of education is invaluable."

"Traipsing around the world sounds like a lot of fun."

"It would be more fun if you were joining me," he said solemnly.

"Don't start, Michel. You know how complicated my life is."

"Yeah, so why don't you let me make it uncomplicated?" He swiveled me around, forcing me to face him—to see the hunger that filled his eyes. He looped his arms around me, pulling me close with a possessiveness that I was too weary—too beaten down to fight. The chemistry between us was undeniable. Simply giving in to the heat seemed easier than continuing to fight a battle I couldn't win, and so I melted into him without protest.

His kiss was intense. Aggressive. His tongue invaded my mouth like a conquering army. Feeling his hard dick pressed into my groin, my body undulated against him.

His hand slid down to my crotch, which he discovered was moist. Breaking the kiss, he looked at me and smirked. His expression told me he wasn't at all surprised that my pussy was dripping with anticipation.

Michelangelo lowered his mouth to my ear, brushing it lightly with his lips. "You know you want me as much as I want you. Am I lying?"

I didn't respond.

Taking my silence as consent, he backed me into the grubby

exterior of the warehouse. The idea of protecting my Carolina Herrera pants suit was the last thing on my mind.

I closed my eyes and tilted my head back in surrender. While his lips grazed my bared throat, his fingers busied themselves, unbuttoning my jacket and deftly unhooking my bra. He cupped both breasts with his warm hands, and I shivered with delight. Dipping his head to suckle, his tongue danced across the nipple of my right breast, rapidly bringing it to a sharp point. I felt his thumb graze the left nipple, drawing slow deliberate circles around it. I moaned and clutched his jacket in both fists as he went back and forth, teasing each nipple in turn, firing darts of pleasure throughout my entire system. One hand pulled away from the sumptuous mounds of my breasts and meandered downward, caressing my thigh, moving slowly toward my hip, and then around to the front of my pants.

Expert fingers unhooked the clasp as I stood trembling before him. His hot hands palmed my ass and then, his fingertips traveled around my waist before wandering to my tummy. He slowly dragged his fingers downward, leaving a line of fire in their wake. They journeyed lower and lower, and then grazed across the velvet texture of my inner lips. I spread my legs, giving his adventurous fingers access to my heated interior. One finger, then two, slid in and out of me gently, but with insistence, until slick, leaking moisture revealed that I was ready for him.

Momentarily insane, I didn't care that we were outside—exposed. I mumbled how badly I needed him as I grabbed his waistband and freed his dick. Freed from confinement, the full length of his shaft speared toward me. My hand closed around its wide girth and I aimed the helmeted head toward my throbbing clit.

Michelangelo bent his knees a little as he drove himself deep inside me.

I wanted more of him. No, I wanted *all* of him, and so I pulled one leg out my designer pants, allowing the expensive fabric to drag the dirty ground. With newfound freedom, I propped my foot on a tall stack of cinder blocks to give Michelangelo more access. He anchored me with his arms wrapped around my waist and then proceeded to work his concrete manhood inside me.

He was hunched over and I met his thrust by standing on the tiptoe of one foot while the sole of the other was planted on the top cinder block. The gentle, yet persistent fuck that Michelangelo had begun, soon morphed into a furiously intense coupling.

My mind drifted a bit above the frenzy, wondering how we must have looked. With me splayed open and straining to meet his height and him bent low as he thrust into me, we must have looked like contortionists from Cirque du Soleil as we slow-fucked in such an awkward position.

Strangely, our awkward position made it easy for him to reach my spot. With every stroke, my stomach spasmed and I drew air in desperate gasps. As I climaxed, the only way to keep the volume of my voice down was to bite my lip so hard that I tasted blood.

Michelangelo came shortly after I did. Groaning my name, his body shuddered violently, but he didn't let me go. In that spinning vortex of ecstasy we had created, he remained an anchor, holding me tightly.

CHAPTER 34

Maverick returned from Brazil with a sun-bronzed hue to his brown skin. Not only did he look exceptionally handsome, but he was also in great spirits. I assumed his cheerful disposition was the result of his slutty adventures in Brazil. Fucking his brains out for seven days straight did for Maverick what a week-long spa retreat did for the average person. I wondered if the hookers in Brazil had put up with his penchant for biting, or was that something only Russian whores were into?

After spending three nights of passionate sex with Michelangelo, I was feeling pretty good, my damn self. Now that Michelangelo had decided to travel the world, he could appreciate not being tied down with one person, and our "friends with benefits" situation was much more appealing to him, now.

For the next few weeks, the two of us were scheduled to do a press junket, which required overnight stays in some instances— like our upcoming photo shoot in Hawaii for *Bon Appétit* magazine. We were being flown to beautiful Waikiki to be photographed on the beach with a spread of delectable Southern cuisine.

I was super excited about the trip. By day, Michelangelo and I would pose for pictures on a private beach, and I'd be able to feast my eyes on his magnificent physique for hours at a time. But our evenings would be even steamier. Staying at the same hotel, we'd have complete freedom to slip in and out of each other's hotel suite and no one would be the wiser. I got goosebumps imagining his large hands awakening my skin—his mouth and skillful tongue teasing me to near madness.

My personal involvement with Michelangelo made me feel less agitated about Maverick's sexual shenanigans. For once, I wasn't the least bit concerned about what he was up to. Had I known that having a sidepiece could be so emotionally healing—so soothing to the soul—I would have gotten one a long time ago. I suppose it took the right person to make me aware that life didn't have to revolve around my husband.

Remarkably, Josh's anger over my breach of contract subsided and he became somewhat friendly. I was initially baffled by his pleasantness, but his unexpected civility made perfect sense after Ellie informed me that she learned from Josh's assistant that the network executives had seen the dailies of my show. They loved my sassy one-liners and the way I had interacted with the contestants so much, they were eager to pick up *Cookin' with Cori* for a third season.

With a stable marriage, a successful career, and a sizzling new love affair, my life was fabulous! My only complaint was the relentless phone calls from Sophia. What a pest! While in Hawaii, I'd be able to get some well-deserved respite from her constant bitching and lamenting. In case of emergency, I'd advise her to contact Maverick during my absence. Maybe she'd shut the fuck up if he stopped by her place and tightened up that pussy for her.

I engaged the incline feature of my treadmill and powered uphill as intense workout music blasted from my headset. In beast mode, I huffed and puffed, sweating like crazy as I got in some last-minute cardio along with a little thigh and butt-toning before my trip to Hawaii with Michelangelo.

The beach shoot was all about displaying my food and showing off Michelangelo's abs. I planned to wear a cover-up in the photos, so I wasn't worried about my body looking perfect in a swimsuit; I simply wanted to be as toned as possible when my boo stripped off my clothes.

I rarely pushed myself when working out, but today I was going to extremes, alternating between running and steep-hill climbing. In a zone, all I could think about was heating up the sheets in Hawaii.

In the midst of fantasizing about sex on the beach, Maverick suddenly came hurtling through the door of our home gym. He was holding up his phone, waving it, and yelling something that I couldn't hear with loud music pumping in my ears.

"What's wrong?" I asked, yanking off my headset.

"What is this shit?" Phone in hand, his arm was outstretched as he stomped toward me.

Confused as to why Maverick was acting the damn fool and interrupting my workout, I turned off the treadmill. He thrust the phone in my hand and when I gazed at the screen, my vision blurred. In freeze-frame mode was an image of Michelangelo and me, kissing passionately. I was so totally unprepared to see photographic proof of my indiscretion that my legs went wobbly. I had to hold on to the handle bars in order to remain steady on my feet.

"Hit 'Play,'" Maverick demanded with a look of rage in his eyes.

Having no desire whatsoever to witness the video, I blinked rapidly as if I had been slapped across the face. I was in such a panic, I was close to jumping off the treadmill and haul-assing out of the workout room. But where would I hide? Mechanically, I obeyed my husband's command and tapped the screen. In a state of shock, I stood on the treadmill and watched a video recording of Michelangelo and me outside the warehouse on the night of the finale. I stared at the footage with my eyes wide and my mouth wide open. We were fucking like two animals in heat, and it wasn't easy to stand there and observe myself behaving like a savage. Suddenly parched, I grabbed my water bottle from the side compartment of the treadmill and took a desperate gulp. Dazed, I needed to lie down, and so I got off the treadmill and handed Maverick his phone. With my mind in a fog, I thought my feet were heading for the doorway, but having lost all sense of direction, I found myself pacing in a circle.

"What are you doing? Stop walking in circles like a freakin' lunatic," Maverick bellowed. He gave me a look of such intense hatred, I stopped moving and physically recoiled.

"How'd you get this?" I asked in a monotone.

"What the hell does it matter how I got it? What the hell possessed you to smash dude from your show—in public—like a dirty ho?"

Being called a "dirty ho" made me flinch, but being curious about who had taken the video and sent it to my husband's phone, my mind wandered. Then it hit me—Josh! There'd probably been hidden security cameras outside the warehouse and that devious queen had gotten hold of the perfect weapon to destroy me. No wonder he'd been acting so sickeningly sweet lately. He knew he was going to stab me in the back the entire time he'd been grinning in my face.

"How am I supposed to show my face around town with that filthy sex tape of my wife breaking the Internet?" Maverick looked down at the footage and then angrily hurled his phone, smashing it against the wall. Then, as if in anguish, he held his head with both hands and hollered. It was a long and loud, plaintive wail.

Seeing Maverick becoming unglued influenced me to pull myself together. "Get a grip, Mav. We have a powerful PR machine. They'll do damage control."

"Nobody can fix this. It's over; we're both done. I used to kill myself on the football field to ensure we had a good life. And after football, I continued to grind. Those endorsements that help us maintain our lifestyle didn't simply land in my lap; I busted my butt to get them. And now your dumb ass has destroyed everything I've worked so hard for."

"You're upset, honey. I understand, but we aren't a hundred percent certain that the video has been posted online," I said in a rational tone.

"Someone sent it to me, so I assume it's everywhere." He yelled out every word and punctuated his tirade by kicking the treadmill.

"Who sent it?" I asked quietly, hoping my calmness would encourage him to take it down a few notches.

"I don't know; the sender was private." He was still livid, speaking through clenched teeth, but at least he'd stopped yelling.

I went into action and used my phone to check gossip blogs, social media sites, and entertainment news. I couldn't find the video or any mention of it, thank God!

"It's not online, Mav. But I have a good idea who's behind this."

"Who?"

"Josh. He's using the tape to blackmail me into giving in to his demands."

"Josh is gay; why would he demand sex from you?"

"It's not about sex. It's about the show."

Maverick stared at me inquiringly. "Why would Josh put something out there that could destroy the show?"

"We've been having creative differences, and I think he wants to replace me with Azaria Fierro."

No longer composed, Maverick punched the wall. "Do you realize that if this shit gets out, I could lose my endorsement deals as well as my position at the network? What the hell were you thinking, fucking around with that kid?"

"He's not a kid. Michelangelo is a grown man."

Maverick grimaced. "I hate that stupid-ass, pretentious-sounding name. Ugh. Michelangelo." He spat out the name as if it were a violation to his very soul. "How much is that motherfucker worth, Cori?" Maverick looked upward as if mentally calculating. "Let's see…he won the competition, so at least he has a few bucks in his pocket," he said sarcastically. "You got yourself a hundred-thousand-dollar man. Wow. That's a hell of a downgrade, Cori. I hope the dick was worth it."

I took a deep breath and closed my eyes. And I kept them closed as if the way out of this nightmare was written on the insides of my lids.

"I don't get it. Don't you get all the dick you need from me?"

I opened my eyes. "Maybe I need more than a hard dick, Maverick."

He shot me a look of disgust. "You could have fooled me. The way you came out of your pants and let them drag in the dirt, it looked to me like you were starving for some dick."

"With all your whoring around, you can't talk," I clapped back.

"The big difference is that I'm discreet. And I've always been honest with you. You're always reminding me about discretion and then you turn around and get with your boy toy out in the open. Letting him raw dog you up against a rundown building—like two vagrants who can't afford a hotel room."

"I'm sorry, Mav. I didn't mean to—"

"Shut up with that lame excuse. You're well aware of the morality clause in my contract. Our brand—Mavcor—is a symbol of wholesomeness and your slutty conduct reflects on me, as well as you. This is so fucked up," he lamented, rubbing his forehead circularly.

"You don't understand how lonely I get being married to you."

"How the hell are you lonely? I take a boys' vacation to Brazil once a year, and I travel sometimes for work, but other than that, I come home to your ungrateful ass every single night."

I laughed bitterly. "You come home, all right. And you bring sluts and whores home with you and fuck them in our bed, and expect me to accept the disrespect with a smile."

"We agreed on an open marriage a long time ago, so don't start complaining about it now."

"I never agreed to an open marriage. I only agreed to your having a sexual encounter once a year on your birthday. You took it upon yourself to take it further with the whores in Brazil. I didn't like it, but since you were doing your dirt outside the country, I dealt with it. But your obsession with prostitutes has gotten out of hand, leaving me feeling inadequate and lonely. Everyone envies us, but we both know there's nothing to envy about our bogus marriage."

"Don't give me that sob story. If you had been honest with me, you could have been with your amateur cook on the up and up, but you made the decision to be a deceitful bitch. If your sex tape gets out, and I'm sure it will, I'm not going down with you. I'm distancing myself from you and your lewd behavior as of right the fuck now."

"Mav! What are you saying?"

"You heard me. I'm packing my shit and leaving. My spokesperson will be making a statement later today about our imminent divorce."

"You can't divorce me. What about our baby?"

"You mean *my* baby. I knocked up the hooker, so it's my child, and not yours. I'll raise my son on my own."

The tale I'd woven about the ripped condom and Sophia getting pregnant by Maverick had come back to haunt me. "That baby belongs to both of us, Mav. Sophia didn't get pregnant by you."

"What?"

"You wouldn't go along with the surrogate birth, so I tricked you into believing the condom broke the night you were with Sophia.

Sophia's not a prostitute; she's our surrogate, and she's carrying *our* child. I set it all up, and convinced her to pretend to be a whore. I'm sorry for tricking you, but you gave me no choice. I was desperate to have a child and you wouldn't cooperate."

"You're a piece of work, Cori. I never realized I was married to such a lying, conniving bitch."

I started to speak, but couldn't think of anything to say in my defense. I gazed at him, hoping to see a glimmer of compassion in his eyes. But his eyes were filled with such loathing, I quickly glanced away.

"That sex tape speaks volumes about your character. No court of law would give custody of an innocent child to an indecent piece of scum like you. Thanks for hoodwinking me into fatherhood," he said, gloating. "But I'm going to be a great father. Being a hands-on single dad will be the key to winning back public approval. I can rebuild my brand and make it even bigger than it already is when I start pushing baby products like disposable diapers and baby food. Maybe I'll write a book about the joys of single fatherhood." He gave a burst of evil laughter. "Mo' money, mo' money," he taunted.

Maverick had been the ultimate dog, fucking anything that moved. I'd only cheated with one person, and yet my entire world was collapsing.

The unfairness of the situation pushed me to the edge. "I won't let you take my child," I screamed as loud as I could. "I'll fight you for my son. And I'll fight dirty if I have to. I'll tell the world about your whores and how you like to bite them. Sophia hates you, and she'll testify on my behalf. She'll reveal that you bit up her thighs, leaving deep teeth marks, like a rabid dog."

He waved me off, unaffected by my threats. "Do what you gotta do, baby. It'll be your word against mine...and after your sex tape goes viral, your word won't be worth shit."

CHAPTER 35

Maverick sauntered out of the workout room and I was left with an awful feeling of doom. Not knowing what to do or whom to call, I gave a strangled, hopeless cry. My husband and I were represented by the same PR firm, and with him being the bigger star and the person responsible for paying their exorbitant fee, it was pointless for me to turn to our PR team for support.

That stupid prenup I'd signed when I was young and dumb would prevent me from getting half his money or any spousal support. I wouldn't get child support either if he won custody of our child. Oh, Lord…my life sucked!

But I couldn't give up. Maybe I could convince Josh not to go public with the video. I'd offer to bow out gracefully from the show if that's what he wanted. My finger was poised to press Josh's number when my phone suddenly rang.

I noticed that the call was from a private number, and I swallowed in fear. Josh was about to make his demands, but I found it weird that he would bother to block his number. With a bad feeling swelling in the pit of my stomach, I swiped the screen, and accepted the call.

"Hello?" My voice came out in a tiny, frightened tone.

"Hi, Cori," said a voice that sounded vaguely familiar, but I couldn't accurately identify.

"Who is this?"

"You forgot me, already? Aw, my feelings are hurt."

Trying to make out the voice, I wrinkled my brow. "Who the fuck is this?" I shouted insistently.

"No reason to get ghetto on me. I thought you were too polished and dignified to go there. Oops, that's right, there's nothing dignified about you. You get down and dirty, with your pants down and your leg hitched up, fucking in public, for all eyes to see. Good thing I had my phone camera handy. Your adoring fans need to know about your fraudulent, fake-ass self."

Suddenly, I became aware of who was behind the attempt to destroy my image and my good name…and it wasn't Josh. "What do you want from me, you malicious little viper," I said through clenched teeth.

"Temper, temper," Ralphie said mockingly.

"How dare you try to blackmail me after all I did for you and your family—"

"You didn't do anything out of the kindness of your heart. You bought my mom some dentures and tried to give her a makeover because you didn't want to be embarrassed by her. You considered her a hood rat and a disgrace to the race. But you fucked up when you played me. My food was perfect and you and those judges conspired together and got me kicked off the show."

"That's not true, Ralphie. I didn't have anything to do with your elimination."

"I heard the words 'goodbye, Ralphie,' come straight out of your mouth."

"I don't pick the winners—"

"That's a lie," he hissed, cutting me off. "I saw Preacher Yancy's name printed on the card you left behind in your dressing room the night of the finale, but you didn't announce it that way. You gave the win to your boyfriend. Obviously, your show isn't about the best cook. It's about who's laying the best pipe in you."

"Michelangelo is not my boyfriend," I said, but didn't sound convincing.

"You could have fooled me. Why did I catch the two of you about to smash on the couch several weeks before the finale? I was the only cook who could beat Michelangelo, and I bet you planned to get rid of me way back then."

"What happened between Michelangelo and me was wrong…it was a mistake. But there was no conspiracy against you, Ralphie. I swear."

"Why don't we let the public be the judge of that after they see the tape? I'm not going to release it until after the finale airs. Then, while Michelangelo is making his rounds and doing TV appearances, I'll be doing the same thing—going on talk shows and discussing what I filmed."

Never in a million years would I have believed that such a seemingly sweet and harmless soul like Ralphie would have the power to blow up my life. His capacity for vengeance was chilling. But I couldn't let a little nobody punk like him publicly humiliate me. I was shrewder than he was. I could outthink him. Despite how upset and shaken I was, I had to pull myself together and outmaneuver that lowlife, orphaned, motherfucking black-acting, white-ass, street urchin.

"Ralphie," I said in the soothing tone of a negotiator speaking to a terrorist in the midst of a hostage situation. "Listen, I can help you with your career."

"What career? Oh, do you mean you can help me get a promotion from the stockroom at Target to a cashier's position? No, thanks, I don't enjoy dealing with the public."

"I'm serious, Ralphie. I know lots of influential people and I can help get you started in the culinary field. I have ways to get you an apprenticeship with some of the most prestigious chefs in the industry. In fact, I'm tight with the owner of one of the top soul food restaurants in Harlem. A place called Bay Leaf that I used to own. I could get you a job as a sous chef. You don't have to worry about housing; I'll set you up in a nice apartment near the restaurant."

"Hmm."

"What do you think?" I asked, feeling hopeful.

"I think you're kissing my butt so hard, *my* lips are starting to hurt."

His insult infuriated me. But being at his mercy, I couldn't curse him out the way I wanted to.

Ralphie cleared his throat. "The way you did me was wrong, but I'm not comfortable being a vindictive person—it's not my style. So, you don't have to worry about me exposing you. Well, not to the whole world, but I already sent your husband a copy. From what I could tell after meeting Maverick when he was a guest-judge on your show, he seems like a good man, and he deserved to know what was going on behind his back."

Maverick was a good man, my ass. Ralphie had no idea of the kind of man-slut I was married to.

"Anyway," Ralphie continued, "as far as the public goes, it's not my place to blow your cover."

Oh, thank God!

"I used to look up to you, Cori. You were my idol. In my mind, you were the most decent person in the world. It's such a letdown to discover how you really are—the kind of person who's so hungry for fame, money, and power, you'd probably throw your own mother under the bus to get what you want."

Ralphie was really going in on me, and I felt like shit. It was hard to listen to what he was saying. Until now, I'd never realized how badly the truth hurt.

"I'm going to take you up on your offer," Ralphie said. "Go ahead and set something up for me at the restaurant in Harlem. Tell the owner I'm willing to start at the bottom—as a dishwasher or whatever. I'll work hard and earn that sous chef position in no time."

Realizing my secret was safe, and that I wouldn't have to live in disgrace, relief washed over me. I would have kissed Ralphie if he'd been within my reach. "You're right, Ralphie," I said, feeling elated. "You'll be a sous chef before you know it. With determination, you'll become a restaurateur one day."

"Nah, I don't have a head for business. Being able to cook for a living will make me happy."

"Whatever your aspirations, I hope you achieve them. I also want to say thank you for giving me the opportunity to redeem myself."

"You're welcome."

I told Ralphie I'd be in touch with him in a day or two. Considering the circumstances, I felt we'd ended the conversation on fairly decent terms.

But I had a lot to think about. It had been as if Ralphie had held a giant magnifying glass in front of me, forcing me to take a hard look at myself, and I didn't like what I'd seen.

I should have been packing for my trip, but I sat on the edge of the bed instead, contemplating cancelling. As badly as I wanted to be with Michelangelo, it would be foolish to leave New York while Maverick was assembling a team of attorneys to help him end our marriage and ruin my life. He had access to the video, and I wouldn't put it past him to release the damning footage himself.

I needed a pit-bull-type lawyer. Someone who was clever enough to find loopholes that would invalidate the prenup I'd signed. But I was between a rock and a hard place, fearing that putting up a fight against Maverick would provoke him into releasing the tape.

My phone pinged with a text message from Sophia, informing me that her lower back had started bothering her. She further stated that she'd heard that prenatal yoga was helpful for back pain and wondered if I'd be willing to foot the bill for yoga classes. *Dear Lord, would this woman ever stop pestering me?*

While grumbling to myself, I was struck by an idea. I quickly called her. She seemed surprised that I'd personally called and was delighted when I told her I'd be more than happy to pay for the classes.

Then, stealthily, I steered the conversation in a different direction. "I need to talk about a sensitive subject."

"Is something wrong, Cori?"

"Yes, I'd like to apologize for what my husband did to you. I don't believe I was as compassionate as I could have been when you told me about those bite marks he put on your thighs."

Sophia sighed. "Yeah, that was pretty shocking."

"I bet it was. I should have been there for you—on an emotional level. But I was so busy with the show at the time. But now that we've finished taping, I'd like to make it up to you, if I can." I cleared my throat. "I bet you were in a lot of pain afterwards," I said, encouraging her to talk about the unfortunate incident.

I was still scheming, and I wasn't proud of myself. But a leopard couldn't change its spots overnight, I reasoned, and then promised to become a better version of myself after the legal battle with Maverick was behind me. In the meantime, my dire circumstances required me to fight fire with fire.

"It was extremely painful. My inner thighs were black and blue with visible teeth indentations for over a week. I don't know how I would have explained those bites to my husband if he were home. Having the doctor at the fertility clinic notice the bites was mortifying."

"I bet it was. Do you think the doctor documented what he saw in your medical record?" I asked, hoping there was a legitimate paper trail that proved Maverick was a sadistic pervert.

"Yes, the doctor insisted on giving me a tetanus shot. He suspected I had been abused by someone, and so he also took photos. I have no doubt that he mentioned his treatment and his suspicions of abuse in his notes."

I smiled. *You want to fuck with me, Maverick? Well, I've got something for your ass: photos of your handiwork and suspicions of physical abuse, documented by a physician!*

"The doctor believed that I was in an abusive situation, and suggested I take photos myself in case I ever needed evidence of domestic abuse for the police."

"Did you take pictures?" I was growing excited.

"Yes, but I would never show them to anyone. I'm your biggest fan, Cori. I would never do anything to create bad publicity for the Mavcor brand. All I ever wanted was for us to be friends. The way you've ignored me has been terribly hurtful."

"I'm sorry, Sophia. Like I said, filming the show was all-consuming. Now that I'm free, I can spend more time with you."

"Really?"

"Uh-huh. Would you like to get together today? Maybe do some shopping?"

"I'd love to."

"Okay, I'll see you in an hour."

CHAPTER 36

I took Sophia on the biggest shopping spree of her life. I bought her a bunch of household goods and spent a lot of money on expensive tech stuff for her son and her husband. I also offered to pay to have her apartment cleaned once a week so she wouldn't have to strain her back.

She was ecstatic, but I felt the money I'd spent was a small price to pay for what I was getting in return.

I called a meeting with Maverick and his group of attorneys. They all smiled condescendingly when I arrived at the conference room of the prestigious law firm without benefit of counsel. But I wiped those smug expressions off their faces when I spread out blown-up photos of Sophia's ravaged thighs on top of the conference room table.

"This is some of my husband's handiwork," I announced.

Maverick went into a coughing fit.

"This photo could have come from anywhere. It means nothing," said the youngest attorney in the room, waving the photos and turning down his mouth disapprovingly. He was a show-off, overly eager and aggressive, and I was looking forward to putting him in his place.

"I figured you boys would attempt to invalidate the photos, so I also brought along a video." I'd deliberately called them all *boys* simply to irk them. My ploy worked, judging by their sour expressions.

"Are you sure you want to have a war of videos?" quipped a pompous-looking, older man with beady eyes, a hawk nose, and badly thinning hair.

I gave a shrug, fished my phone out of my purse, and confidently pulled up the video.

When Sophia appeared on screen, sitting in her living room, dabbing tears from her eyes, Maverick dropped his head. His team of high-priced attorneys exchanged confused glances.

My husband, who is serving in the Marines, and who is currently deployed in the Middle East, is a fan of Maverick Brown. He has followed Mr. Brown's football career since he played football in college. As for myself, I've been a super fan of his wife, Cori, ever since I bought her first cookbook. Naturally, I was honored to be chosen to be the surrogate mother of their child. I trusted both Mr. and Mrs. Brown, implicitly, and it's difficult for me to come to terms with what Mr. Brown did to me. I can't express how stunned I was when the man I knew as a sports hero lured me to a hotel under false pretenses. Once he got me inside, he pounced on me like a wild animal. I've never been so frightened in my life.

"She's fucking lying," Maverick exploded, jumping out of his chair. "That bitch pretended to be a prostitute and lured me to the hotel."

A portly lawyer with several chins frowned at Maverick. "That's not something you want to say out loud. As your counsel, I have to advise you not to repeat that the accuser reeled you in under the pretext of being a prostitute."

"Yeah, you're right. That sounded messed up," Maverick agreed and quietly returned to his seat.

On the tape, Sophia continued: *My image of Maverick Brown was shattered on the night of June 23, 2015 when he violently attacked me. He savagely bit my thigh, and then after the vicious mauling, he raped me.*

"That's a damn lie. With my money and looks, why would I have to rape that homely bitch?" Maverick lashed out. One of the lawyers gave him a stern look and gestured for him to quiet down.

I saw a doctor the next day and received a tetanus shot. Mr. Brown left his teeth marks on my inner thighs, which the doctor documented in his medical report. He also photographed my injuries. It is my belief that a rapist usually strikes more than once, and if there are other women who have been savagely raped by Mr. Brown, I urge you to come forward and join me in seeking justice. In my opinion, Mr. Brown is not only a violent rapist but also a practitioner of cannibalism. Had I not fought him off, there's no doubt in my mind that he would have devoured pieces of me…he would have eaten me alive.

The word "cannibalism" caused a collective gasp from the attorneys.

Maverick was livid, standing again, and this time he pounded the table. "I'm going to sue that whore for defamation of character."

"Hold on there, Maverick," the chubby lawyer said. "I hate having to put you in an uncomfortable situation, but I have to ask, did you bite that woman?"

Maverick dragged his fingers down his face. "Yes, but it's not what you think. She was into it. She loved every minute."

All three lawyers groaned.

I rubbed my hands together gleefully. "You're putting the nails in your own coffin with that statement, buddy. Opposing counsel will eat you alive for saying that a victim enjoyed being ravaged and raped."

"But it's true," Maverick persisted. "I didn't do anything to Sophia that she didn't want me to do."

The young, aggressive lawyer jumped into the fray. "Maverick, are there any other women who could possibly get on this bandwagon? Anyone else you can think of who might accuse you of raping and, uh, biting her?"

Mute with embarrassment, Maverick could only shake his head.

"What about Katya, the Russian escort?" I piped in.

The beady-eyed lawyer jerked his head toward Maverick. "Did you bite a Russian escort?"

Maverick groaned and lowered his head, apparently too distressed to speak.

"I have the Russian escort on speed dial," I offered. "And there's Tamara, our former chef. She's also been attacked by Maverick and I'm sure she has a few war wounds to back up her story. When word gets out about my carnivorous husband, women will come crawling out of the woodwork to get themselves a piece of a multi-million-dollar class-action suit."

The young, aggressive lawyer flipped through the photos again, and then looked up at Maverick. "This doesn't bode well for you, Maverick. It looks particularly bad that your accuser is the wife of a military man, serving his country in the Middle East. Add the fact that she's making the sacrifice to be a surrogate for your unborn child, and I'm afraid she'll come off as extremely believable."

I smirked as I glanced at Maverick. "You need to settle privately with Sophia and keep this thing out of the media. Seriously, do you really want your name associated with cannibalism?"

"Will you stop using that word?" Maverick shouted.

"Certainly," I replied with a catty smile. "I'll stop using the word and Sophia will be satisfied with a moderate payout if you tear up the prenup and pay me what I deserve for putting up with your shit for ten long years."

Slumped in his chair, Maverick mumbled, "Whatever you want, Cori. I'll do whatever it takes to make this go away."

"Oh, I also want full custody of the baby; you can have weekend visitation."

He nodded his head.

I left the lawyer's office feeling powerful. The way I had deflected the negativity from me and placed it on Maverick was brilliant. I'd singlehandedly outsmarted Maverick and his dream team. I was sure Grandma Eula Mae would have been proud of me.

Azaria Fierro ended up getting my show, after all. And she didn't do anything nefarious or underhanded to get it. I gave up the spotlight and all the trappings of fame willingly. I wished her all the luck in the world. She was going to need it being married to my ex-husband. Well, they weren't married, yet. But they were engaged and planning the wedding of the century. Maverick and Azaria were the latest power couple in the entertainment field.

Busy keeping up his golden-boy image, Maverick rarely had time to spend with our eighteen-month-old son, Ryker. Although we both lived in New York, I would say that Maverick only saw the baby approximately once a month. It was a good thing I'd won full custody, otherwise, Ryker would have been raised by a parade of nannies.

Before putting him down for the night, I rocked my son in my lap as I read *The Velveteen Rabbit*. Being fussy, he kept yanking the book from my hands and flinging it to the floor.

I knew exactly what to do to get him to settle down. With Ryker on my hip, I crossed the room and searched through the collection of his favorite DVDs.

I popped in a DVD and the moment Michelangelo appeared on the TV screen, Ryker squealed happily, "Daddy!"

"Yep, that's Daddy," I affirmed. He referred to Maverick as Mav and called Michelangelo, Daddy. In my son's mind, Daddy was the one who put in the time.

Ryker and I settled back in the rocking chair. Together, we

watched Michelangelo as he stood on a boat, bare-chested and wearing swimming trunks. He explained that he was about to jump into the green ocean of the Bahamas to forage for shellfish. While putting on his gear—fins and snorkel mask—he said he would be diving fifteen feet down and while below water, he'd have to flip over huge rocks to find hidden conch.

"That's Daddy when he was in the Bahamas," I explained to Ryker. "When Mommy's able to travel, you and I are going to start joining him on his adventures."

Seeming to understand, Ryker grinned up at me.

Michelangelo had made such a great impression when our Hawaii photo shoot hit the newsstands, his Twitter and Instagram followers surpassed a million followers. After season two of *Cookin' with Cori* aired, his fan base shot up to ten million and he was offered his own travel show, *Diving and Foraging for Food*.

For his show, Michelangelo traveled to various locations around the world where he sometimes trekked through dense woods carrying a backpack and shovel as he dug for wild-grown herbs, mushrooms, and berries. He once went on a truffle-hunting expedition in an ancient village in Croatia where the foraging required specially trained dogs to sniff out the coveted prize. Once the dogs had led him to the location, he carefully dug truffles from the ground. Even sweaty and covered in mud, Michelangelo was a big hunk of rugged handsomeness.

When he wasn't digging in the ground for elusive ingredients, or trekking through mountainous terrain to pick wild-grown vegetation, he was jumping off motorboats and yachts, searching for seafood.

The second segment of the show featured him using the foraged ingredients to prepare a meal, which he cooked outdoors on a crude manmade stove, oven, or grill. Unlike the glamorous life of the typical celebrity chef, Michelangelo went off the beaten path and got his hands dirty while searching for unusual ingredients.

His show was a huge success and got the highest ratings on the Travel Channel. Not only was he delicious eye candy, showing off his rugged masculinity as he traversed rough terrain, climbed mountains, and swam the raging sea in a quest to find food, but he also possessed an earnest charm that dazzled TV viewers.

The backstabbing, contract disputes, network strong-arm tactics, and other forms of Hollywood politics that were part of the entertainment industry, had all become too much for me. Once I became a mother, I yearned for a simpler lifestyle and had gladly given up the bright lights of show business.

Michelangelo wasn't the only breadwinner in our household. Contributing to the family income, I penned a new cookbook that featured healthier eating, and I was looking forward to its release. Though I had only agreed to minimal promotion, the presale figures were more than my previous cookbooks.

It turned out the painting that Grandma Eula Mae had left in the attic was worth a fortune. The artist, Horace Pippin, was right up there with African American greats like Jacob Lawrence, Romare Bearden, and Henry Ossawa Tanner. I split the profits with my mom, aunt, and cousins, and still came out with a large sum.

With the addition of my multimillion-dollar divorce settlement, we were doing quite well.

When Ryker finally fell asleep, I put him in his crib and tiptoed out of the nursery. Michelangelo would be arriving home soon from filming in Amsterdam where he had foraged for rare herbs in the heart of the city.

Known for its red light district, Amsterdam was famous for its brothels and sex shops, but I wasn't worried in the least about bae sampling the human merchandise of women who displayed their wares in the red-fringed window parlors. Michelangelo was a faithful partner, and for the first time in my life, I was experiencing what it felt like to be cherished, respected, and loved.

"Honey, I'm home," Michelangelo called out when he entered the apartment, and my heart fluttered with love. I rushed from our bedroom to greet him. He collected me in his strong arms and then broke the embrace and bent over my protruding tummy.

"How's my baby girl?" he asked, rubbing my abdomen.

"She's been kicking like crazy all day. I think she was excited because Daddy was coming home."

"And what about my boy?" he asked, grasping my hand and tugging me along as he made his way to Ryker's nursery.

With Michelangelo's arm around my waist, we stood over the crib, smiling down at our son. Yes, *our* son. Though Michelangelo wasn't Ryker's biological father, he was proving to be more of a father than Maverick would ever be.

Speaking of biological fathers…I had yet to reveal to my mom and Aunt Chloe the true identity of their dad. I had no idea how they'd take it, and I wasn't even sure if it was my place to tell them.

Grandma Eula Mae was my guardian angel. Through the hard lessons she'd learned, I was able to stop making the same mistakes. Her audio recordings had redirected me from the superficiality of show business and guided me toward what really mattered in life. With Maverick, I had been attracted to the money and fame, but with Michelangelo, I had found real love for the first time.

"Hungry, babe? Do you want me to heat something up for you?" I asked my beautiful man.

"Yeah, I'm a little hungry. What are you going to heat up?"

"It's a surprise dish." I threaded my fingers in his and led him out of the baby's room.

In the hallway, he kissed me passionately, groaning as he ran his hands beneath my clothes. "Ooo, I missed you, baby."

"I missed you, too," I responded, tearing off his shirt, and planting kisses all over his beautifully sculpted chest.

"Fuck heating up food; I'm hungry for you," Michelangelo said, tugging me toward our bedroom.

Our desire for each other was palpable, and I became keenly aware that the only thing that was getting heated up tonight would be our sheets.

ABOUT THE AUTHOR

Allison Hobbs is a national bestselling author of twenty-seven novels and has been featured in such periodicals as *Romantic Times* and *The Philadelphia Inquirer*. She lives in Philadelphia, Pennsylvania. Visit the author at:

AllisonHobbs.com

Facebook.com/Allison hobbseroticaauthor.

Twitter.com/allisonhobbs

Instagram.com/allisonhobbserotica